The

Quiet Travels

of Marjorie

Paris Blatecky

Published by Paris Blatecky

Marietta, Georgia

ISBN: 979-8-218-71983-8

Editing by Jennifer Twomley, thependwells.com

Cover design by Paris Blatecky

Cover illustration by Alice Negri, alicenegri.com

For more information, follow Paris on Instagram @parisbwrites

A Note About This Book

While a work of fiction, *The Quiet Travels of Marjorie* is set in the real cities of San Francisco, California, and Marietta, Georgia. Many places take inspiration from real businesses, events, or locations. All characters are original to the story, except for fictionalized versions of historical figures mentioned such as James J. Andrews, The Gartrell sisters, The Goodmans, and other founding families of Marietta.

You can learn more about the city of Marietta by visiting the Marietta History Center, the basis for the museum in the story, located in the old Kennesaw House at 1 Depot Street. To see archives of San Francisco in the 1960s, I encourage you to check out opensfhistory.org which showcases individual streets and neighborhoods throughout the decades, thanks to photographs shared by residents, past and current.

The Quiet Travels Playlist

Please scan the following code for a curated playlist for your reading experience! Enjoy tunes that inspired the book featuring The Platters, Lana Del Rey, Frankie Avalon, The Shirelles, Stephen Sanchez, and more.

For Papa and Grandma. Everything truly started with you both.

It's been long understood that the veil between spirits and Earth is lifted on the 31st of October.

But does that veil fully return when the day is gone?

Here we follow one of the few whose existence traverses both, fueled by place and times.

Marjorie Estelle Valdez, born November 1, 1993, minutes past midnight.

Marjorie, 1959

At 1:07 p.m., a woman walked into Hunt's Ice Cream and Restaurant on Marietta Square, wearing an orange silk scarf around her head and sporting tortoise sunglasses that made it seem as if she was a starlet far off from Hollywood. To the waitress leaning back against the counter, there was a good chance she might have been—with many of the usual townspeople strolling through on these cold February days, she had never seen her before.

Her name, unbeknownst to the waitress, was Marjorie, and upon opening the door into Hunt's, she looked around before darting straight to one of the open seats at the counter. The waitress came up and placed a menu down just as Marjorie was removing her sunglasses and draping her blue coat across her lap. "Welcome in, darlin'," she said before looking up to Marjorie—she stared longer than Marjorie would have liked before she continued in her initial pleasantries. "Want to start with anything to drink? Coffee?"

Marjorie shook her head. "No, thank you, I think I'm going to go for a milkshake." She ran her finger down the menu toward the ice creams. "Could you please make me a mint chocolate chip shake with whip?"

The woman continued to stare at her, but soon nodded and walked toward the back. Perhaps it was the notion of something cold on a chilly day—or because at that moment Marjorie looked around and, not to her surprise, everyone but her was white. She sat with her back straight but arms folded, trying to not act too nervous. The narrow restaurant was so familiar, with the same cream ceiling medallions and wooden floors, although a bit darker in varnish than she had seen it earlier that morning. Had she not just waltzed back into 1959, she would have never known this was the same building she'd only walked out of minutes before. Something by Dion and the Belmonts floated across the airwaves. Looking back out to the front she could see it was overcast, early afternoon, according to the big clock on the back wall that said HUNT'S with ice cream cones at every half-hour mark. The waitress came back with her shake filled to the brim and topped with whipped cream. "Sixty-five cents, please." Marjorie slid a dollar over and sighed at such a beautiful price. "Thank you very much," she said. "Keep the change."

She sipped up the shake, listening in on the few conversations between the other diners: two ladies at a booth, an older man chatting with the waitress, a gray fedora set beside him at the far end of the counter, and a young couple giggling in the booth by the window. But her ears wandered back to the sounds of the radio as it now played Elvis's "I Want You, I Need You, I Love You," her favorite tune of his and what she considered vastly underrated.

The bell above the front door rang and in came a young man in a big gray wool coat, clutching what looked like envelopes and a newspaper. She thought it was a cigarette behind his ear, but a second glance and she realized it was a pen. "Good afternoon, Miss Alice!" he shouted, waving to the woman who had taken Marjorie's order.

"Curtis Fuller!" she exclaimed. "Now I hope you're here for your usual chili dog and Coke and *not* a job—Mr. Beales from Hodges already phoned me for a heads-up, and I've told your mama we're plain full here."

"Oh, Miss Alice, 'suppose you could just take in one more spare hand around here?" He pulled up to the seat next to Marjorie. "Mama didn't say anything to me, so how was I supposed to know? And Mr. Beales didn't even read these letters, which I know is a mistake you won't be making."

"It's a mistake unfortunately I'll have to make. And you know it's not my call, but if I were to talk to the man himself, I wouldn't hear the end of it about scheduling and, Lord forbid, upping prices to cut costs. I'm sorry, Curtis, we're not looking and I can't budge, no matter how often it is I see you and your family here and that it would break my heart to say no to any of y'all."

"You sure won't, ma'am." He sighed. "And I'll just have to accept. Well, while I'm here you can fix me one of those dogs, if you please, and ooh!

Excuse me, ma'am—" He turned over to look at Marjorie, straw between her red lips and chocolate on the corners of her mouth. "But that looks pretty good. Mind if I ask you what it is?"

Marjorie quickly gulped and pursed her lips tightly. "Not at all, it's mint chocolate chip."

"Swell! I'll take a mint chocolate chip shake as well, Miss Alice." While Alice disappeared, Curtis turned again to Marjorie, his smile still as wide and uncracked as when he had first walked in. "Thanks again for the inspiration," he said cheerfully. "It's just what I needed after a long day."

She laughed. "It's only one o'clock."

"I know! And a beautiful day like this shouldn't have a guy like me feeling beat. But I gotta keep moving on, persist and look for something in this miserable town. But first, a refuel." He held out his hand. "I'm Curtis Fuller, and you are?"

"Marjorie Valdez," she replied, taking his hand and gently shaking it. "Nice to meet you, Curtis."

"Valdez, huh? Spanish?"

"Filipino."

"Oh, no kidding! I know we're pretty friendly with the Filipinos. But you sound like a Yankee, are you not from the Philippines?"

"Nope, born and raised in the States. Full on American, if you can believe it."

"Oh I do, ma'am. Say, *you* know anyone who is hiring?"

Marjorie shook her head and smirked. "I do not—I just got barely hired as is. It was my first day, in fact."

"The way you say that makes me think it wasn't the best first day."

"It could have been worse. Mind you, I haven't been in such a people-facing position in a long time."

His face perked up even more than Marjorie thought it could. "Do you think they'll need help, at your job?"

"Unless you'd like to be a receptionist, I doubt you'd want to help."

"Oh, I'm not picky, although reception isn't what I was aiming for since it's mostly for ladies. Just something fun, quick, hands-on, and pays good. But I've only hit up half of the Square for prospective places, so there's still hope! Sounds like you and I are having quite a day, though, when it comes to earning our keeps. Where are you as a receptionist?"

"A hair salon, but I don't think you'd know it."

"On the Square? My mama and sister go to Miss Birdelle's down the street from here."

Marjorie shook her head. "No, it's not here on the Square," she told him. "When I get more settled, I plan to look around for something more fitting to my skills, but until then, I hope I can keep this job."

"What makes you so doubtful about it now?" he asked as Alice came back with another shake and slid it over to Curtis. "Being a receptionist can't be that tough."

"Oh, it can. When you're trying to check out two clients back-to-back and then the phone is going off, right as a mother with two rowdy kids walks in without an appointment—like, if you were me, how would *you* have handled it?" Curtis was sipping on his shake as he laughed a little.

"Goodness, I couldn't say. What did you end up doing?"

"Well, since screaming into my hands wouldn't have solved anything, I focused on the people in front of me, told the mom to wait, and I let the phone ring out. But that's just one curveball thrown at me for my first day—there were others."

More sips. "And what were those?"

"I miscounted the cash drawer, and some stylists weren't tipped right, one not at all—she was missing twenty-two bucks. We figured it out later, thank God for Alex, who'd been doing my job along with haircutting before I came along. The real kicker was the two Matthews."

"Two Matthews?"

This time Marjorie didn't sip on the straw but put her lips to the glass—the whipped cream was a melted film on top that she drank down with ease. "So Matthew Collins, he booked for eleven this morning with our owner, Nelson. And mind you it was such a busy morning! Everyone had a person in their chair. Well, in comes a guy practically on the dot, and he said he's Matthew for Nelson, so I brought him over to the chair and Nelson came out, no problem. Only just a few minutes after the actual Matthew Collins walks through, apologizing for how late he was."

"So, who was the other Matthew?"

"Matthew Rogers. Can you believe not just the timing—of all Nelson's other clients, another Matthew?"

They were both now laughing, with Curtis holding out his shake to cheers with hers. "That is some rotten luck, or a darn good coincidence! So Matthew Rogers just waltzed in thinking his barber was available, huh?"

"Nope. Turns out, Matthew Rogers did book for an eleven o'clock but the following Wednesday. He'd booked it online and didn't even double check the date."

"Booked online?"

"Oh! Online, it's uh—a special system that we have. Very new and limited, but I'm sure it'll be everywhere in the future. Anyway, that was my day. And when you land your job here on the Marietta Square, I only hope you have half my luck!"

"Thank you, Miss Marjorie. I've been in school for a while and haven't had a job in a few years, but I like to think I'm a fast learner! I'm determined to land something. I need to save up some money if I'm gonna try and transfer out west. I wanna study political science." He looked around and lowered his voice. "At Berkeley."

"I'm from Berkeley! Well, just outside of Oakland. I lived in San Francisco for a while, and I think you'll find the Bay Area a wonderful place. Is Marietta too small town for you?"

"I love it! It's home. But I want to go far and be adventurous. We just got our forty-ninth state and I reckon I need to visit them all at some point in my life. And also change some things if I can help it. The South is going through so much right now with all these stupid old laws, and no one gets that it's unnatural to keep any American citizen apart, no matter their race. These changes are supposed to move the country forward for the better! Lots of folks around here don't think it best to try getting into civil rights since we've got a lot in our own lives to still figure out, but if there's a place I can go and learn to fix things for the better then take me there as fast as I can. Once I have the money of course."

"Well, sounds like you're just what the country needs. We may not have our stuff all figured out, but I can see you have a big heart and bravery for trying to do more and move out of here."

"Why thank you, Miss Marjorie! Say, do you have another minute to tell me about California?" Alice came back with a steaming plate of a chili dog and fries for Curtis, and while he pulled the plate closer to pour some ketchup, Marjorie looked up at the big clock.

"I wish I could," she responded with a sigh. "But I'm terribly sorry to tell you I need to get going. I might be late for an appointment."

"I understand. Just make sure it's an appointment meant for you and not another Marjorie."

She laughed, getting up and slipping her blue coat back on. She turned to Curtis and held out her hand. "Curtis, it's been a pleasure and I wish you all the luck on your journey. And I hope to see you around here working behind the counter somewhere after all!"

"Likewise, Miss Marjorie. Our conversation gave me the confidence I need for these big plans. I'm heading over to Johnny Walker's and Atherton's on the other side of the Square to see what luck I might have with them. But I won't keep you any longer, I enjoyed our talk and hope to see you again!"

She smiled and headed toward the door and out back onto Church Street. She walked to the edge of the sidewalk and closed her eyes. Taking a big breath, she felt a cold sting as the temperature dropped, and she turned around to look back at Hunt's. But the small restaurant had disappeared—in its place the same building that had been covered in a cream stucco before now had its brick exposed, the windows still wide but revealing not a diner but instead two rows of six salon stations along the walls. Overhead hung a neon green sign that read NELSON'S just turning on as the sunlight dimmed at a little past five. The large scissors that hung over the door confirmed that Nelson's was indeed a hair salon. One, in fact, that had opened eleven years ago in 2012 on the Marietta Square.

Just like that, Marjorie was back in the present.

Chapter 1

She'd already missed her first Pie Night. The full moon had been last Tuesday, but Marjorie was so overwhelmed with the last of her unpacking to remember. One tradition she wanted to begin, and she'd already missed it. Well, starting Pie Night on a Friday night was certainly just as good of a start.

When she'd found Dogwood Daze advertised online for lease back in January, she knew she'd have wonderful times on that wide front porch. And with haint blue on the ceiling, no less! The porch, with soft pistachio shutters on wide windows leading up to the peach-colored front door to the right, won her over even before seeing the interior. There had never been a porch in her twenty-nine years of life, not when growing up, certainly not at relatives' houses out in Daly City, and especially not the Grant Street apartment—it had a wide, covered stoop, but who sat around the stoop of a big apartment complex in the middle of a city like San Francisco?

Thinking back on Grant Street, she remembered the costume party she scrambled together one Halloween, her studio being a perfect pregame spot before everyone went down to the bars off Columbus Avenue. Dressed as Wednesday Addams, she had an enthralling, wasteful night with people she held dear in those years they all worked side by side at that stupid startup on the Embarcadero. And then the next morning when she was alone, about to walk on her usual morning coffee run, she stepped out of her apartment and looked down. There at her feet was an empty Newcastle glass bottle. It would have freaked her out had she not remembered the evening before seeing Steve Yu chugging and dropping it by the tree at the bottom of the complex's front steps. Fear turned into embarrassment, realizing her neighbors had simply picked up the mess for her to clean herself.

Marjorie hoped these new neighbors wouldn't act in such passive aggressive ways. This was the South after all, and she set her sights on some of that renowned hospitality. It'd only been a few weeks, and now that the moving was coming along, actually living was next—starting with pie on this porch. She layered two wool blankets on her lap and placed on top a paper plate of Pecan Bourbon pie. In a matching paper cup nearby was some coffee, heavy on the cream and brown sugar—as Marjorie herself joked, she loved her sugar with coffee. *Proper china,* she made a mental note for her next jaunt to Goodwill. She had just gotten comfy but grunted, realizing that she had forgotten the other essential—the vinyl. She reached over to her red Crosley portable player and put the needle down to play *The Platters Greatest Hits*.

She took her first bite of the pie and scanned the sky, making sure that the moon was in view—it would have been ironic to observe a pie night if you couldn't even see the pie in the sky. It was barely illuminating through the big tree across the street in her neighbor's yard. Officially a perfect night after a week of unboxing, calling her family, setting up the cable and internet. Surprisingly in an old house like this, getting the Wi-Fi in place had been the easiest task. Now, she looked down at the Crosley, "Only You" crooning softly into the night, loud enough to echo through the tall ceilings of the porch but of no real disturbance to the surrounding houses.

She wondered if it would happen tonight, with the record player out. It had happened before with music. Perhaps it was the raw emotions that melodies drew from the energy field or within herself that sent her back to those forgotten moments. And if tonight was a traveling night, she felt anxious. Her landlord, Caroline, told her only so much about the house's history—built in 1907, three different owners, and the last having been a gentleman who grew up in the house, and died in it back in 2015. She could meet him tonight, get a glimpse into the life that had unfolded before her arrival.

She just had to give it time. After all these years, she still had never figured out the logic of any of it—let alone why this talent or gift or whatever it was had been bestowed upon her. She learned to stop killing herself over the many questions and resigned to just going with the flow—in her case, the flow backward. Minimal manipulation or interaction was one single rule she made, but her travels seemed not to have any real effect or change on the course of time, as far as she knew. A sip of her coffee, another bite. The record skipped but smoothed itself out, and the serenade continued. Another sip. How the heat of the drink melted and merged with the creamy smokiness of the pie, that's what really warmed her up on a cold night such as this.

Suddenly, she felt the cold grow densely around her and the music began to fade. The sky seemed lighter and an old Chevy truck drove through Morris Road, still paved but brown and dusty in the dimming light. The truck didn't look too old, sharper around the edges, sometime in the early seventies. Up the street, a neighbor's '72 Ford was parked in their driveway. Learning cars had been her best bet at understanding exactly what year she was in.

The Platters stopped playing as the faint murmur of a television from inside the house grew loud behind her. Keeping in mind that she was no longer in *her* house, she got up from where she sat and crept away to the side and out of the light—she was unsure how these owners would act should they come out and find a stranger reclining on their big porch. She could be there all night. How long she would stay across the decades was never certain.

But suddenly, like an echo, a faint buzz began to grow in the silence. Marjorie looked down at her phone, forgetting it had been tucked away in her skirt pocket. Her muscles relaxed as she looked back at the porch and hurried over to the folding chair that now sat where she had left it in 2023—any trace of Dogwood in 1972 had instantly disappeared.

"Hello?" Marjorie answered her phone.

"Honey!" said her mom, Julia, on the other end. "What are you up to? You OK? I called four times."

"Sorry, I was inside the house," Marjorie told her. "Everything OK, Mommy?"

"Yeah, your dad and I are fine. You scared me though, honey, what are you doing tonight? You're not out, are you?"

"No, of course not, I just said I was home—eating pie."

"Hmm. Well, instead of being alone in a strange place you could be out with friends or hanging with your dad and me—Eileen's bringing the littles over, and we're always sad you can't be here to play with them."

"Oh, they're gonna be fine! I'm gonna try and come back in May for Daddy's birthday, remember?"

"That's still so far. Daddy's still upset you're not here. It doesn't make sense when you only moved out there for a job that got cut weeks after."

"It doesn't have to make sense. I am an adult, Mom, and I made my decision. I want to stay here for a while."

"You can't even support yourself with that job—you didn't go to college for four years to be a receptionist!"

"Well, everything's super cheap out here, I'll manage. And even before I got laid off, I was burnt out and stressed out like hell, but I'm getting peace of mind right now. With this job, this town, taking things easy while I can afford to."

"But Marietta? I don't even know where that is."

Marjorie let out a big sigh. "It's just outside Atlanta. The opportunities are still here! I'm just not looking for them right now."

A long pause on the phone passed before Julia began, "Just all a waste of time. And money. You need to come home soon, Marjorie."

"This *is* home," she retorted. "It may not feel that way to you, but this is where I need to be right now, Mommy. Believe it or not, I'm over San Francisco, the big city—this place is beautiful, and I'd hoped you and Daddy and Eileen could come see it for yourselves."

Another pause. "Doesn't make sense at all," Julia said stiffly.

"Well, Mommy, I gotta go now. I'm trying to enjoy this night, and you ranting and raving on the phone isn't helping."

"What's to enjoy when you're all alone?"

"Ugh, Mommy! I'll call you before I go to bed. I love you."

"I love you too, honey. We just miss you."

Marjorie missed her family too. As peaceful as Pie Night was here, home was not a place to feel lonelier. She'd like to make friends here, get settled, and turn these tiny new traditions of hers into moments enjoyed by others. From all she had seen of this town, past and present, she could see it being home.

But there was something– someone – in between the roads and building pieces of the past that brought her here. She had to still keep looking—and keep traveling.

Chapter 2

Just off the town Square where Duncan Road and Moss Springs Road intersected along the train tracks was perhaps the best variety of pies in Marietta.

Marietta. The musical sound its name made even as it was whispered could make your heart skip a beat, charming for a town here in the heart of Georgia, where Marjorie was ready to start anew. A place like this, rich in history with so much of the town preserved since its founding in 1834, got her excited, thinking about where in time her gift would take her. But until then, she had to get into a morning rhythm—little things like brushing out her rolled hair, putting on a dress, and getting coffee before starting her days at the new job. By now, she'd gotten her walks to town down and figured cutting through the nearby cemetery shaved off a mere four minutes. Old headstones scattered on her stroll seemed like dull pearls in the morning light; when she had enough time again, she planned to lazily walk by them all and learn more about the souls who lived and thrived before her.

A bare tree marked the corner of Caroline's Pie and Other Loves, with red bistro table and chairs set across the wide front windows that popped against the shop. She crossed the tracks and headed inside, coming face-to-face with the long pie display and butcher block counter seating, the scents of toasted coconut and fresh-brewed coffee lingering in the air. Some pies were pure green with dollops of whipped cream and graham cracker crumbles, others darkened by flambéed egg white peaks on top of dark, flaky crusts. Chocolate was drizzled in a webby coating on the fluffy chocolate mousse one that Marjorie couldn't take her eyes off.

"Good morning!" greeted the young woman behind the counter. "Let us know if you have any questions."

"Thank you! I will," Marjorie said. It had gotten stuffy, and she removed the red beret that was hung on her loosely flipped curls. "You know what, I'll have a slice of this one, please," she followed, tapping on the glass where the chocolate drizzle pie was. "And a cup of coffee too. I was also wondering, is Caroline in today?"

"Great choice, and yes! She is. Can I let her know who would like to talk to her?"

"Absolutely! Just let her know it's Marjorie Valdez, please."

She sat down with her slice of pie and coffee at a small enamel kitchen table by the front window where red gingham curtains fluttered overhead. The walls varied in light blues and soft yellows, while all the tables and dishes were vintage and intentionally mismatched, and the chairs painted in the same red shade. It was as if you were grabbing some pie in your friend's house rather than a renowned local establishment that had won the Best of Cobb award for dessert consecutively since the early 2000s.

A short-haired brunette woman wearing a linen apron over a red Fair Isle sweater emerged from the swinging door on the back wall and smiled as she hovered over Marjorie's table. "And look what the cat dragged in!" she exclaimed. "From one of my doorsteps to another. How's everything? The place doing alright for you?"

Marjorie had taken a bite but quickly gulped it down and dabbed her lips on a napkin, careful not to smudge her crimson lipstick. "Hello! Thanks for coming out here. I didn't mean to bother you if you were busy but just wanted to say hi. Oh, and this pie—"

"New creation!" Caroline excitedly interjected. "Well, not new, but tweaked. Peanut Butter Drizzle with more chocolate than before. Perfect balance, wouldn't you say?"

"Perfection indeed. I'm just happy to finally stop in when you were here, and fate would have it that I chose the right slice today. I'll definitely be coming by more to take them all."

"Don't feel like you have to, darling! You already are paying for the house. But by all means, I won't turn down extra cash coming my way." She winked and took a seat opposite Marjorie.

"That house is worth every penny. I still can't get over how spacious it really is! I don't know what I'm even gonna need the two extra bedrooms for. But that gas fire is a nice addition and gets so hot! Not that that's a bad thing with these current temperatures."

"Good, good! Yeah, the house was in pretty bad shape when we got it. That fireplace's brick was just crumbling, but glad we could save that mosaic mantle. I like to think I'm a considerate landlord—it makes my blood boil thinking of how many just cheapen their places by painting white over *everything*."

"You truly are. I really enjoy the original fixtures you managed to preserve. Didn't think I'd get so lucky to find a place so historic."

"I always assumed many people your age don't really care about aesthetics or fixtures. Good reception, plenty of outlets, hot water, yes. But not old fireplaces or beadboard panels on the walls. I didn't even know what beadboard was until you said it on our first walkthrough."

"Oh, hot water is a must! But the charm is a huge bonus. The front porch light is flickering, though, if that's something of concern?"

"I'll get Cameron to go over there and fix it in the next few days. But glad nothing else seems to be falling apart. You have my number, though, or you know, just come down to the Square and get pie."

"Exactly! One less thing to worry about. It's off to the Square right after here, I haven't really seen it besides passing it on the way to work."

"How's everything at Nelson's so far?"

"An even quicker walk than I expected, and all the stylists are sweet. It's really nice to have found something right downtown, and to live close by as well is a miracle. Although Nelson's been so booked that I barely have time to really talk to him."

"You don't miss much, darling. He's always quiet, but very active in the Merchants Association, him and his wife, Lara Jean, who you'll meet if you ever pop into the History Museum. They always bring coffee and Krispy Kremes for us at meetings—that says a lot to me. But that's just me, where the way to this woman's heart is through anything sweet." Caroline finally stood up and slyly grabbed the crumpled napkin Marjorie had left on the table. "Glad you stopped in and enjoy your day on the Square. You have my number for anything, remember!"

A deep bellow of a whistle sounded in the distance, and seconds later the pie shop rattled softly against the train rolling by. Marjorie didn't want to miss the full spectacle and finished her pie quickly before heading out to the back trail by the tracks. Rusted containers latched to the beds of the passing CSX engine glided by only a few feet beyond the iron fence, giving Marjorie a sense of thrill and fear that one of the cars could easily derail in a second and fall over on her.

She continued walking along the back trail after the train passed, crossing over to the farmer's market pitched in the parking lot on the other side of the tracks. She was about to head over to pick through a stall of wildflower bouquets but was distracted by the sound of little yips and woofs. Cobb County Animal Shelter had set up a small pen nearby to let a few of their available dogs wander and mingle with people. She lingered over and admired the few puppies and small mixed breeds and the one big mastiff that wagged its tail in a slow, steady motion as he went from person to person sniffing. She planned on getting a pet sometime, but it was too soon to make that call. He made her miss Carl. That was the big Dalmatian-Lab mix that she had grown up with, and he always reminded her that there were thousands of dogs out in shelters that needed a home. Once she'd figured out the hang of things with her job and getting Dogwood Daze in order—she hadn't even asked if a pet was OK with Caroline—then she'd think of adopting.

She was turning to leave when she looked up at the mobile van that had other dogs displayed on side enclosures. Her eyes became fixed on something slightly moving in the bottom left window and went over to find a powder-faced black dog with sleepy brown eyes and frosty caramel brows between small floppy ears. His head kept moving left and right to look at all the commotion and it was as if he were smiling at the hope of any human looking over his way. Taped to the inside of his window was all his information:

NAME: DOC

AGE: 10 YEARS OLD

GENDER: NEUTERED MALE

BREED: MIXED

INTAKE: OWNER TURN IN

That last note got to her. She placed her hand out as old Doc drew his snout close to the glass to sniff her. *Such a darling old man*, she thought, and how heartbreaking that someone would give him up so late in his little life. She took a deep breath and looked around her for an assistant. "Hi there!" she said to someone emerging from the van. "I'd like to meet Mr. Doc, please."

...

There was no doubt now that Marjorie needed to get a car quickly. Doc was still spry and energetic once he was out of the van, and now that they were walking across the tracks and back toward the Marietta Square, it was apparent he was a puller. It had been years since she'd handled a dog on her own, but he was old, and she firmly held on to the green leash that the volunteer had given her and pulled lightly back when Doc would try to go faster. At the intersection of Moss Springs Road and West Square Street, he led them both up the red brick sidewalk and aptly relieved himself on a tree. It was a long pee, and as she waited for him, Marjorie could only think of how long he'd been holding it stuck in that crate. She saw a door between the smoothie and boba shop that looked like it went to the upstairs floor. Outside a sandwich board had in big chalk letters BOOKSTORE OPEN TODAY – BRING IN YOUR FUR BABIES.

Up the creaking stairs, she found a central round room where a table of featured authors for Black History Month were displayed. A back hall led to the register and in the two front rooms stacked floor to ceiling in books were large bay windows overlooking the west side of the Square. A bookstore in town, as if she couldn't love this town any more! While other people were scattered around the rooms browsing, a woman with her hands full of books made her way to the front and warmly greeted Marjorie. "Let me know if you or this guy needs anything!" She bent down to Doc and smiled. "May I say hello?"

"Of course!" said Marjorie. "He's very sweet and friendly. I actually just adopted him today."

"Did you? That's awesome! He's so well behaved, I got a soft spot for old dogs. From the farmer's market, right? I can't make it over there without bawling my eyes out and wanting to take all those dogs back home when I really just wanna go get some bread."

Marjorie liked this lady already. She seemed her age, or at most early thirties, with long dark blonde hair and a green turtleneck over patchwork denim jeans. "Basically! I figured if I had to pick one, it'd be this guy. Always heartbreaking to see seniors being the last to get noticed."

"Well, thank God for people like you." She kept her gaze on Marjorie, eyes wide. "Dude, you live in my neighborhood! I've totally seen you around these past weeks walking, and you're always dressed up! The cute, colorful headscarves and the long coats. You're like the Jackie O of Morris! Is that just your thing or are you a model?"

"You're so sweet, I'm no model, though. But a small world! I live in that white house with the peach door. Are you close to it?"

"Ah, that's a cute place. Yeah, I live with my sister a few houses down across the street. I'm Benny, short for Bernadette. Nice to meet you, neighbor!"

"Likewise, Benny! I'm Marjorie, some call me Marge."

"Wow, never hear that name anymore! But then again, when have you met a Bernadette?"

"At first I thought it was short for Benita, my great aunt's name. But still, yay us!"

"Aren't we special! But hey, I'll let you guys get back to looking around, I'm here if you need anything—or just stop by the house whenever you're feeling neighborly!"

"Thanks! Actually, I was curious if you have a special section or books that focus specifically on Marietta or Cobb County history? Being new to town, I could definitely use some of those."

"If you're looking to get familiar with Marietta, I'd say follow the city Instagram or join a local Facebook group, girl! But yeah, we have a few specifics. In the history shelves in the back room, under Georgia History."

"Perfect. It's nothing current I'm looking for. The history for me has just always been a good place to start to get a feel of the place. Read up on its bones."

The book she did find, a compilation of photo archives from the *Marietta Daily Journal* dating from the 1880s to now, was a great start. She sat in the Square with its neatly arranged paths that intersected past the big bandstand and ornate little gazebo with its green roof and met at the dark iron fountain at the center of the park. She thumbed through the book and looked down at Doc, who was lying at her feet, still smiling, looking around until his face met hers.

"And so it all begins," she said to him with a smile, rubbing his head behind his tiny ears. "For the both of us."

Chapter 3

What luck that Saint Patrick's Day fell on a rainy Friday. In shades of green, the salon felt more cheerful than the day outside, and mood was all that mattered to John Nelson. Marjorie herself was glowing in her jade sheath dress with a pop of pink beads strung around her neck. It was a hair-up day since she'd washed it on Monday and the curls were loosening—the full effect had her feeling a little bit like Joan from *Mad Men*. Thursdays and Fridays were Nelson's busiest days of the week, but it made the hours go by fast toward a calm weekend.

The rain didn't deter clients, but just a few arrived late. Marjorie was getting comfortable with her own rapport of greeting clients and anticipating who was for which stylist based on the calendar. She had just walked over Addie's client to her chair when she saw clumps of hair scattered about Jeff's and Nelson's stations. She took up the broom and dustpan to sweep in quick sharp jolts, like a hockey shot—there was something so therapeutic about doing it that way. She was wrapping up when she felt a tap on her shoulder and turned to see her boss.

"Lunch today," Nelson said, taking off his Wayfarer glasses to wipe on his dark green flannel shirt—to Marjorie, he looked like a silver-haired Buddy Holly. "I'm going to need you to head to the Merchants Association Assembly at one, since I'm booked through three."

"Oh! Absolutely," she responded. "And where do they usually host it?"

"It's just down the street at The Strand. Lara Jean's coming by here before so you both can walk together."

"Perfect! Glad I can help. Anything I need to speak about for the salon?"

"Nope. Nothing today. Just take notes. It's gonna be fun—you'll be meeting the finest of Marietta's own."

Marjorie waited at the front desk as one o'clock approached, looking around the salon and thinking back to that first day. The medallion ceilings still loomed high above and exposed brick peeped through all the walls where Nelson had hung up various old advertisements for cars and local businesses. It was rustic but clean; had old touches but was not stuffy. Nelson's was an inviting place to come in for a haircut, and a bit of history too.

Marjorie's heart pounded when a green '48 Chevy pickup truck pulled to the curb in front of the salon, and for a second she thought she was traveling again. But a tall woman with long black curls waved to her through the window—it was Lara Jean Nelson, Nelson's wife and the director of the Marietta History Museum. It made complete sense that history enthusiasts like her and Nelson would drive around town in a classic car—it was actually how Marjorie landed her job, having seen it around the Square in those first few days she'd moved to town, with NELSON'S SALON ON THE SQUARE painted in big letters on the truck doors.

Lara Jean didn't bother to take her coat off when she came in, only greeting Marjorie with an enthused "Hello my dear! You got an umbrella, I hope?"

"I didn't think it'd get this bad today," confessed Marjorie, grabbing her trench and headscarf. "But I'm prepared to run!"

"Oh hush, you can share mine! We don't have too far a walk anyhow. Excited for your first MMA?"

"Nelson only told me so much about it. Does it get really busy?"

"Depends on the businesses. We have our usual cluster of reps, but if someone's busy sometimes they don't show at all. This is gonna be an interesting day, Saint Patrick's in the rain. Who knows what we'll get!"

Beneath Lara Jean's clear umbrella, they walked in the rain back down Church and left on North Park Square toward The Strand Theatre right on the corner. Its grand marquee was marvelously splashed in red and gold and dotted with bulbs that glowed overhead. A digital screen had WELCOME MARIETTA MERCHANTS displayed below where the STRAND letters stood, its neon lighting switched off. Inside it felt like an old movie house should, Marjorie thought to herself as they made their way past the concessions stand with its high ceiling to the stairs leading up to the mezzanine level. The theater itself was grand with the tall stage and a white screen dropped before rows of red seating and flanked by red walls paneled in gold art deco shapes. The mezzanine hovered above, although most merchants were huddled in a cluster of seats right before the stage, close to where an old organ was raised and looked lonely to Marjorie. On a long table off to the right of the stage were boxes of donuts and hot coffee ready to be poured into paper cups.

Marjorie followed behind Lara Jean, who began greeting people and ushered her to two seats toward the middle. Next to Marjorie was an elderly Black man in a tweed three-piece suit and dark green driving cap, and in the row in front of him sat Caroline herself.

"Of all the gin joints in the world!" she said to Marjorie before turning to Lara Jean. "I figured you'd drag her to one of these things, LJ. Nelson backed up again, I take it?"

"Mm-hmm," replied Marjorie, "I'm just here to take notes. I recognize a few faces already, but it'll be nice to formally meet everyone."

"Speaking of everyone, Marjorie, that distinguished fellow next to you is Art Martin from the menswear store Art of Threads, just a few doors down from Nelson's."

"That is true." Art spoke up and held out his hand to Marjorie's. "A pleasure, Miss Marjorie, we're happy to have you as our neighbor. Nelson's a fine hairdresser, no one can deal with curls like that man can." He lifted his cap to show Marjorie.

"And no one can deal with your unannounced pop-ins like my husband does," Lara Jean teased. "You've been warned, Marjorie, this man never makes an appointment."

"That's the beauty of being neighbors." Art laughed. "And most of the time Nelson can always squeeze me in."

"I will not be surprised for the future then," Marjorie responded with a smile.

"I hope you're liking our little town. Pretty, and plenty to do around here like the art festivals and the concert series in the summer. You're gonna love those! All the festivities will make you forget how hot and sticky it is."

"And for those hot and sticky days when you do want to listen to music inside somewhere cool," began the gray-haired man with glasses and a navy blue pullover on Caroline's other side, "You can just pop on into ours for a good time. I'm Alvin, or just Al! This is my husband Ken." He patted Ken on the back, who Marjorie could tell had a big smile under his thick red mustache as he shook her hand. "And we own Aloud Records and the Marietta Mercantile on the south side of the Square."

"Well, the Mercantile is my baby," Ken added. "I love my local artisans and Alvin loves his records."

"Well, I've got a small record player and an even smaller collection, which I'll need to build up with your help, Al," said Marjorie, beaming at him.

"Who you got in your collection so far?" Al asked with raised brows.

"I mostly stick to older artists so I don't get overwhelmed trying to buy newer stuff. Dean Martin, The Ronettes, Beatles, Frankie Valli, Linda Ronstadt, Elton John—to name a few."

"Those are oldies but goodies! The classics just hit differently on vinyl. But I am always happy to help you expand and give recommendations."

All the chatter across the different sides of the room began to quiet down as one woman ascended the stage and raised her hands for everyone's attention. She wore a yellow sweater dress with emerald earrings and wore her honey-blonde hair back in a braided chignon that showed a few gray streaks.

"Good afternoon, y'all!" she began, speaking through a mic. "It's good to see a lot of you again, and a few new faces, which we'll know soon enough after we all go around the room. Welcome back to our monthly Marietta Merchants Association Assembly, and for those who don't know, I'm Luanne Sullivan, Marietta city commerce manager, who leads these gatherings and kicks them off with updates straight from the city. There is nothing new, in fact, other than the brick replacement around the south side of the Square is still going on until next Thursday, and closures are still in effect for Moss Springs Road, so if you could, we recommend letting your clients, shoppers, or diners know that until then, there is no street parking or throughway for another week."

A soft groan from Caroline.

"And moving on into spring, it's just around the corner! And so the city will be replacing the mulch in the Square along with all the tulips that line the paths leading up to the fountain. This should be started and completed the week of April third. Alright, let's go around the room with all your announcements before we circle back to last month's business and public safety!"

Other businesses present were Molly's Stationery Shop, The Australian Bakery, Brennen-Hoffstadt Art Gallery, Daffodaisies Children's Store, The Pop Shop Soda & Candy, Eddie's Magic & Costumes, and Four Aces Tattoo & Piercing. It soon came to Marjorie's turn to speak, and after her quick introduction, a few welcomes were spoken up to her before she quickly sat back down and was patted gently on the back by Art, who then stood up and began his updates. In a few minutes, it was back to Luanne, who wore a big smile.

"Thank you everyone for sharing! And Marjorie, I want to personally welcome you to Marietta, and I'm sure you can see for yourself, but know that you're in with a good bunch. We're always happy to take care of our own here. Which brings me to"—she looked down to a pile of papers laid out before her and thumbed through an email she had printed out—"a debatably hospitable announcement. Following discussions from our last assembly in January, Northfield Properties have officially taken over ownership of the northwest block of Church Street between Wells and Polk. They assured the city not much is going to change for tenants, despite perhaps some exterior updates and backlot parking renovations later in the summer." Luanne's stiff smile said much in the awkward silence that followed the announcement. Nelson's was a part of that block of buildings she mentioned, and Marjorie wondered what changes, if any, might come from this new ownership—and if Nelson was already aware. Based on the disgruntled mumbles around her, it didn't sound like Northfield was good news.

Luanne then turned to the police officer standing next to her on the stage. "And now to Officer Dennison on public safety updates." Officer Dennison was an older, muscular man with thinning silver hair beneath the aviator sunglasses he pushed up on his forehead. He had a pleasant smile, though, that put Marjorie at ease and a high voice.

"Well, it's a new year but old problems that I'll address first. Since last Chalktoberfest the loud horde of street preaching youth seem to have doubled down at all our sidewalk events, more on each corner, and they seem to have gotten bolder with the use of amplifiers."

"Jesus, how are they even powering it?" asked Kevin.

"Well, it's just a Bluetooth and mic, Kevin. Technology is new and to them so is the gospel, but the disruption is being heard loud and clear by concerned citizens who continue to remark on how loud and aggressive they're getting."

"Isn't there like a noise ordinance?" Caroline chimed in. "Or a solicitation violation?"

"Soliciting, yes, which is why they're on the corners or in the park. But it's tricky, there is a thing called the First Amendment, after all."

"I believe there is a permit that is needed for the use of external tools or equipment like those speakers," Luanne added. "The city can look into it and confirm, but until then just record all intakes from the city."

Officer Dennison nodded. "And now to new concerns." He turned to the small projector set up on the other side of the stage where he had pulled up an image of a man on the sidewalk near the Marietta Pizza Corner entrance on the west side, only the man was standing in a terracotta pot and covered in a costume that basically resembled army camouflage with artificial twigs and leaves. "No complaints from citizens, but we're keeping an eye on a prankster who sits idly as a bush until popping out at unsuspecting passersby. He moves around, so that's been hindering our efforts. If he's sitting more than thirty minutes in front of your business, take note or give the city a call. While just harmless now, this could turn into an unexpected escalation."

Marjorie couldn't help smiling a little. Growing up with family visits to Fisherman's Wharf or Union Square, she was feeling nostalgic for San Francisco's infamous Bush Man, and now of all places, she found herself in a town with one of their own. It didn't sound like a safety concern—to her, it was a comfort.

She heard a snicker next to her. "Oh, come now, Walt," began Art. "If there's been no complaints, just let the man be."

Dennison looked to Art with narrowed eyes. "None yet, Art, but you don't want to wait until it is too late."

Art turned to Marjorie. "There's some TikTok video showing the prankster startling Mr. Dennison here," he revealed. "New Year's Eve. All laughs, except for you, Walt! Just 'cause you got pranked—"

"I am just saying, what if someone who was actually violent started beating the guy, or worse, pulled a gun on him?" Art chuckled a little while Dennison continued, "And as for that video, for the record, I was off duty that night and just gave the man a stern warning. I'd hope he'd adhere to my words, but it seems he thinks he's above the law."

"But you just said you were off duty," said Al. "So, it wasn't like you gave an official citation."

"Regardless, he still should not be harassing our Square!" said Dennison. "As soon as he gets one of you guys, I'm sure you'll be feeling the same way. Well, that's all my updates." He sat down to let Luanne take the floor once more, and she broke the lingering silence with a graceful laugh. "Don't we love our town!"

After the meeting was over, Lara Jean stayed back to chat with Officer Dennison while Marjorie felt the need for some air. As she went past the concessions and opened the door to go back out into the rain, she nearly collided with Benny, who was walking in. "Oh fuck!" Benny cried.

"Benny!" said Marjorie. "What are you doing here?" Her neighbor rested her hand against the door and took a few slow breaths before she flashed her a big smile.

"Hey! I just hauled ass over when I realized what day it was. It's over, isn't it?"

"Yeeahhh," Marjorie admitted. "I mean, I can let you see my notes if you want?"

"Nah, save it! Just come by for wine or something later. I'll walk back with you!" She reopened her emerald-green umbrella that seemed large enough to fit almost a dozen people.

"I probably should wait for Lara Jean. She's just talking with some people inside the theater."

"Miss Lara Jean! You're besties with one of Marietta's first family dames now?"

"First family?"

"Uh-huh. You've got the Brumbys, Northcutts, Archers, Rambos, Hunters, Coles, McCollums, and Clearys. Street signs, buildings, and people—they still pervade the town. Before she married Nelson, Miss Lara Jean was a Cleary, one of the more prominent families with quite a few successful Black businesses here in town way back in the day."

"Had no idea. That's pretty cool there's still the old families like that around here."

"It's even better to be on their good side and have the pull with them. Sounds like you're making moves fast, meeting the who's who around here." Marjorie slightly smiled at this revelation—in all her travels, she really never had met anyone famous or of some local stature.

"Would have liked to have met some of the chefs or restaurant owners, though."

Benny laughed and looked over Marjorie's shoulder. "Most of the restaurants never come to these things," she said. "Anyway, you don't need to meet them—you just have to go eat!"

Chapter 4

Spring finally came to Marietta. Happily Marjorie kept the bedroom curtains drawn back so that the soft light of the dawn could seep in through the blinds and cast an awakening glow. Doc wasn't bothered by it—with the peaceful sprawl among the disheveled blankets without fuss from his human, he wouldn't have minded much. But spring mornings, Marjorie had waited for them with eager joy. Dead branches were resurrected with bright green buds that would bloom into small pink and white flowers, the cardinals would start singing again, and for herself, the sundresses were about to come out in full force.

She had her travels to thank for her eclectic wardrobe from the fifties and sixties, heightened by the occasional chunky earrings and scarves tied at the neck when she was feeling playful. Today, she crept over to open the window and determine the temperature that the beautiful April day would bring. It felt cool, but the golden sunshine made the passing breeze comfortable. She turned and leaned over Doc to graze his belly with a few good rubs and an aggressive kiss right behind his ears. Just a small grunt from him, but he wasn't stirring. After heading to the closet and choosing a floral swing skirt and a dusty blue short-sleeved sweater for the day's look, Marjorie went downstairs and got her coffee going while she flipped through the records. Lana, Dean, Sam, Billie, Freddie—the winner was The Platters, again. The needle hit on the track for "Enchanted," fitting for the gentle morning. She poured hazelnut creamer into her cup and stepped out on the porch into the rays that felt like a big hug from your oldest friend. The smell of magnolia and pine floated in the air while she opened the window to let the sounds of the record flood through, the wicker rocker feeling cool to her touch as she sat back into its curve. Rocking back and forth while sipping on the steamy cup, she smiled and looked around at her home and at the other bungalows starting to wake up in the light.

It wasn't long after that Benny came around the corner of the porch, dressed in a striped collared shirt knotted over jeans and chunky white tennis shoes, a corduroy fanny pack draped across her waist.

"Well, good morning, neighbor!" she greeted, walking up the steps. "Aren't we all set for the day, as I expected you would be."

"How'd you figure?" Marjorie smiled.

"Your music. I could already hear it from ours, and I envy your don't-give-a-fuck-about-the-neighbors way of doing it."

"What psychopath would get mad over The Platters being blasted? I think they'd need to check themselves."

"No, that's what I'm saying! Keep doing you, boo-boo. Seeing that you're up now, still wanna go to Westside Antiques?"

"Sure do! You want some coffee to go before we walk over?" Loud scratches on the door announced Doc was finally up and ready to join the humans in the sun. Marjorie let him out, where he promptly greeted Benny with hand licks. "And is there any particular reason for the trip?"

"No thanks for the coffee, and nothing really other than browsing. I probably shouldn't be buying stuff and bringing it home for Morgan just to give me shit about it. I don't buy a lot, but when I do I go big, obviously."

"Well, happy to be your chaperone for today, so long as you keep an eye on me for buying something within my budget. Let me get Doc situated and then we can get walking!"

"Why don't you take Doc with us? He's pretty mild, and I don't think he's gonna break anything. I can help walk him too if you want."

"You're sweet! I think I'll be fine, and if it's not gonna get much hotter, I think he can handle the long walk." She looked down at the old dog with his grizzled straight stare back at her with sleepy eyes, his tail wagging fast. A good spring walk to the Square for all of them, and as Benny pointed out, what trouble could the old boy get into at the antique mall?

Dogwood branches prickled in bright blooms reached out to the women from over the cemetery's iron fence as they made their way along the back road by the train tracks. For a silent morning like this, Marjorie knew it only meant the town was overdue for the next train to pass. Past Caroline's they went toward Westside Antiques, which had pastel crepe paper and Easter egg cut-outs pasted onto its wide windows. Westside looked the same as any antique mall with its many turns and narrow twists past booths divided into small peg-board rooms, but as all seasoned enthusiasts knew, no two antique malls were identical. With the beauty of treasures bygone acquired by a cast of characters from God knows where, whatever you found on a given day in a booth wasn't guaranteed to be there the next time around—and Marjorie was always careful to pick over every space, crack, and crevice. She'd gone into Westside many times now, but lazily meandering through what seemed like miles of treasures thankfully never initiated any travels. Maybe the overabundance of items from across the decades canceled out the lingering energy in the building that would have sent her back in time.

To her relief, Doc was on his best behavior, just following along at her pace and only sniffing whatever was low to the ground. For all her meticulous picking through, Marjorie herself never really had an idea what it was that she wanted. She liked rustic summer items like plaid Thermos picnic bags or paint by numbers in bright colors. She found herself gravitating toward a long, yellow headscarf detailed with a swirling pattern in shades of pink and white.

Suddenly, Doc was pulling her to the booth across the narrow aisle. She tried nudging him back to her, but he was bent on sniffing the old red Coca-Cola crate stacked atop old suitcases and filled with what looked like a random mess of ephemera. She walked over and was careful not to knock over a naked dress form next to it, taking the crate down and placing it on the ground as she knelt beside Doc, whose small black ears remained perked as his nose dug deeper through the papers, postcards, and old restaurant matchbooks.

"Baby, you're gonna ruin the stuff!" she whispered to him and tried gathering as many of the items as she could away from his wet snout. Some bulkier items remained at the bottom, like cassette tapes and a pair of cracking leather driving gloves that had been the culprit. He kept his nose on the gloves, but Marjorie took them out of the crate and placed them higher on one of the booth's shelves near a box of mismatched sunglasses. "No gloves, I'll get you a proper toy."

She began putting all the papers and postcards back into the crate when her finger touched something else at the bottom behind the cassette tapes. A few 45 records lay there, some in sleeves and scratched ones without tucked in between them. She took the 45s and began looking through each one. So funny that these little vinyls had been everywhere at one point, and nowadays, unless you had a converter or a jukebox, you were out of luck listening to them. She didn't recognize the name of the singer on the first record, but the second one was a Firestone Tires exclusive compilation from the 1960s that had various artists featured from Nat King Cole to Kay Starr and Guy Lombardo—*Five All-Time Greats on One Album* said the sleeve. Then she flipped over to the next vinyl, removing it from the yellowing ripped sleeve—and nearly dropped it.

It wasn't scratched and it looked like it could have been from a home recording. But the inscription in the middle suddenly had Marjorie shaking, for it was handwritten in the simplest of words that felt heavy on her heart as she read them:

"Oh My Angel"
S.G. 1966

She couldn't breathe, and she instantly turned to get up and find Benny, who was only a few booths over. "Everything OK?" Benny asked when she saw Doc and her approach.

"I don't know," Marjorie confessed. "I—I've gotta go home. Just something I realized I need to do that I forgot about."

It felt like forever before Marjorie could get back to Dogwood Daze that afternoon, walking mostly in silence and trying to convince Benny that she was alright and that she needed to be alone for a bit. Benny gave her a big hug before she asked her once more, "You sure?"

"Yes. Please, I'm so sorry—it's just something I need to think over before I get back to doing it. Just a call to my mom about some stuff my sister is going through."

"OK girl. I hope you guys can figure it out. Message me later, yeah?"

When Benny had disappeared around the corner of the porch, Marjorie waited a few minutes in her rocker before she brought out the Crosley. She plugged it into the side of the house and pulled out the 45, placing the adapter in its center. And then for the big reveal, she set the vinyl in place and dropped the needle down.

The pops and cracks of the first few seconds were suddenly followed by the sounds of guitars being plucked and the ascension of chords on a keyboard, some men mumbling. But then, the voices were clear and sharp.

"Alright, guys, give us a few minutes, we're gonna play something," one man said to the other voices. "Shh, OK let's go Simon. I've got it recording, you ready?"

There was a chuckle and another voice spoke up, that familiar gentle voice thick in a Southern accent as it responded, "Yes sir, I'm ready to begin. Tell me when to start."

The brief silence then gave way to a tune, familiar to Marjorie, a melody from a moment she had known once and never forgot, now finding and serenading her across the air as that voice she knew too well sang the verses of "Oh My Angel," singer Bertha Tillman's forgotten single from 1962. Smooth, deep, and almost crying out—at least how it sounded to Marjorie—and only accompanied by the soft strumming of a guitar.

She sat still on the floor beside the record player with her ear close to the music, her face staring blankly at the street. Finally, Marjorie drew a big breath and looked over to Doc, leaning over to hug him tightly as tears started to fall, then getting up to go into the house. On her vanity, surrounded by necklaces draped around the mirror and old photographs of family pinned in between the glass and the frame, she gently grabbed a small folded paper, which she brought back out to the porch. It was a receipt for a restaurant, St. Francis Fountain, San Francisco—1964. At its center was a big signature, Simon Grace. Marjorie stopped the music and placed the 45 by its side.

Him. The S.G. on the record. Same swirl and slants in the right angles. Her hand softly caressed the writing on the record, and let it rest there.

He remembered me.

Simon, 1964

To Simon, this was exactly what a summer day in San Francisco should be always. Not the chilly, fog-drenched one Mark Twain talked about, but one without humidity for which he thanked God every second under his breath.

He woke up late in his apartment off Valencia and Eighteenth, which only had one fan that he plugged into the wall to keep him cool—here in San Francisco, they had radiator heaters aplenty, but warm days you were left on your own. His roommate Ernie, a Hispanic man from the valley, was already out, having gone to his waiting job at Sears on Union Square. Sometimes when Simon got in right before the lunch crowd, Ernie could sneak him a plate of the food at a good fraction of the price at the farthest table in the back, just outside the kitchen, which was generous of him as Simon was using his own savings to support himself and had to cut financial corners when possible. But he was aching from the night before when they both had gone out, and for being in the city for only four months, he couldn't quite remember in what neighborhood they had overdone it. No matter—he was too tired to get up for food at Sears, but at least he was back home and in his bed.

He turned the radio on to a brief forecast for that Friday before switching to Roy Orbison. Just what he liked. That, and the highs of eighty degrees across the whole city, minimal cloud coverage, sunshine for hours and a slight breeze. He looked in the mirror at his tousled hair and took a cool shower to kickstart a day of possibilities, changing into a white button-down that he tucked into his slacks and, just in case, his faded blue cardigan. He went into the kitchen and found his small notepad and pen on the table alongside some dirty dishes. He tucked the notebook in his cardigan pocket and put the dishes in the sink before moving over to the stove where the coffee maker rested on a burner.

It still had some day-old brew in it, but Simon decided that he needed something fresh and hot, and to get some fresh air. Before leaving to go grab coffee elsewhere, he glanced once more at his reflection in the mirror by the front door—his hair seemed to have gotten a little longer and it was just how he liked it, unkept and one less thing to worry about, and trendy at that. *Who cares if The Beatles are looking sloppish*, his sister Annette would say. *You're not a musician, you're gonna be an architect. An American one!*

The street was bright and buzzing with the passing cars and groups of young men and girls heading past Simon in the opposite direction, presumably toward the park with their wicker baskets and blankets in hand and sunglasses pushed back on the top of their heads. Smartly dressed women in day dresses and pillbox hats walked along 18th Street with their children not far behind as the sidewalks seemed to shine like silver beneath the clear sky, and a fair number of windows from the towering apartments were propped open, their fluttering curtains reaching through the wide gaps as if beckoning to Simon. He got his coffee to go and turned back toward home—but as he reached the steps to his place, he found himself walking past and on to the park.

Dolores was more than a lush knoll, stretching out far and happily away from the noise and crowds of downtown for the quieter pleasures of San Francisco. The skyline on the horizon and the cool fog magically conceded to the warm sunshine that rarely poked through the other parts of this strange city that had bewitched the small-town boy from Georgia. Simon made his way up the grass past groups gathered on mismatched blankets, their coolers with beer cans and transistor radios scattered beside shoes the girls had kicked off and the shirts the men had tossed onto their bikes lying nearby. Cigarette smoke, laughter, and the occasional crooning of Sam Cooke or siren call of The Supremes filled the air as he reached an empty bench near the top. For the decades to come, Simon was sure this place would remain the Eden that it was in this very hour—for the careless, the young, the uninspired souls that would soon enough either run this town or desert it.

He sat and sipped his coffee. There were class assignments, the telephone call to Mama at one, laundry to start, but Simon was bent on ignoring all these duties—well, except the phone call home. It was the least he could do to put Mama at ease that her only son would move so far away from her, from a life that was practically all sorted out for him. He didn't need San Francisco, he could have continued school at UGA, but Berkeley was a luxury that he was determined to make work, with his own savings, and especially for his best friend, Curtis. If only he could see where Simon had ended up now! He was not about to neglect this perfect warm day in a city that fascinated him, with its steep hills and bustling waterfronts flanked by two breathtaking bridges, and best of all, the Victorians. He'd never seen so much splendor sprawled across a densely populated city such as here. He took another sip of coffee and pulled the notebook from his cardigan pocket. On a clear day like this, he had to draw it all.

Straight across the sea of green and gatherings, Simon could see the stiff skyline with few buildings starting to take form against the few clouds speckled in the blue. At the bottom of the park's edge, the old Mission High School, designed in a looming Spanish Colonial style, sat empty but like a pearl beneath the sunlight. To its left, a bell clanged and moving up the tracks that dotted the park's west side was the green Church Street streetcar. Once the skyline was finished, he started tracing the people with their bikes, their limbs flailing about in the grass, the few dancing to the music on the radios. Suddenly he had begun tracing the edges of an arm, then the flow of dark curls that flowed from above it followed by a yellow-colored sweater down on the ground.

A woman was lying down alone in the grass across the park—one arm tucked underneath the curls on the back of her head while the other arm remained spread out over the white trench coat she had put beneath her like a blanket. With her yellow sweater and what looked like cream capris, she was over layered for the day, and he couldn't tell if her eyes were closed from so far away, but she looked peaceful. He continued sketching, his hand slowing as he finished her outline and began going for the details that he could just make out from his distance. The brown hair was pushed back by a white headband, and she might have worn a crimson shade on her lips. The pen stopped. He could only imagine these details of her lips—their shape, what color they really were, how they might have felt if they were pressed against his.

His pen continued tracing on the page, and he looked back up to the woman. She now was sitting up, turned at the waist, and looking directly his way.

Chapter 5

I love how you love me.

It was days like this where oldies like The Paris Sisters floated up from Nelson's jukebox around the small space and would bring Marjorie back in time—in this case, just in her mind. She thought of those faraway places, to the people she'd never meet again who had lived and died, and the facades long gone after she'd seen them at their peak, periods only few could say they were lucky to have been alive for. San Francisco, 1916, was the first spot, and it would always be her favorite. But there was a charm about watching the old schooners glide across the Atlantic when she'd gone with her college roommate Jessica back to her hometown in Cape Cod that spring break sophomore year and actually seeing a first edition of *Little Women* in the window of the bookstore there in 1869, less than a year after it had been published. She was obsessed with *Midnight in Paris* and spent her semester abroad wandering the streets of 1922 looking for Hemingway and the Fitzgeralds. No luck, but she got to stand a few feet from Josephine Baker just outside the door to the club she'd been dancing at when she was turned away from a packed house that night. But New York, 1945. No one alive now would know the feeling she had when walking around the grandeur of Penn Station while the world around her erupted in cheers, rejoicing at the end of the war and the return home of many good men. Though the time with the boy from New Jersey whom she'd met on a work trip was short-lived with a few dates, she was glad to have not turned down his tickets for a concert at The Garden that same day.

Marietta was smaller in scale but just as rich in history as those places she'd been to, and sitting in her chair by the front door of Nelson's, she looked out and wondered if she'd ever return to Hunt's again. She never seemed to return to the same time period twice. Noting this, she hoped that the young man Curtis had settled somewhere not long after their meeting.

It had been a hectic morning at the salon but now that things had calmed, she pulled up the Museum website and looked for their hours. She needed to get serious about her search for Simon, and any steps further would have to involve actively learning the history of the town. A Saturday she would pop in, perhaps this coming one. Next, she called Westside Antiques and got the email of the booth vendor, who she quickly messaged about the origins of the record. The owner, a local woman named Roberta Hamilton, might not remember where she found it, but it was worth a shot. Now she had to wait. Alejandra came over from the back room and leaned into the sunlight flooding from the front windows.

"You're like a plant," Marjorie joked, as Alejandra, or Alex as she preferred for short, closed her eyes and tilted her head back to absorb the rays. The stylist, with her red velvet colored hair, was only twenty-eight but was one of the longest remaining stylists on Nelson's staff and had been the first to greet Marjorie on that first day. "I'd like to think I'm more like a cat," Alex responded, "but sure, I'll take a plant. A beautiful, blooming fig tree!"

"The kind of attitude we like to hear." Marjorie looked over at the schedule pulled up on the computer. "Want me to call Josh? He's not quite fifteen minutes past."

Alex remained facing the sun but shook her head. "Nah, don't bother. He's always like this, and he'll call and apologize profusely and then he'll do it again. Think we might just need to put him on walk-in only basis now."

"I'll make a note in his profile."

"Thanks, girl! Ugh, I'm over all the delays this week. But the usual suspects—I should know better by now and not expect them to show up. If Josh weren't one of my oldest clients, I'd be more pissy. Nice guy. Just always late."

"That and the good head of hair I guess is going for him," Marjorie chuckled. "Maybe go on a walk if you can and really get that sun—I know I'd be asking to do so if I didn't have to watch the desk."

"I'll just keep you company! It's a drag being up here for hours alone, I know. But I'm antsy, maybe you're a better fit for this."

"Honestly, it's the people part I feel rusty on at times. I was working remote for so long that when it comes to people, I feel like I'm scaring them."

"Oh my God, definitely not! Since you've been here, everyone's always asking about that girl at the front in all the dresses and the big hair. It's like you got a cult following. A good front show, that's what matters, right?"

"Gee, thanks. Cult leader has always been my dream." Two men suddenly appeared passing by the big front window and entered the salon; it was Art Martin, dressed today in a tweed suit with a dark red shirt and followed by a near spitting image of him, but younger and thinner, with overgrown curls that fell over his big brown eyes that looked around the salon with curiosity.

"Well, well, Miss Marjorie," declared Art, taking off his fedora and setting it down on the desk. "How are you doing today? I was hoping everyone's in a good mood to forgive my son Stephen and I for coming in without appointments to get a few trims?"

"You're actually in luck!" she said, turning to Alex, who smiled at Marjorie and shrugged. "Alex just had a cancellation, and Nelson is just finishing up his client early. I think we should be able to fit you both in."

"Just perfect! I'll take a seat," he said, and turning to his son, "Stephen can go on ahead with Miss Alex. Is that Miss Luanne I see over there? Hello, darling!"

Luanne Sullivan sat at Jeff's station in a red smock with foils in her hair and waved back at the gentleman, seeming unphased in such a vulnerable looking state. She called out, "So you finally realized that you had to take care of the bird nest atop of your head, Art?"

Art gave out a good laugh as he made his way over to one of the vacant seats in the waiting area. "Yes ma'am! Gotta do some spring cleanup, I suppose. Coming in for your usual golden glow, I see?"

"Every eight weeks on the dot! Don't know what the town would do without me if they didn't recognize me—consistency is key!"

"That it is, that it is. Miss Marjorie, does someone here do your hair? It's always so neat and big! You definitely give me flashbacks to my own mama way back when."

Marjorie blushed and pulled at her hair, gathering the wavy flipped ends off her shoulder. "Nope, it's all me! Years of trial and error and YouTube videos. I just feel good with my hair like this! The volume balances out the wide face."

"Wide face? Luanne, did you hear her? I can't believe you! No ma'am, you are just a doll, one that reminds me of my youth. It wasn't the best of times, don't get me wrong, but to be young is to be stupid, and rightfully so, because sometimes we feel our best when it's in the throes of an adventurous life. And you know what adventure is, Miss Marjorie?"

"I don't particularly. What is it?"

"It's as you said before, trial and error. And then you move on. The same courtesy doesn't apply when you get old."

Alex came over with Stephen when it was time for them to leave, and to Marjorie's relief they were both laughing and smiling at each other over something concerning the upcoming Shaky Knees Festival in Atlanta. As they set out, Art tipped his hat to Marjorie and Alex. "Until next time ladies, dolls of the town!"

Stephen smiled too and looked back to Alex as he remarked, "Hope you get to go. It's gonna be amazing!"

"I hope so!" she exclaimed, a smile lingering on her face as she watched him follow his dad out of sight. "That wasn't as bad as I thought it'd be. People with thick hair scare me, but that was decent."

Marjorie giggled. "Seems to me you weren't paying all that much attention to his hair."

Alex flushed and nervously grabbed at her wavy hair to pull behind her ear. "He's a music guy! An artist! Fun to talk to, what can I say. He just got his master's at SCAD and is doing photography around here now."

"I'm guessing he's going to Shaky Knees to get some photos?"

"Nah, he's already working a wedding that weekend. My friend knows someone who can get us passes for that Saturday but I'm on standby until she gets word of how many tickets they have. He likes a lot of the same acts I want to see that day! Hopefully it works out."

The ease of the day continued until her meetup with Benny, who came by later that evening with cabernet that they enjoyed on Dogwood's porch in mismatched antique glasses from Westside. Benny was always prone to laughing, but tonight she seemed more quiet, listening and giggling at anecdotes of the day's clients. "At least the day seemed busy enough to keep it interesting for you," she mused, "and I wish it was the same with the bookstore today. So dead. If it wasn't just me today, I would have stopped by the salon to hang with you."

"As someone who works at a bookstore," Marjorie said, "I would think you'd easily fill your time up with some reading."

"Not exactly. No, even if I read, it's just my mind that's not sitting still. I don't particularly want to be alone right now, stuck in my head."

"Why so?"

Benny sat up straight in the wicker bench she'd been leaning back in, pulling the quilted throw blanket she had at her feet over her whole legs as she took another sip of the cabernet. "I was in Athens but moved in with my sister about a year ago after a breakup. I know, in a year I should be well over it, but when it's just me, I keep thinking about her. Us. I can't afford to find a new therapist, and I thought just being with my sister would help things. But she's now seeing this guy, and recently it's been getting to me how often they hang out—which is cool, totally happy for her—but it just gets me all fucked up, you know?" She took another sip. "I'm sorry I brought it up. It feels good to just come out with it, though! I don't mean to be a wet blanket tonight. But quiet days at the bookstore are bad. Worse when it's just me."

"I'm so sorry, Benny," Marjorie said to her. "Don't feel bad! I'm glad you could talk to me about it. Come hang with me more whenever you like—no one should feel alone."

"I just don't feel like that's good enough, or healthy. Avoiding the real issues here." Benny finally gave out her signature chuckle. "That's what got us in trouble in the first place, I think. Just not being honest with each other. About when we were bored or too busy—or just not in love. Fuck—I honestly think I'm still in love. Her … apparently, it'd been months before she finally told me those feelings were long gone."

"Jesus."

"Amen to that!" She was about to take another sip again but lowered her hand. "That's the real shitty thing—she saw how happy I was and wasn't even going to tell me, or end it. I don't know how I feel about that. Sometimes I wish she had gone on just pretending things were great. I mean, if she was fine with it. But that's not fair to her too, I know. God, listen to me! I'm sorry, Margie."

"Girl, please don't! Let it out. Anything I can do, I'm happy to be here." Benny had been staring off to the distance as she'd been talking, but now she turned to Marjorie and smiled.

"I appreciate that so much. It's so good to have a friend close by." She looked around for Doc, who was lying on his side on the floor, and called to him in a sweet high voice, patting the seat next to her on the bench. He obliged and jumped into the spot, curling up with his back right against Benny for her to rub. "I'm here for you too. If there's anything you ever need, or want to talk about, I'm your girl. You've been such a trouper for moving here solo and making your bones in town, job and house and all. You got a fucking dog too! You're iconic. But being strong can only carry so much weight if it's just you. I know."

Marjorie sipped her wine, looking up to the stars in the clear sky, and then turned to Benny with a smile. Benny was right about the burden of loneliness, the longing feeling that crept in when one was alone. But the aches of her particular solitude were something that she couldn't ever really explain to anyone.

Marjorie, 1916

August, 2001. Though usually this time of the year in San Francisco had been referred to as "Fogust," Marjorie and her mom lucked out on their day in the city with bright skies and hardly a breeze. Since Julia Valdez had a dentist's appointment that morning and had called out for the day, she figured she'd take her younger daughter on a little adventure. Her dentist was in San Leandro, but they drove over the Bay Bridge for another fifteen minutes into the city, and from downtown's flat streets, headed up to where Julia's old neighborhood lay among the hills on the outskirts of Noe Valley. Rows of Victorian houses ran up and down the winding roads alongside Spanish Colonial duplexes that dotted the main strip of 24th Street. Marjorie and her mom managed to find a space just outside the bookshop with its yellow stucco facade and blue-tiled big windows and walked up 24th to kick off the late morning with some Frappuccinos at the corner Starbucks. She'd been to plenty, but there was something charming about this location that excited eight-year-old Marjorie. The jade green brick and wide corner windows within a big Victorian complex with red-trimmed bay windows above looked like how she imagined a castle would.

After the Frapps, some cupcakes from the bakery up the street, and then a sunflower-filled posy picked from the florist next door, Julia led Marjorie back down to 24th and Noe where they turned right and up the hill on the next street at 25th. This street was much quieter, still more Victorians but smaller, wider almost, with their lower levels converted into garages and painted to match the exteriors as best as they could. However, the one exception to these rules was the very house that Julia stopped in front of with her daughter. It was a purple square Victorian that seemed taller without the sharp gable that its neighbors had, with long stairs going up to two identical doors off to its left side. Gold numbers of 4055 and 4057 were stuck atop both doors, respectively. On the right side the two bay windows were stacked above the garage on the bottom level, and a black Buick was parked in its driveway.

Julia opened the box in her hand and handed Marjorie her vanilla cupcake with sprinkles. "So, this is where we first lived when your grandma, me, and Auntie Liz finally came to join Papa."

"It's so pretty!" cried Marjorie with a mouth full of cake. "How old were you and Auntie Liz when you guys left the Philippines?"

"That was back in 1966, so I was three and she was just one. Grandma was so nervous on the trip. Planes weren't easy for traveling with little babies then. But we did it! And then we stayed here, and Papa's sister and her family lived in the bottom apartment. On days like this we'd be on our bikes up and down the street or drawing on the sidewalk with chalk, and when your Uncle Kevin was born our cousins, your Uncle Ed and Uncle Vincent, would try to teach him how to toss a football."

"Was there an ice cream truck that came through here?"

"There was, but the hills were tough to drive for a truck, so he wasn't here that much. Besides, we had the drugstore nearby, which we all just walked to and got sodas and ice cream there. The first time I ever had Chocolate Malted Crunch."

Marjorie's jaw dropped. "My favorite! You guys had that even back then?" Nothing beat a good three scoops of Thrifty's famous flavor for Marjorie, wishing she'd had that now instead of the cupcake.

"We sure did, honey," Julia continued. "Well, we'd get our ice cream and sit on the sidewalk, and watch the cable car come down the hill and drop off, pick people up."

"Can we go see the cable cars?"

"They're not the old ones you see downtown, sweetheart, but they still have new trains come by. Yes, let's go see if that drugstore is still there." They walked down the street and Marjorie looked back at the purple house. Nothing else seemed so spectacular as it, as unique. It made her sad, thinking that so long ago it was once home to her mom.

"Mommy, why did you all leave San Francisco?"

"Well, we were still quite a ways out from where Papa worked in the shipyards at Mare Island. And after your Uncle Kevin and Auntie Sophie were born, it got too cramped. Then Papa bought the new house out in Clayton and then we moved there."

"When did you all leave?"

"We left the apartment in 1972 and lived with your Papa's brother and his family for a while in Oakland. Then Papa's house was finished in 1974, and they've been there ever since. You realize how wonderful it is to have a bedroom of your own after sharing for so many years."

"I sure do! But I hate how Eileen still just comes into my room and never knocks. I hate it!"

"I'll tell her again that it bugs you. Oh wait! I have to show you this house." Julia stopped and turned to point up at a home on the corner. It was square and sharp like the purple house, but it was a proper house with three levels and the garage off to the side. It was painted cream, almost a soft lavender hue, and the rectangular bay windows shot out overlooking both streets. A lush garden seemed overgrown around it but contained tall white roses behind a thin iron fence, with creeping thyme like beads strung on green threads spilling over the concrete steps that led right to where Marjorie and her mom stood.

"This is the witch's house," Julia whispered.

"A witch!" Marjorie exclaimed.

"Not really, but as a kid we thought a witch lived here with all these big trees and bushes behind that fence. Maybe it is a witch, but truthfully we never saw who really lived there."

Marjorie kept looking up at the windows in hopes of glimpsing the witch or other resident, but a soft bell chimed in the distance, prompting her to turn around as the sound grew louder. She was surprised to see that the street covered in trees was rather neat, with dirt roads spread throughout the block and no cement in sight. The cars parked along 25th had vanished while a horse turned the corner and came round at a steady pace, drawing a wagon that had a sign for ICE pasted on its side. Beyond the horse on the wide street that was Church, Marjorie saw a crowd of men shoveling out mounds of dirt while an old-looking contraption like a construction crane dragged slowly over the ground, clearing what looked like a large chunk of railroad tracks.

"Mommy, a horse!" she said and turned to her mom. But she stood alone there, in front of the same house, now white with brick red trim around its windows, and the gated garden containing mostly bushes with yellow and pink roses. Marjorie's heart began racing, realizing that the witch inside must have cast some spell that took away the cars and cement and her mom.

She panicked seeing some people walk by. There were two men in suits and wearing hats that looked almost like ones she'd seen her grandpa wear but larger; one man had a very large mustache unlike any Marjorie had seen before. They gave her strange looks but kept walking on. A woman wearing a long red skirt and a big sun hat over hair piled on top of her tiny head was crossing the street toward Marjorie, with packages wrapped in brown paper underneath her arm, coughing and covering her mouth with her gloved hand as she disappeared up the street. It was rather dusty right now, with all that construction work getting louder and the men shouting as their work seemed to intensify. Marjorie looked around, not realizing that she had walked backward and suddenly bumped against the fence of the witch house. She heard a faint sound and turned toward the house—the front door was opening. Marjorie wanted to run.

But the witch that emerged wasn't in black, nor was she very old and gray haired with a green complexion. Marjorie wasn't even sure if she was a witch—her dress was very smooth and flowy, a crisp cotton in a light yellow color and with a beaded square neckline. Her golden hair was fluffy and wrapped into a loose big bun at the nape of her neck, and Marjorie could see pearls dangling from her ears through her strands. She couldn't help but stare into the woman's eyes, even if she was a witch and should have known better—they were hazel and looked like they shimmered in the sunlight.

"Hello, miss," the woman said to Marjorie as she made her way to the gate and gently leaned over to get a better look at Marjorie. "Are you lost?"

Marjorie didn't say anything just yet, still nervous and confused. Finally, she shook her head and simply said, "My mom is gone."

"Oh dear, where were you both coming from? When did you last see her?"

"She was just here."

"Were you both coming from a shop? Perhaps she is still there!"

"We were at a bakery and then we walked over here and then all of a sudden she disappeared. But she couldn't have run back to the bakery, it's far."

"What did she look like?"

Marjorie was about to answer, but then she felt frozen again. What if this witch had kidnapped her mom?

"If you tell me what she looked like, I can send a servant to go find her with you. She can't have gone too far. What is your name?"

Marjorie got her composure back and flatly responded, "I don't speak to strangers."

"Indeed you shouldn't, miss! But if your mother is lost, how can I help you find her if I haven't the faintest idea what she looks like?" The woman stepped back and sighed as she pulled the gate back to open it. "I am Emily Axford, and this is my grandfather's home. I'd love to help you. Won't you come in, dear? I can get you some lemonade."

Was it a trick? Should she accept the invitation? Everything was strange—felt old. But new also. As she looked around again Marjorie still saw Victorian houses winding up the street and carriages making their way up and down the dirt road. A completely different, yet familiar, world.

Marjorie was about to answer Miss Axford, but she felt a tug on her arm.

"Marjorie, what's wrong!" her mom's familiar voice nearly shouted. "Pay attention, are you daydreaming?"

"Huh?" She looked up at her mom whose face was full of panic but also irritation, with her brows knitted in frustration. "You weren't responding to me. You can't just space out, even when I'm here. We have to particularly pay attention to our surroundings in the city, you never know."

Even though her mom was upset, Marjorie was thrilled to see her and hugged her. "I thought you disappeared!"

"What? What are you talking about—I've been right here."

"But there was a lady in yellow and horses, and there was dirt—"

"No, we've always been right here, Marge. I knew it was too early for sugar."

Julia wasn't wrong. Marjorie looked around again and she hadn't left, not really. But in the confusion of that moment and how vivid everything in those few minutes had seemed and then disappeared just as quickly, Marjorie held her mom's hand the rest of the day. It wouldn't be but a few more months before her second travel happened but years for her to understand exactly where she was traveling to.

Chapter 6

A few days after her initial email, there was finally a response waiting for Marjorie in her inbox. She didn't check the email in full until she got back to Dogwood Daze, where she made herself an evening coffee and read the message while it was brewing.

Hi Marjorie, it began, *Thank you for reaching out regarding the item you found at Roberta's booth. Roberta is my aunt, and I am currently helping her run it given some recent health issues she's been having and am happy to find out what I can regarding the record. I did ask her about the box you found it in and if she possibly remembered the estate sale she was at where she picked it up, but unfortunately, she couldn't, other than it was from last year in Marietta. If she does happen to remember anything new, I will be sure to follow up, or provide any resources that I can in hopes of locating the original owner, which I understand is what you're looking for. Sincerely, Daniel D'Amato.*

She sighed and sat at the kitchen table with her arms folded, feeling exceptionally tired now with this dead end. Doc was nearby watching her with his tail slowly wagging back and forth across the wooden floor while she stirred cream into her cup and took sips. Maybe a walk would do both of them good. The evening was still light out, but a coolness had settled in the air, so she put on her trench and hooked Doc to his leash. They made their way down Morris toward the cemetery gate. The sprawl of graves that gradually got older and more faded as they made their way up the rolling little hills didn't scare Marjorie nor raise any concerns of traveling—cemeteries seemed to function in the same way as antique malls, a neutral ground. But the peace of these spaces provided the quiet and mindless strolling that she needed to keep her from going crazy at home. While Doc strutted along casually and tried his best to pull toward the occasional grave to sniff, Marjorie had to think of her next plan. They were walking farther up and deeper toward the headstones that predated the Civil War when she looked behind her and stared down at the big knoll on the west side of the cemetery. It was mostly grass and hardly any gravesites, the same open space where she'd taken Doc a few times to sit leisurely with a blanket and look onward at the newer homes built along the other side of the cemetery gates. Only now, she saw it as a familiar ghost in itself, the cascading green calling her back to a sunny day nearly sixty years ago, in a city that was once home and now so far away.

In her lifetime, it had only been five years. Five years and she had nearly forgotten him—put him out of her mind at least while she focused back on her career when her enthusiasm had begun waning— but it was Simon after all that had ignited the spark again, especially for San Francisco. But as the years went on, San Francisco was still the dull gray city masked by a false sense of innovation and inclusivity that she fell out of love with; nothing compared to the sunny day they shared together in 1964 on the edge of free love and true new energy in the city that she left behind.

It was practically a sign that she needed to go to Atlanta when a recruiter had reached out about a new opportunity. With the incredible benefits and salary offered, that was a good enough excuse for family and friends about uprooting on a whim. But the real reason—it ate Marjorie alive as she flew across the country, kept her head down, found a modest apartment near the office while figuring out how far away Marietta was from the city. *Just maybe I could track him down,* she kept thinking, *meet him again, if he did go back to Georgia at all.* She was here, and she was sure he was too. Maybe in the ground, maybe still above it—and if it were the latter, she wanted to make sure that everything had gone according to his plans. Her heart ached to stare at the grass, and she walked on with Doc.

She decided on giving the booth at Westside Antiques one more glance for any additional clues. Three days later she managed to find time to go during her lunch when the salon wasn't busy. Thanks to another cancellation, Alex accompanied her. She darted off on her own adventure toward hat boxes towering near the checkout counter, but Marjorie went straight ahead to lose herself in the clutter. She saw the booth ahead with the chipped red Coca-Cola crate jutting into the aisle and the bare mannequin form pushed against the old suitcases. Approaching, she thought about either carefully twisting around the crate or just pushing it in, but before she could decide someone emerged from out of the clutter and startled her, knocking her into the crate altogether. "Shit!" she spat before she caught the crate from hitting the floor.

"Oh, I'm sorry about that!" said the man who was there. "I didn't mean to scare you." Holding old LIFE magazines in one hand, he stepped out of her way into the aisle and had his other hand hovered in case he needed to catch anything that fell. He was tall, and for a warmer April day he wore a blue knit button-up polo and beige chinos. He was maybe her age—but with his dark hair combed neatly back off his face like an Old Hollywood star he might as well have been her age seventy years ago. She was struck by this stranger's look but caught herself. "You're good! I didn't see you there. Sorry if I scared *you*!"

"Oh don't, wasn't you. You come into a place like this and kind of expect running into a ghost at some point. Here! I'll get out of your way if you were coming in."

"Unless there's been any porcelain dolls or paintings from eBay recently added here, I think we're safe from ghosts."

He laughed, showing a gorgeous, toothy smile. "It was lucky to be you then that I crossed paths! But I won't be in your way, unless there's anything I can help you look for here?"

Before stepping in Marjorie narrowed her eyes. "Are you Daniel?"

"That's me."

"Oh my God, we were just emailing about the record! I'm Marjorie." She held her hand out and he took it in his for a brief shake, and his face only seemed to brighten.

"Marjorie, yes! Wow, it's great to meet you. I'm sorry I haven't gotten to your last message—"

"Oh no! This isn't anything pressing. I was just coming in, actually, to see if by chance I might find anything else like another record I missed or more labeled things."

They both looked toward the towering stashes of items for sale, but Daniel shrugged. "Well, I'm here if you would like help, but honestly when my aunt gives me her new items it's everything mixed in, no matter where she got it. I could try to ask again, but for being seventy-eight she wouldn't probably remember at this point. She could have had that record here for years, despite what she said."

Marjorie let out a deep sigh. "No, I appreciate you trying, though, and true—she probably wouldn't remember. I honestly don't even know what to look for right now or what I thought it was I would find."

"Hey, help yourself and don't mind me! I wish I could do more, truly. Pulling up the Shazam app would be so handy right now, but I doubt its catalog for unknown singers from the fifties is deep."

"It's not even that—I mean, I *know* who sings the song. I'm just trying to figure out the source to know how *they* got it."

"Are you a historian? I might know some people to help down at the Atlanta History Center who could try and—"

"No, no, it's personal, and hard to explain. I'm sorry, I'm probably complicating all this, and you've been sweet to humor me."

"Again, happy to try and solve this mystery with you since it began with me, or my aunt at least. I was stopping in today to clear some older unsold stuff if you wanted to check really quick? Somewhere to start." He set the magazines down and picked up a box of old photographs, mismatched transferware, and a big wooden statue of an equestrian rider on horseback. "I'll get out of your way so you can rummage around at ease."

She couldn't help her smile as she looked up from the box. "Thank you again, Daniel, this has meant a lot."

"Glad I ran into you and met in person," he assured her. "If you leave before I'm back, it was a pleasure, and hope you do find another clue to your singer."

"I sure hope I do too!" Back she was among the various old dishes and framed advertisements and records that left no other traces of Simon. Alex found her and tried stepping in behind Marjorie, but seeing how cramped the booth was she stayed in the aisle and gave her some room to back out.

"Anything good?" she asked Marjorie, who shook her head.

"Nothing I had to have on the spot."

"That's always a nice feeling, isn't it? Being able to walk away."

They got back to the salon where they found Luanne waiting around taking pictures, while Lara Jean sat in the waiting area on her phone.

"Good afternoon, ladies!" greeted Marjorie. "What brings you both in today?"

"Well, besides your ray of sunshine, Miss Marjorie, we are just waiting until Nelson's done with his client," said Luanne excitedly. "We gotta finalize some logistics with him for the Taste of Marietta."

"Is it about the cars?" Alex asked. "He's said he's ready to go! And he got confirmation that four other buddies will be bringing theirs also."

"Which is fantastic!" exclaimed Lara Jean, finally looking up from her phone. "Sorry, so much I'm trying to email back and forth with vendors and the board about Taste of Marietta. But about the car display, would there be enough room? There are some pieces from the Museum we'd love to showcase alongside them. We wanted to just look at the street again just to be sure."

"That sounds amazing honestly," said Marjorie. "But definitely a Nelson question." They all looked over to Nelson who was just about finishing with his client. Suddenly, Marjorie remembered to ask Lara Jean what had been on her mind that morning, turning to her. "I do have a question for you, though, Lara Jean! Would there be any way that I could sit with you or stop by on a Monday when we're off, to browse the exhibits?"

"That shouldn't be a problem. I'd be happy to come in on a Monday myself and show you around. In fact, are you free the second Monday in May? We're going to start our work on this year's benefit event, and it's mostly all archive digging, looking for a theme that would resonate with attendees. Another set of eyes and hands would be wonderful for that!"

"Sounds like a plan that benefits us both. I'd be happy to help! When is the benefit?"

"It's not until fall, but for these sorts of things we've already got the cogs turning at the beginning of the year. You should absolutely come and check it out—if you love history, and dancing to classic rock and oldies, you'll be having a grand time all while supporting historic preservation."

She left work that evening as the sun still lingered on the edges of the faded blue sky. Crossing through the Square, she saw the fountain, the water glistening like crystals and reflecting the glow of the twinkle lights dotting the rooftops of the buildings around the park. Teens sat on the surrounding benches with to-go cups of boba chatting and laughing, and across the way in the gazebo a couple leaned close together on the railing looking out. A sleepy but enchanted dusk was approaching, the chime of the bells from both the Methodist and Baptist churches on opposite ends of the Square sounding off in unison. If she didn't have to get back to Doc, she would have stayed to take it all in a little bit longer. She felt a bit more hopeful now, and tonight, compared to when she had been staring at the grassy hill of the cemetery earlier that week, she could watch a park scene and feel sentimental about the laughs she heard, the couples scattered around. As she passed another couple, she smiled seeing that their faces were so lit up being next to someone that only to them in that moment was special—she knew that feeling all too well.

Simon, 1964

Simon was frozen where he sat. Surely she could not have spotted him or what he was up to from so far away. He closed his notebook and tried to look down and away from her. His eyes looked back to the corner of Church and Nineteenth where a dog walker was nearly being dragged by seven dogs in varying sizes and breeds toward the park. The man got what control he could to pull them back, and when they all brushed past Simon, he looked their way and then over at the woman. She seemed to be laughing as her head followed the dogs and the poor dog walker at their mercy. Simon felt some relief as he saw her readjust forward and stare off toward the same skyline of downtown San Francisco. Besides her coat, she had nothing else with her. No purse. No picnic. Not even a proper blanket.

He closed his notebook and stood up, not realizing that he'd started making his way across the grass, his feet carrying him with ease but his heart beginning to race. She didn't notice his presence, but he slowed down as he got closer to where she leaned back, careful not to startle her. He paused and fixed his eyes ahead at the skyline. He wanted to say hello, but he was at a loss on how to begin.

"It's a little hot for a coat, isn't it?"

She turned to look up at him, using her hand as a visor over her face. In the bright sunlight before shading her face, he realized that she was Asian.

"Pardon?" Her voice was soft but not high, and she sounded just like any other Californian he'd met since moving here. He pointed to the coat on which she was positioned and smiled.

"I, uh—didn't mean to bother you, but I couldn't help noticing that you brought your coat, ma'am."

"Well, yes, I did. I mean, you can never be too sure in San Francisco. The fog is always creeping in when you least expect it."

"That's very true, ma'am. Anyways." No other words came to mind. And with his Southern accent, he probably was coming off as a simple hick, as some locals down at the grocery store jokingly told him. "I hope you enjoy the rest of your Friday. I apologize for being forward. But just everyone else here has blankets and here you were with a coat."

"And it bothered you that much, I suppose," the woman responded, dryly but more amused than irritated. She sat up and crossed her legs in front of her. "And it is a beautiful Friday. I guess I underestimated how pleasant it would be when I stepped outside this morning. We don't always get blessed with summer days that feel, well, like summer."

"Indeed, ma'am. Back home in Georgia, it's sticky and unbearable with the heat right now in August. But this…" He looked around him and smiled back at her. "This is just heaven."

She returned the smile. "What brings you to Dolores Park?"

"Same as everyone else today, I guess. Just enjoying the weather and the views. Nothing beats this spot. Well, I don't want to take up any more of your time. I just thought I'd—"

"Come say hello, no, that's perfectly wonderful." She remained still, smiling. "What is your name?"

Simon sighed with ease. "My name is Simon, ma'am. And you are?"

"Marjorie. You're welcome to join me to admire the view if you'd like, Simon. Unless, are you with friends or—"

"Oh no, no, it's just me. But some company would be nice, especially for a nice day. You're very kind, Miss Marjorie." He pointed to a spot for approval to which she laughed and nodded, and he sat down, keeping a comforting distance between them.

"Did you say you were from Georgia?" she asked him.

"Yes ma'am, from Atlanta. Well, a little town just outside of it. Marietta? Ever heard of it? Doubt you have."

She shook her head, and her dark brown curls danced slowly about her shoulders. "No, I haven't. What brings you so far from Georgia to California?"

"School. I'm getting my master's here. Architecture. There isn't a better city—well, maybe New York—to see so many different styles and buildings than San Francisco. Are you from here?"

"I am. Well, I'm like you. I was born and raised in Walnut Creek, a city across the Bay. Doubt you heard of it also."

"What brings you here from across the Bay? Are you visiting or do you live here?"

"I live here now. I'm working downtown."

"Oh, where at?"

"I don't think you'd know the company, they're a local business. Business-to-business stuff."

"Imagine, one of the most beautiful cities is in your backyard. I'm jealous you were born close by and got to move here. Atlanta is nice, but it's got nothing like San Francisco. That feeling, the thrill of possibility and dreams."

Marjorie took a deep sigh, looking at the skyline before them. "She sure is beautiful. That feeling is exactly what she is."

"I would love to stay out here after school, find a job—but who's to say, with my family back home they think I'll be back too. I'm not so sure."

"You're in no rush. You just got here, didn't you?" She looked over and smiled at him. Her eyes were brown, enhanced by black eyeliner in the cat-eye style that a lot of girls were doing, and she had a brick red color on her full lips. He hadn't scared her away, thank God. Not yet.

"No, you're right. Be present, take each day as a blessing. I was originally going to come out here with a friend—but he passed before we could make it together. So, I'm here alone."

Marjorie turned to him with a sudden look of sadness, her smile gone. "Oh, I'm so sorry," she said. Her sincerity loosened him up, but he awkwardly shrugged and shook his head.

"Thank you, really. This was really more so his dream—I was just tagging along for adventure, to be honest." He hadn't really talked about Curtis's death since it happened.

"It must be hard out here on your own—have you really gotten to know your classmates or make friends with anyone?"

"Honestly, just the occasional drinks out with some guys from school, and my roommate. I usually keep to myself as I figure out this city. But you're definitely someone I feel easy to talk with. I don't mean to make you feel uncomfortable."

"If I was uncomfortable, I would have said so. Then I guess that makes me one more person you know now, right?"

"Yes ma'am. This is a sure beautiful day, and I'd consider myself sort of a loner—but on a day like this you gotta enjoy it with good company. Oh God, I apologize for just jawing off about myself. You've been so kind letting me go on. I'd like to know a little more about you. Do you enjoy your job?"

She was giggling as she said, "I do. I'm in the marketing department, and it's almost like I get to tell stories every day. By that I mean I get to be strategic about telling the story of the brand through my work, mostly creating lots of marketing materials from ad copy to tote bags. I've been there a few years now, and I'm so grateful that it brings me back to San Francisco. I never feel quite like who I should be anywhere else, but when I'm here—I'm certain about everything I do. Who I'm about to become. I like the adventure that every day seems to promise."

"Do you think you'll live here forever?"

"If I do, that's not so bad. Of course, I've been to other places—Paris, New York—but like you said before, I was lucky to have grown up here, so close. Why go far when family, work, and adventure is here? I try to take one day at a time, though. I tend to think I live too much in the past." She said so with a smirk that confused Simon. "But also not to promise myself anything for the future."

"So you just came out here today with no plans other than sitting in a park by yourself?"

"Basically." She kept her eyes on him. "I don't know what I'm doing next, but I wouldn't mind if you came along." She pointed to the kids' playground at the bottom of the hill. "Swings? Party crashing? Bank robbery. What's your pleasure?"

Simon laughed, running his hand through his long hair, which had fallen and clung to his forehead in the heat. "You know, I was reading about a robbery out on Guerrero and 14th in the papers—and I'll tell ya what, you do fit the description. I could turn you in, or, could I offer to treat you to something to eat?"

Marjorie thought about the proposal, twisting her lips and playfully turning her eyes to the sky. "We can find a place. No need to treat—I'll just split the bank money under the table with you and go Dutch." She leaned closely toward him. "No local authorities need to get involved."

"Offer accepted. Keep things less messy and more time to eat." He was feeling pretty faint having only had that coffee all day. He looked at his watch and stiffened. *Fuck*, he thought, *Mama*. It was 12:32.

"Oh Lord, I'm deeply sorry!" he nearly shouted. "It's almost one—I call my family every day at that time—I have to go home. Miss Marjorie, I'm so sorry—" He paused, and then spat out, "Would it be strange if I were to ask you not to leave here? I'm having such a great time with you—talking with you— but if I miss this call, it'll be hell to pay and—"

She started laughing again, drowning out his pleas. "Wait, wait, I'll stay. Yes, go make your call. I'll be right here."

"You will?"

"I promise. I told you, I have nothing else to do! How long should I expect to wait here for you?"

"Twenty minutes max." He stood up, a bit relieved, as weird as it was to ask this girl he'd just met such a desperate request. But he didn't care. He asked and she didn't flinch. As he wiped off his pants, he felt his back pocket. Suddenly he had another proposal.

"Or," he began, sitting back down. "We can already go get lunch, and I'll make the call from a pay phone on the way. I've got some change on me." Marjorie's face lit up at the idea.

"That works for me! Actually, I'll do you one better." She stood up, looking away to the east, and said, "What if I told you I knew a spot that had a pay phone inside?" She held out her hand, which Simon took as she pulled him up, his smile meeting hers, admiring her brown eyes and high dimples beneath the shade of his shadow.

"Is it far from here?"

"A little ways, but if we walk fast, twenty-five minutes tops? It's one of the oldest spots in the city!"

"Oldest spots, you say?" This young woman named Marjorie said she lived in the past, and maybe it was nothing special, but in Simon's mind he thought it was an honor that she now was sharing one of these special places with him. How could he refuse? "Let's get started then."

And then she walked forward, but for a second turned back, stretching out her hand for his again.

Chapter 7

A few magical things happened on that last weekend of April in Marietta: on Friday the summer concert series in the park, followed by Taste of Marietta on Saturday, an annual tradition that the town took much pride in by showcasing the most flavorful dishes and treats from local restaurants in stalls across the closed streets of the downtown. As a treat and always in support of the local festivities, Nelson had already purchased a handful of tickets for everyone, including Marjorie, to use on their lunch break.

For the concert, a Beach Boys cover group would be taking the stage that Friday on the wide bandstand of the park's north side, flanked by large round tables at the very front of the stage that would be filled by some concertgoers, while others crowded behind on whatever patch of grass was available to set out their blankets and lawn chairs. When Marjorie was walking to Nelson's that morning, she was shocked to see that so many people had already staked their claim on scattered spots with their chairs already folded out—they must have either come late in the night or early that morning to secure their good views. As she waited outside of Nelson's for Nelson or Jeff to arrive and open up the salon, she saw another woman with a blanket and chair beneath her arms walking past. So, this is how you knew summer was coming. Along with the sunshine, the town was coming out in full to welcome the warmer days ahead, and Marjorie was ready.

Jeff was the first to arrive and unlocked the front door as he and Marjorie and the other stylists piled in and began their day. The air was cool inside, and the smell of citrus and vanilla wafted over to the front desk while

Addie washed Jeff's hair, a regular ritual among the stylists before hours– after all, where was there a better place to get ready than at the salon?

Nelson finally showed up, cup of coffee in hand and a sort of grimace on his face when he removed his glasses to rub his eyes.

"First concerts," he muttered when he came over to add more cash to the drawer. "I leave the house early and still people act like they've never dealt with a street closure in this town."

After work finished, Marjorie got Doc settled before heading back to the Square to meet up with Alex and Addie for drinks. While she waited for them, Marjorie decided to walk around the block. The closed-off streets were crowded now with Marietta's own in their chairs or standing around with drinks in hand—it reminded Marjorie that she could go grab a drink and bring it back to the park. On the same block as The Local Spoonful was a seafood bar that had an outdoor to-go window for cocktails, and she wandered over to see what was on the menu. Her eyes were drawn to The Sun Glow, a boozy frozen lemonade topped with flambéed meringue in a frosted plastic cup—it sounded perfect. She sipped as she waltzed back up to the park that was overflowing with concertgoers crossing through and sitting by the fountain or in the grass—an elderly group had miraculously stolen the gazebo as their own and set up a delightful round table for themselves with a gingham tablecloth and stemless glasses of red wine. On a bench lining one of the paths, she took a seat and could finally enjoy the whimsical evening of a fleeting April.

She was watching the band address the crowd and kick off their set with the familiar riff of "Surfin' USA" when she felt someone hover close to her. "Good evening," she heard a familiar voice say cheerfully as she looked up to see Daniel D'Amato's big brown eyes meeting her own. "I thought it was you from across the park!"

"Oh, hi!" she exclaimed. "Great to see you again! Were you at Westside or just coming out to see the show?"

"I was there today, but mainly just hanging out a bit to check out the music with my aunt. She's chatting to some friends she spotted nearby." This time he wore a crisp white button-up with short sleeves and dark fitted slacks. He had a few paper bags in one hand.

"How lovely! It's a beautiful night to be out together. Do you also live in Marietta?"

"Actually no, I'm over in Midtown. I'm staying the night with her, though, she only lives off of Whitlock Avenue. She's excited I'm going to be here for the Taste of Marietta tomorrow ."

"That is tomorrow, isn't it? Well, I'm sure I'll run into you both again—I work over at Nelson's Salon, and during the festival there's gonna be a classic car show right in front of it on Church Street. Definitely check that out when you're stuffed and need to walk the food off!"

He smiled and nodded. "We sure will." The song came to an end and the Square erupted into applause. As Marjorie looked toward the stage, she caught out of the corner of her eye Alex and Addie walking toward her.

"I have to get going now," she said, holding her hand out, "but it was great to run into you again, Daniel. I hope to see you and your aunt tomorrow, so I can formally introduce myself."

"Likewise, Marjorie. And call me Danny! I promise to bring her to the show tomorrow. Would you like me to bring you something from the food fest?"

"Oh, don't worry about it, but that's so nice of you. I hope you both have a fun evening!"

His smile never ceased as he turned and headed toward where his aunt was still caught up in chatter. Maybe it was the Sun Glow, but her face felt warm. She was still smiling. That wasn't the drink.

...

From one festivity to the next—Taste of Marietta was all set up with its stalls lined up around the Square and various dining spots set up by the time Marjorie was back en route to work. Nelson made a point to get there before seven as his truck was already parked right at the front of the salon facing outward toward the street. A few other classic cars were already parked, belonging to some friends of his and Lara Jean and donors to the Museum, with the truck flanked on one end by a light blue 1956 Bel Air and a salmon pink 1958 Cadillac from across. She stopped to admire them both, thinking how well restored they were, like when she'd seen similar models in their actual heyday.

As Marjorie sat at her desk, she began observing the foot traffic grow on Church Street as people made their way toward the Square and all the dishes that were lined up and ready to be sampled. Nelson stepped out as the last car, a red '46 Buick, pulled in and parked. After getting the car and its driver settled, Nelson came back in and held his hand out for a high five. "It's all yours," he said to Marjorie, who jumped to her feet and tagged herself in with a smack to his hand.

The draw of the car show was pretty solid, and Marjorie enjoyed the time walking around as Nelson's liaison between the spectators and car owners, dropping back into the salon for questions or passing along information when Nelson would pop his head out with a message. She felt good waltzing around in her blue floral sundress, with her teased hair pushed back with a blue headband. A steady, busy day, and warm—it was a pleasant Saturday, made all the better when at last she saw Danny walk through the gathering and toward where she stood by a baby blue convertible '62 Thunderbird.

"As promised," he greeted, pushing his black Wayfarer shades up to the top of his head. "It's good to see you!"

"Likewise," returned Marjorie. "It seems you lost your aunt again!"

"Oh no, she's close!" He turned around and waved to a woman not far behind who waved back, in a flowy, long polka dot dress and with a gray bouncy bob at her shoulders. She had a wicker shoulder bag filled with some flowers, which whacked a passing man as she hurried to where her nephew stood. "Aunt Roberta! I'd like to introduce you to Miss Marjorie, the one who was asking about that record from the shop."

"Well!" exclaimed Roberta. "You are just a doll, my dear! Marjorie, what a pretty name—old-fashioned too, you don't get many Marjories now, or Robertas, if we're being honest."

Marjorie laughed. "It's wonderful to meet a Roberta! I really am glad I came across your shop at Westside. I can't help myself around good antiques and old things."

"It warms my heart, darling, to hear that straight from a customer! Daniel told me you found something pretty unique too, an old record of a singer you know?"

"Something like that. I just wanted to see where you got it from, but it must have been forever ago, which I completely understand. All the same, I'm so happy to have found it. I wish I had money to open my own little storefront like you!"

"It pays most bills, that's for sure. But antiques and estate sales are a passion of mine. Nothing like turning what you love into income. But these!" She turned to look at the Thunderbird behind Marjorie. "Now I'd never part with one of these. Me and Daniel's grandma, my sister, we grew up with a Cadillac and, boy, did we feel spoiled! I wish Daddy had kept it, but Lord knows the maintenance that would go into a car like this now! So, these are Nelson and Lara Jean's friends, eh? I used to get my hair colored at Nelson's, a girl who no longer works there, but she got my hair to a nice strawberry blonde for a while, before I decided to embrace the gray. Are you a hairdresser there, Marjorie?"

"No ma'am, I'm just the receptionist. The current stylists are lovely, and Nelson has been great about telling me about Marietta. I've learned so much in the few months since I've moved in."

"I'd love for you to tell me all about what you like about our town. Come to lunch with us today! When do you have a break?" She had such a wide grin on her face, and Danny behind her was seeming a bit sidelined by his aunt's suggestion but smiling just as well at her sweet gesture. Marjorie would have loved to, in all honesty—after all, if it weren't for this woman, she wouldn't have heard Simon's voice again.

"You know, I would love to, but," she began, "the salon is so busy today, and I'm not sure I can wander far given that I was put in charge of the show until four. I'd love to take a rain check, Miss Roberta, if your nephew doesn't mind the next time—"

"If it's willed by Roberta, what will be done will be done," Danny assured her. "But you're working and we understand. I promise we'll catch you next time!"

"Or maybe we'll have to come to you, Daniel," suggested Roberta, turning to him. "He's the Operations Director at The Georgian Terrace. I've had the loveliest afternoon teas there, and I'm sure Daniel can make arrangements for us to get the most pristine table at the restaurant. It's so grand! Have you been, dear?" She looked back to Marjorie, relaxing her smile.

"No, I've never been. I only just moved to Georgia, but there's so much I'd love to check out in Atlanta too!"

"Well, if you love historical places and things like my nephew does, you'll fall in love with the hotel. I could tell you all the music he listens to and the stories about Atlanta—he got most of it from me, his original babysitter."

Danny laughed a little and nodded. "Auntie, I think we have to leave Marjorie back to work. But yes! Please stop by—in fact, take my number if it's easier to contact."

Her hand went to her side before she also realized she didn't have her phone on her—not having pockets in vintage dresses was one of the world's more simpler forms of evil. "Could you take mine?" she suggested. "My phone is inside."

"Absolutely." He got his phone out and took down her number, turning then to his aunt. "Shall we, Auntie?"

"Let's have a look at some of these cars first," she said and turned to Marjorie once more, clasping both hands around Marjorie's. "So nice to meet you, Marjorie, and I hope you can find more of what you're looking for. If I can remember anything about that record, I sure will let you know—well, I'll tell Daniel to tell you."

They walked off and Marjorie was back alone among the cars of another time. She could have been thrust back in time and wouldn't have known the difference. But seeing Danny look back and smile once more, she was reminded of the date, happy to be where she was supposed to.

She hadn't felt that breathless since sixty years before.

Chapter 8

Surreal was the word for those moments when Marjorie had been completely immersed in one place in the past and revisited it back in the present. It was always the comeback that took her off guard, with all the changes that had happened in the years to follow, familiar but not—a strange déjà vu but only in her case—she really had been there, done that. When her grandma passed and Papa was selling their old house in Clayton, Marjorie and her sister went with their dad to check in on the renovations they were doing before it went on the market. The wood paneling had been stripped, leaving blank white walls that made the house feel wider than it ever had, and the carpets were ripped up and awaiting new vinyl flooring that Daddy said looked and felt like real wood. Grandma had been a big collector of porcelain figures and ornamental gold fixtures like lamps and side tables—those were all now with her aunt or other relatives with taste just as daring, leaving this house she'd visited so many times on weekends and holidays a cold, unwelcoming shell.

She wouldn't say that's what the History Museum felt like now, walking through the vestibule and into the lobby, but it was still strange. Historical artifacts and photos greeted her upon entering—nothing like the elegant, comfortable feel of Fletcher House Hotel that once was thriving here during the Civil War. On one of her first travels here in town, Marjorie had found herself standing outside of the hotel in 1862, and nervously entered it, discovering inside the elegant lobby where **a red Persian rug lay across the dark parquet floors and kerosine lamps lit up a lively reception area near the long staircase that guests were traveling up and down. A few women waltzed in between rooms, and Marjorie couldn't help but admire their fine muslin dresses with wide skirts and woven bonnets tied with satin ribbons around their delicate** faces. She'd been mistaken for hired help and was led by a bellman toward the back when she accidentally brushed shoulders with a handsome gentleman with a big beard. He kindly smiled at her before he stopped by the reception desk, where the clerk greeted him, "Good afternoon, Mr. Andrews."

Back in the present, she turned left and up a few steps into a low-ceilinged gift shop with old-fashioned candy in jars, postcards, and birdhouses built to look like The Big Chicken. A head of dark curls turned the corner and Lara Jean appeared, carrying a box with a notebook on top. Her face seemed to brighten when she saw the young woman in a flowy shirt dress with a blue embroidered cardigan over it.

"Good morning, Marjorie!" she greeted her. "Glad you could be a part of us today. Follow me! We're mostly going to be among the stored archives on the third floor today with Safiya. She's already begun piecing through things."

Lara Jean led them back out to the lobby and into the elevator that went straight to the third floor. Upon opening, it revealed a narrow hallway of closed doors on either side with old photos of the town throughout the centuries displayed at intervals along the walls. A door on the left was open and some rustling was heard. Following Lara Jean in, Marjorie saw it was Safiya, the facility manager, in a blue PROUD MUSEUM PERSON T-shirt stacking big binders on top of one another before pushing them off to the side of the long rectangular wooden table at the center of the room, itself looking like an antique from the building's bygone days.

"Look who's here, Safiya," Lara Jean announced, and Safiya nearly slammed the binder in her hand down to walk over and hug Marjorie. It was her first time meeting her.

"Yay!" she nearly shouted at Marjorie. "We're happy to have you today. I agree with Miss Lara Jean about a fresh pair of eyes to fine-tune this shindig. Want some coffee? I'm about to go downstairs and get a refill."

"Please," Marjorie responded. "I never say no to a hot cup!"

"When she's back with the coffee, Marjorie, you can just jump into these boxes," Lara Jean continued, waving her hand toward a shelf by the window.

"So, what exactly is it that I'm supposed to be looking for?" Marjorie asked. Her eyes wandered toward a cluster of framed photos at the edge of the center table, all black and white save for one.

"Go in and look through everything. The news clippings, the documents, the photos, old ads, awards—do that first and then go through them backward. That usually works for me when I want to find a theme. Something profound but sentimental, and of course as it relates to Marietta."

"What have been some themes of the previous years?"

"Adolescence in Marietta, Loved and Lost Local Hangouts, Marietta's Political Influences, Celebrated Cobb Artists—those kinds of threads. You find something good, just say it out loud!"

Marjorie dived in, opening the first album to a page where at the top was a black-and-white photo with a tag at the top of its pocket that read WEST ATLANTA STREET, 1940s. A single road stretched into the distance of the photo's center along a train track where a steam engine was about to pass by a large water tank, and on the left of the road a familiar hillside with rows of graves behind tall red cedars. The Marietta Cemetery. The same path she would walk from Morris onto this road where the bike path led over a walking bridge into town, nonexistent right before her eyes in another time. *Pathways*, she thought, looking for a theme. *All Roads Lead to Here.*

Another photo from the 1940s showed a long brick building that reminded Marjorie of a castle shrouded in large trees. MARIETTA HIGH SCHOOL, the pocket was tagged, ERECTED 1924. From having driven around town since getting her car, she remembered that this old building was now Marietta Middle School, as Marietta High was moved into a larger, brand-new campus up the road on Whitlock Avenue. *Reduce, Reuse, Recycle?* Never mind, a lame theme. She looked through a few more photos before glancing over to Lara Jean, still working in silence as she rummaged through boxes, sipping the coffee that Safiya had finally brought back for them before she stepped out again. Marjorie's eyes then turned toward the table to the framed photographs left on the table. The single color photo right away caught Marjorie's attention, of a Black woman in a beautiful, flowing tulle cocktail dress.

"In case you were wondering," Lara Jean said, catching her stare,

"That's my mother."

"Oh, she's just darling in this photo!" exclaimed Marjorie. In the background behind the grinning woman raising a highball glass to the camera was a full Christmas tree adorned in tinsel and pink and gold ornaments. "Christmastime?"

"Christmas of '52," explained Lara Jean. "I wasn't born yet, but she had that dress way in the back of her closet. I'd try and put it on, but it was always too out of reach on the hanger, so I'd just touch the skirt and pretend I was Cinderella or something. There was one time she did let me try it on—my Senior Prom. She said I'd look lovely if I wanted to wear it—but it was the eighties, and as a young teen I wanted something new and trendy by that time.

But I did love how it fit me, and the seafoam green felt like you were a floating cloud. I wish I did wear it more."

"Why don't you wear it to the gala?"

"Oh, I don't even think I could fit it now! I think that window's passed, anyhow, to look good wearing it. I'm too old."

"I don't believe that. I think you'd look incredible, just like her! Make Nelson fall in love with you all over again."

"Come to think of it, had I known Johnny in high school I feel like he totally would have loved the green dress more if we went to prom together. He's always been an old soul and historian. We always joked he just wanted to marry a Cleary instead of just me."

Safiya walked back in with more boxes from the next room for the three of them to continue sifting through. "Just about the last few items from the seventies to the nineties," she said. "I'm sure we'll get some good color photos from these!"

In the next hour Marjorie cleared two more albums, but no new themes—or names—popped out to her from her work. She saw a snapshot of Regina Rambo before she became the first woman to drive around the state of Georgia in a car, horses carrying cotton bundles to the local merchants during the 1890s summers on the Square, the breaking ground of the new Kennestone Hospital in 1957. She couldn't help but smile getting to a more recent photo, from 2014, when a heavy snowfall had really hit Georgia and cars stuck in heavy traffic by the Big Chicken were slowly being caked by snow. Glancing over at her progress, Lara Jean snorted as she remarked, "Nothing can take down The Big Chicken. And Lord, did they try! Back in '93 a storm nearly destroyed it, and the city was ready to just raze the poor guy, but everyone fought back and were up in arms about it. Even pilots from the airport and officials at Dobbins Air Force Base spoke out, the Chicken was one of their biggest focal points to know how close they were to Atlanta."

"That makes sense."

"It's a real service to the people that so much of Marietta's bones have been saved from the perils of time. I think it's why Marietta has met the future with such enthusiasm. We can blend the old with the new seamlessly. Every step, every day you walk to the Square and see the same buildings that we're looking at in these old photos from the eighteen-hundreds and onward, it's a celebration for the richness and community of this town."

It hit Marjorie then and there. "That's an idea!" she said. "A celebration—that should be our theme—with a throwback prom aesthetic? Crepe paper streamers, photos of the youth throughout the decades at the soda shop or watching movies at The Strand, the town parades—Marietta, forever young."

The cogs in Lara Jean's mind were slowly moving as she kept silent. "I do like that," she finally said, "You know what, I'll pitch it to the rest of the board. I think you're onto something there, my dear." She paused and smiled again, nodding at Marjorie. "I knew it was a good call to have you here with us!"

Marjorie was relieved, smiling to herself as she looked down and ran her hand over the next page of photos. It was a collection from 1963, Halloween and November. Her smile faded as she observed in each photo the ruptured, messy shell of a corner building that looked torn apart like a shirt ripped at the seams. "What happened here?"

Lara Jean came over and looked, biting her lip. "One of the city's worst tragedies," she began. "An explosion at the Atherton Drugstore, where the pizza parlor is now near Westside Antiques. An accident, gas leak—and on Halloween of all days. The force was so powerful it blew out the windows and sent tables and chairs and lots of candy as far as the park."

"Oh God! Did anyone get killed?"

"Oh yes, nine, and many more injured. They were open that night, and given it was Halloween the town parade was happening too. The street level fell into the basement and the concrete collapsed on eleven people inside. An ungodly perfect storm." Folded in one of the pockets was a copy of a newspaper clipping from the *Marietta Daily Journal*. For a moment Marjorie panicked, fearing to read the list of those killed or injured—until she remembered that it was 1963, not 1964. Still, she pulled out the paper and scanned it. "Do we know anything about the victims?" she asked Lara Jean, sitting down to read the clipping in full.

"Not really. I do know that one of the women killed was in fact the mother of the Daily Journal's editor at the time. But little else is known other than what eyewitnesses had seen, like a regular who would stop in to buy a cigar or a father who brought his son in to get him a mask for the parade. And of course, the employees themselves. Marietta didn't do anything related to Halloween for the next twenty years out of respect. The accident still felt raw."

Marjorie read on, coming across the names of the deceased: *S.A. White, Mrs. Ralph Fowler Sr., Mrs. Leslie Barfield, Mrs. Betty Carlisle, Mrs. Otelia Scott, Joe B. Carter, Terry Carter;*

And then she gasped at the last name listed. *Curtis Fuller.*

She closed the book and took a deep breath. Softly, she said, "I'm so sorry for everyone."

"It was so long ago," Lara Jean said. "But it doesn't feel like it sometimes. Like I've said, Marietta is not a place to forget. It's how we move forward, especially with the tragedies."

Marjorie felt like she finally caught a decent breath of fresh air as she exited the Museum, just as another train horn signaled the passing of an oncoming freight line in the distance. The sound of the train soon drowned out her sobs as she walked along the tracks toward the Square, along the same road where the Halloween tragedy occurred decades before she even came into the world. A simple, clean corner pizza parlor now overlooked the park out of the same building where destruction and loss had brought the town to its knees—and it nearly did for Marjorie too.

He had been such a sweet soul, genuine and inquisitive, inspired by her own journey as he was about to take on his own. A comfort to her first few travels in Marietta, which was complete uncharted territory at that time. Poor Curtis. She had hoped to run into him again and see if he did remember her in whatever time they crossed paths again. But it wasn't to be. She wondered if they were to cross paths again before that tragic night, if she might warn him—she could try. As much as she tried to not meddle with anything in the past, it only felt right to try to tell him not to take that job. That was, if he did remember her at all, or if time would let her go back at the perfect moment.

For all her efforts, she knew Simon's death was a possibility in her search. But her gut feelings were telling her otherwise. No matter what she'd find, if she could find anything new at all, she had to keep her focus. Simon was still out there, and she would find him, if she hadn't lost him already.

Simon, 1964

He should have just gone home for the phone call. But any chance to extend this day with Marjorie meant going to unnecessary lengths to meet his mother's demands as well. Mama would be more furious than concerned that Simon didn't call. Thankfully there was a phone booth at St. Francis Fountain. He'd never been to this ice cream parlor but figured that you'd seen one and you'd seen them all. Marietta had five drugstores, just on the Square alone. He would have suggested a drink or lunch, but the thought of alcohol made him nauseous and restaurants were mostly overcrowded right about now. So no, a soda shop it would have to be.

The walk was pretty far from the park, but Simon didn't mind the extra steps and seconds with Marjorie. She did seem not quite there at times, looking around her as if waiting for someone or something to come jump out at her. Maybe she was running away from someone? Even so, she was still very engaging, talking about her other recommendations in the Mission District and other neighborhoods Simon vaguely had heard about. At times, it even seemed like she was in wonder looking around them at the drugstores and record shops and small theaters that dotted along Mission Street, smiling at the cars going by. A rather odd girl, but genuine. And she still held his hand—that was shocking, but a blessing. He could just hear his mama and Annette raving on about the impropriety of such a gesture for only knowing a boy for barely half an hour. But these California girls—they really were relaxed, thrilling.

They turned off Mission up 24th Street and kept along this route past the apartments and corner stores. They were coming up on a corner crowded with people out the door. "La Victoria," Marjorie pointed out. "Great pan dulces!"

"I can see," said Simon, his eyes still glued to the lines as they walked past the bakery's facade. "And again, this soda shop you said is the oldest in the city?"

"Uh-huh! We've got a few more blocks and then we'll be in."

"You go there often?"

"Once or twice before. But it'll be great!" Somehow it felt like she was more excited to get there than he was, and he was starving like hell. A block away he could see a towering vertical marquee for a movie theater, THE YORK, and was expecting to pass it on their walk when Marjorie pulled him off to the right before hitting the intersection. "Here it is," she announced, as they both looked up to the dull unlit red letters of the neon sign that said ST. FRANCIS - SANDWICHES, FOUNTAIN, LUNCH over the door. Inside, it was a narrow soda fountain and wasn't too crowded, but the booths, all toward the back, were filled. Only one gentleman was sitting at the counter with coffee and a half-eaten tuna sandwich. On the opposite wall of the counter seats was a glass display of candy in jars.

Simon scanned around to find where the pay phone was, when Marjorie nudged him to sit with her at the two swivel chairs at the counter. "I'll order if you want to go make your call," she said, and pointed to the right. "The phone is around the corner there!" He smiled and nodded before leaving her, turning around the counter and coming face-to-face with a private phone booth that matched the rest of the cherry-stained wood panels on the walls and booths. He knocked, listened in against the frosted glass, and pulled open the door slowly. Seeing it was free, he went in and closed the door behind him.

After connecting with the operator, it felt like minutes before a familiar voice answered. "Miss Lucy!" Simon exclaimed, happy to hear the warm voice of his mother's housekeeper. "How is everyone this Friday afternoon?"

"Mr. Simon, so good to hear you," Lucy said joyously, "We're staying cool, we can't complain. Annette is over with the baby and they're just sitting on the back porch with your mama."

"Oh good! I'd love to talk to Annette too."

"Actually, the ladies are doing some catch-up for their fall Junior League benefit. I'll be sure to let them know you did call, Lord knows how your mama gets if she thought you never even bothered to try!"

"Absolutely. We can't forget how furious she was the week I forgot. Thank you, Miss Lucy, I'll try again on Sunday if that would be better, right after church?"

"I'll be sure to tell her you plan on doing exactly that. What else have you got going on for today?"

"It's funny you ask—I think I'm on a date with a girl. Well, we just met."

"Darling, what! Well, I don't suppose you'll have time for me after catching up with your mama on Sunday, so you'll have to tell me about it in your next postcard, I love those. The last one of the park with that big conservatory, it looks like a diamond."

"I pick only the best for you, Miss Lucy. Tell everyone I love them, until Sunday!"

"Until Sunday. Goodbye, Mr. Simon!"

When Simon returned to Marjorie, she was sitting straight with her arms folded neatly on the countertop, in front of them a chocolate milkshake heavy on the whipped cream and fudge drizzle, untouched. She grinned at him. "That was quick."

"Turns out, my mama and sister were too busy for me," Simon explained with an exaggerated sigh. "I'll try them back on Sunday, though. Thanks again for humoring me and letting me call, even if it was for nothing."

"Hey! It worked out, and no time lost, right? I'm glad I remembered this place and its phone. Now," she said, patting the stool beside her, "let's have some food." He followed her lead and sat, staring at her milkshake. "Want one too?? She asked. "It's a chocolate orange."

"Plain chocolate is good for me. Let me see what they got." He took the paper menu she handed him and scanned their meals, finally settling on a bacon tomato sandwich. "That should be an interesting pairing," he said, with a shrug. As they waited for his order, Marjorie pulled her shake close. "Is it alright if I start? I can wait, I just figured that I put an order down while you were in the booth in case the guy got weird about me just taking up space. I didn't think he'd make it so quickly!"

"Go on ahead, I don't want yours to melt. How is it?"

Marjorie bent over and sipped from the striped red straw, a look of joy overcoming her face. "Shit, that's good!" she declared, but then covered her mouth with a small snort. "I mean, wow! I'm sorry, you didn't hear me say—"

"Shit?" Simon started laughing. "And here I mistook you for a lady. Must be that great of a shake."

"Yeah, really. Sorry, I've got a secret sailor mouth. When I'm alone with my thoughts I let the words fly. But really! It's amazing."

"I can't wait for mine. Ah, so quick!" His shake came sliding toward him from across the counter. He took an exaggerated slurp and nodded his head as he turned back to Marjorie and said, "Well, shit!"

"Right!" she exclaimed. Together they drank more of their delightful drinks in silence and not long after the bacon tomato sandwich came out. "So," Marjorie continued, "Do you think your family will ever come visit you out here?"

"It would be nice if they did. See all the places I've fallen in love with. But my sister just had a baby, and my mom's practically a pillar of our town, busying herself in committees and ladies aid groups—we honestly never spent much time together when I was living back home, but now she acts like her life has fallen apart since I came out here. She's just doing the same things, whether I was there or not."

"Sorry to hear that. As her only son she should want to become more involved in your life and interests. But I guess she's more the molding-you-into-her-way-of-life type."

"Yes ma'am. But I do understand why she'd want to keep me close. My father passed away in the war and my sister's only been married a few years and lives a few towns over. She's lonely, really, and I love her. But I had to see this through and not keep thinking *what if*."

"Have there been any times when you've woken up and thought this was all a mistake?"

"Truthfully? Yes. But not a mistake exactly about moving. I'm here for architecture and while I'm fascinated by buildings, I'm not sure if it's still what I want to do since I've been here. It's more of a personal interest, but no longer a career I aspire to. I think about going back home sometimes and how I'll just be doing something with the town or finding a job at a firm, but I made it all this way so I might as well do something worthwhile. But I'm not sure if school is it."

"What is it exactly then you see yourself doing instead?"

Smiling at her, he took a breath. "I'd love to sing. Write songs. I've never really told anyone it's what I'd like to do instead. I've written things down, lyrics, melodies—I can play guitar and piano and my daddy would always get me and my sister to sing to Mama on holidays. Something about how it reminds me of him that really gets me going."

"Kind of like honoring his memory with music."

"You could say that. I've just always had music in my life. And how I would love to do something like Eddie Cochran, God rest his soul, or even Bob Dylan. Maybe more upbeat than him."

"The West Coast is definitely a good place to be for music. Maybe go to LA? That scene I feel will be blowing up in a few years."

"You think so?"

"I'm sure of it. Maybe not next year, but I think by the late sixties we'll see an interesting array of acts from there. And who knows—maybe you'll be one of them!"

"I'm not ready yet. If I am gonna start making music, I've gotta start performing and figuring out my sound, neither of which I'm ready for. I'm listening to everything now and trying to figure out what I like first."

"You said Bob Dylan, that's a start."

"Yes, but not too folksy. I'm honestly more sentimental, soft." He looked up, hearing the music flowing from the jukebox toward the back of the soda fountain. "Let me find a few songs for you to give you an idea," he said. "I'll be right back." He went to the jukebox and as the current song, a new hit from The Four Tops from that summer, "Baby I Need Your Loving," was fading, he scanned the codes for the next tune. He passed some Percy Faith and Doris Day, fixated on Dion, but then he saw another title. He didn't expect to find this song, but he had to play it. He pressed C7 for Bertha Tillman's single, "Oh My Angel," from a few years ago—he remembered his sister had it on vinyl and had played it over and over nights before her wedding day—and Simon liked the song the more it floated through those hot summer evenings from her bedroom window down to the porch where he'd been smoking in secret, away from Lucy's disapproving nose.

Sauntering back to the counter where Marjorie waited, Simon held out his hand. "Would you like to dance with me, Miss Marjorie?"

She started blushing as she shook her head. "Oh, come on," she protested, "There's no one else."

"No one else yet. And so what? It's a nice song, we can't let it go to waste." He leaned over on the counter and came close to her, playfully adding, "It'd make this lonely soul the happiest one in San Francisco if you did." She laughed at his persistent smile as she finally gave in, taking his hand once more and wrapping her arms around him as they got to the center of the walkway. He lightly placed his hands around her waist and led their slow steps in place, turning slightly with the soft beat of the song that filled the air around them. She was looking around, smiling nervously and giggling a little, but as she looked toward the other diners, he could only look down at her.

"What is it?" he asked, joining in on her infectious laughter. "Am I doing this terribly?"

"No, you're wonderful," Marjorie assured him, returning his gaze. "I'm enjoying this with you, and generally I'm an unbothered gal who does dumb stuff willingly. But God, get me to dance in the middle of a crowded lunch counter and I feel like the stupidest person."

"No, not you! They're the stupid ones for not dancing along. It's a lovely song, and lovely things are meant to be enjoyed." His hair once more fell down over his eyes, and before he could try and move it, Marjorie reached up, gently grazing his forehead with the soft touch of her fingertips as she pushed the hair back, laughing some more.

"It's a bit too sappy for me," she admitted. "But I guess you wouldn't know a lovely thing if it wasn't enjoyed with the right person."

"That seems to be the theme of today." Her eyes now didn't leave his and as the song wound down into its ending notes, he leaned his head down and onto hers, pulling her in a little more to him. They'd only met at Dolores Park that morning but dancing here and now at St. Francis to what seemed like a silly song to Marjorie, they took in this fleeting little moment, that feeling growing warmer and comforting at the phantom possibility that maybe they had known each other for decades, other times perhaps. Even if it wasn't true, it at least made Simon feel that everything was right—he was meant to be here; he'd always belonged.

The song stopped. As they slowly came to a halt, Marjorie remained with her arms around Simon, her head still against his. "Well, shit," she murmured.

Chapter 9

The Sunday morning began with a phone call to her mom. The line rang a few times before Mrs. Valdez picked up, and Marjorie put her on speaker while doing her makeup at the vanity. "Good morning, Mommy!" Marjorie exclaimed. It was only seven in the morning on the West Coast, but her mom had always been an early riser.

"Good morning, Marjorie," said her mom, awake and rather lively. "What are you up to, sweetheart?"

"I'm getting ready to meet with some friends to go to an estate sale, and brunch after. I'm bringing Doc with me too!"

"Oh, will the sellers allow dogs?"

"Probably not, but one of us could watch him and take turns going in to look around. It's nice out and not too hot, so I didn't want to keep him cooped up."

"That's good. He's such a cute old man. Your dad would love him!"

"He'd be an easier grandkid to watch, that's for sure. Is Daddy still sleeping?"

"What do you think? Got caught up on YouTube until four in the morning watching old Warriors highlights."

"Oh boy, from what season?"

"2017."

"Geez, well I guess it's better to watch 2017 than go see them at Chase Center this year."

"We almost did. But he insists it's not worth those ticket prices when he can yell at the TV at home all he wants for free. But the weekend in Carmel is a better birthday for him anyhow. He's sad you couldn't come out after all, but honestly, it'll be a nice mini vacation just for the grandparents." She and her daughter both chuckled.

"Wish I could be there," Marjorie replied.

"Me too, sweetheart." Marjorie held her breath, hung up on the next words her mom might say, something probably belittling or critical about not affording the flight or time off. But neither of those things came. "Just check up with us later when you're back from the sale. Don't go too crazy, you gotta call me later so we can go over some bills you still need to catch up on."

"Yes, will do."

"Send me pics of what you do find! I can share them with your Aunt Liz, you know how much she'd get a kick out of it." Marjorie had gone to her first estate sale with her Aunt Liz when she was eleven—her aunt's idea of babysitting. It was a house in the Berkeley Hills, in an old Craftsman bungalow with dusty blue shingles and low ceilings that made it feel like going inside a hobbit hole. The one item that she did take away from the sale—a medium-size framed paint-by-numbers of a red lighthouse by calm turquoise waves—now hung on the front room closet door of Dogwood Daze.

"Maybe I'll get lucky and find you a pair of designer sunglasses again. Ooh, a Hermès scarf?"

"I think your luck ran out when you snagged that Dior pair for me. They're the only ones I ever use!" She heard her mom exhale, and sipped what she was sure was coffee. "Have a good time, sweetheart. Glad you're making plans."

Whatever the plans that she might have been talking about, Marjorie was relieved she didn't nag like before. After they hung up, she smacked her lips together to press the red lipstick firmly in place and smiled.

...

Nothing was more exciting to Marjorie than antique stores or estate sales. Some might have found them morbid, the stuff of dead people, but they fostered her burgeoning sense of identity all throughout college and even her twenties when she first moved to San Francisco. The world she built with the items she found was unique, not to be replicated or mocked. Each item had a story—if not its own exact provenance, then the story of how she came across it. Most of these same items curated through the years now adorned Dogwood Daze, and Marjorie loved the idea that they added a new patina to the already deep roots of the house.

What she loved most of all about her collection was how every piece *felt* like she was traveling, when she wasn't.

She hoped to find more lovely things on this hot morning with Benny, Alex, and Doc as they headed to the sale in the Cherokee Heights neighborhood, just north of the Marietta Square. Benny took Doc around the block while Alex and Marjorie made their way to the house, a brick Colonial with jasmine climbing around the front portico of the door and pink roses planted along the lower-level windows. Inside was the familiar sight of items piled about and tagged with different-colored stickers, and both women were armed with giant reusable shopping bags and Marjorie already with her hair wrapped in a headscarf to protect today's bouffant from the dust. She took off her sunglasses to have a better look around, and after making her rounds in the backyard, she headed back inside and found Alex in a bedroom upstairs, grasping two old striped hat boxes. "What's that you got there?" she asked. Marjorie had found an old ice cooler with chipped red paint and PLEASURE CHEST written in big letters across the front. "Oh my God! Love it."

"I could use a cooler out on the porch," Marjorie said, setting it down. "I practically live on it."

"I don't know if you will be with this humidity," warned Alex. "You're gonna be sticky and begging to stay inside, I guarantee."

"Mmm, we'll have to see. Even so, all the more reason to have something for cold drinks! What's in there?"

Alex lifted the lid on the top box as she said, "They're empty, but they'll be good to store some model heads when I practice my cuts! I think I'm gonna call it and go check out downstairs, then let Benny know she can come in."

"Sounds good! I've yet to go through the upstairs, so I'll catch you outside." As Alex disappeared into the hallway, Marjorie got back to rummaging around the rooms, picking up a headscarf with daisies printed on it and a heart-shaped ceramic frame with a blue bow and strawberries swirled around the border on a vine. She thought of a cute photo Benny had taken of her and Doc on the porch during Pie Night a few weeks ago that would be perfect for it. She placed the items carefully inside the Pleasure Chest and made her way into the next room, where she found to her amazement Roberta Hamilton in her element, picking through items that were most likely to end up at the Westside booth.

"Miss Roberta!" she nearly shouted, giving the older woman a bit of a jump as she looked to Marjorie and then held out her arms.

"And look who it is!" Roberta said as she hugged Marjorie. "I'm not surprised to run into you here! How are you, dear? Found some goodies?"

"Sure have. I can't wait to see what you'll bring next to the store. Are those stained glass?"

"Beautiful, aren't they? Not often you find panels this small and with such colors! This foxglove design is my favorite."

"You should keep it for yourself, it is lovely."

"No, I've gotta let things go to move forward and live comfortably. Besides, the things worth keeping in my life are my meds and my nephew. We all still need to have that lunch together, you know."

"I haven't forgotten! How is Danny?"

"Daniel is well! But it's about to be summertime in Atlanta, so what should be a dead season somehow makes him even more busy nowadays. People are trying to get out of this place and away from the humidity, but I don't know—he's always at The Georgian Terrace now!"

"I really would love to see it sometime. It sounds like a grand hotel!"

Benny was just coming up the stairs, already in her hands a tall pile of books she must have picked up downstairs. "Hey!" she said, grinning at Marjorie and then Roberta. "Pretty much found what I wanted already."

"Lucky!" exclaimed Marjorie. "I still have the rest of the rooms up here to case. Benny, this is Roberta! She runs one of the booths at Westside."

"Oh sweet! Great to meet you, ma'am."

"And you too, dear! Any friend of this young lady's is a friend of mine. I won't keep you both but I'm sure I'll run into you again, Marjorie. And lunch with Daniel, we'll be in touch!" She winked as she walked past them and down the stairs, Benny looking back after her.

"With *whom*, she said?" She was clearly curious to know, especially now that Marjorie blushed a little.

"I owe her and her nephew a lunch date is all," she explained. "They've been very helpful in tracing some antiques I came across at her station."

"Uh-huh, and is he cute?" Benny kept her grin. "I don't see why you need to expand your family circle out here, Marge, when you've got me and my sis and Doc! Unless her nephew is cute."

"Oh stop!" Marjorie chuckled, picking up the Pleasure Chest. "Maybe a little."

Done with their hunt, the girls packed their finds into the trunk of Marjorie's car and drove down the street to Bextor's Bistro, inside a whitewashed brick building planted in the middle of all the beautiful old homes a few streets over on Sessions. They got their coffees and briefly watched the current string of train cars whizz by on the hill behind the cafe that was crawling with kudzu, before strolling down past Victorians with their grand porches and large oak trees that created a cool canopy arching over the street. Marjorie leaned to pat Doc who was lapping up water from the to-go cup she put on the ground between her and Alex. "I'd say it was a successful hunt," she said, and both girls nodded.

"Oh fuck yes," Alex exclaimed. "I never can find hat boxes in that *mint* condition. I'm telling ya, Nelson should just put all our practice mannequin heads on display in the front window. It'd surely draw me in to see what the hell is going on inside. But until then, I gotta hide my gals away from the public eye."

"That could just be you," Benny said, "but Marietta does have its share of fuddy-duddies who'd be clutching their pearls at a sight like that."

"*But* it is Nelson," Marjorie pointed out. "You might as well be charged with treason to protest anything he'd do in this town."

"He and Lara Jean seem so occupied, though, with all the stuff they gotta do for the Museum benefit," said Alex, "and honestly, I don't think he'd notice if I put a few heads on display. How else am I gonna show off my handiwork?"

"TikTok?" Benny suggested.

"Ugh, don't get me started! I'm offline for a while, both TikTok and Instagram. I've got too many mutual friends with my ex, who I've been trying to avoid since he moved back in the area. I mean, Powder Springs isn't close but still too close for comfort." She turned to Marjorie. "Say, that guy you were talking with at Taste of Marietta, the Alain Delon type, is he single?"

"I didn't think you saw that," Marjorie said.

"Oh, we all did. Nelson especially. He remembers the woman who was with him too, Roberta, I think?"

"Yeah, she used to get her hair colored at the salon, but it was years ago. That was her nephew."

"We ran into her upstairs at the sale!" Benny nearly shouted, smacking Alex's arm. "You missed it! Sounded like he's single, but sorry Alex, I think he's already smitten with Marge here. They have a lunch date apparently."

"Oh God, stop!" Marjorie said, growing red and gulping more coffee down. "With his aunt too, the *three* of us. It's not a date, it's a courtesy luncheon to discuss antiques."

"All I'll say is that no man I know would willingly sit through a lunch to talk about antiques, of all things," said Benny.

"I concur," piped in Alex. "So, you're not interested in him then?"

"Hey now, what about whatshisname Martin? Art's son? He's come in twice now and once was for a beard trim—and let me tell you, Benny, that boy definitely does *not* have a beard."

"Argh!" Alex cupped her face in her hands. "OK, yes, Stephen is gorgeous, and he's got great music taste. However—" she paused. "So he told me he's got a girlfriend. But I don't know, I get weird vibes about it when he mentions her. They've been together a few years, but they've known each other since high school. But I digress. Not trying to get in the way of anything."

"That's fair," Marjorie said. "Well, that being said, I can find out if Danny D'Amato, that guy, is single since I actually don't know, and I'll see what kind of woman—or man—he likes. Who knows. I surely don't."

Doc took a pause from his sniffing along the fences and stretched out, coming over to Marjorie and booping her hand with his little wet snout as his tail wagged steadily. "Aw baby, you want another pup cup?"

They turned around on Sessions to go back to Bextor's, just as a woman in a blue jogging set and a fluffy brown Shih Tzu were approaching them. At the sight of the small dog, Doc was already perking up to go say hello. "Is this a friend, Doc?" Marjorie said to him playfully, then turned to the woman. "Hello!"

"Hi there!" said the woman. "My Lola spotted y'all a mile away and wanted to come say hi! This might sound weird, but I think she recognizes him—is his name Doc?"

Marjorie blinked before responding, "Yes, that's him! How did you know?"

The woman smiled. "I used to see him up at Lewis Park, but he was always with a man. I'd recognize that face, though, anywhere, such a playful boy and still handsome after all these years!"

"Oh, he sure is spry. I've only had him a few months; I adopted him from Cobb Shelter. How long has it been since you've seen Doc there?"

"Is that so? He used to be there every Sunday in the late mornings with an older gentleman up until last year, I believe. I hope the man is OK, if he had to surrender the poor guy. But I'm happy to see he's in great hands, a happy boy! Bring him to Lewis Park sometime, it'll be good to see him again." The woman gave Doc a gentle rub on his head, before she turned around. "I hope you ladies have a lovely rest of your day," she said before leaving with her little Lola.

Marjorie kept her gaze on the woman, and then turned to Doc. He stood looking onward, too, at the woman and Lola, tail wagging, but a glimmer of youth in his eyes.

"Interesting!" Alex finally said. "Crazy she knew Doc's owner."

"Not really, it seems," responded Marjorie. "But still, small world. I forget that Doc's been here longer than me."

"If only he could tell us about his younger days," Benny added. "Wonder what happened to his old owner."

They passed a sign overhead that showed an arrow leading to Lewis Park. Marjorie looked back at the sign—she wondered, but she wanted to do more than that. She could do more, and for Doc, she absolutely would try to find out.

Chapter 10

The Sunday brunch crowd started to swell in Livingston's around ten thirty, but Daniel D'Amato was ready to leave work. He already did his part, going over the summer menu changes with the food and beverage director and finalized the Instagram story strategy with the marketing manager that would be implemented from the morning's festivities. This wasn't just any brunch crowd after all—having pushed for months to have the hotel host its first ever extravagant jazz brunch featuring local drag performer and accomplished pianist Miss Cuppa Joella, he was finally given the green light. The day had come, and contrary to what his manager thought, Miss Joella proved to be a big hit to the ever-evolving crowd of Atlantans who now flocked to Midtown. Everything was in place, and he was ready to retreat to his office behind the Grand Ballroom. But first, coffee. He'd been at The Georgian Terrace since seven and was starting to feel an itch for a second cup. He went back toward the new coffee shop on the front terrace; they were always stocked up on their creams and milk, as they should be. It was never the case in the staff cafeteria, and Danny was getting sick of plain black coffee.

The air was warm and the door to the terrace was open for the gentle cross breeze that swept up into the café and made the crystals of the old chandelier dance over the register. The new barista gave Danny a cup in the largest size, and he made his coffee at ease, taking a gentle sip after mixing in the heavy cream. He headed out to the farthest table on the terrace, overlooking the magical facade of the Fox Theatre across Peachtree Street. How lucky that this was where his life had ended up, back home in Atlanta working at one of its treasured landmarks across the street from another. The Grand Dame of Peachtree Street. Danny never thought that all those times Aunt Roberta had taken him into Midtown to visit places like Martin Luther King Jr.'s home and the Oakland Cemetery, that they would lead to him finding a career at one of his favorites. He'd left Georgia for New York when it came to college, to see the fascinating monuments of Manhattan for himself and maybe more of the world right after graduation. But the rusty streets of Brooklyn and Queens, where his actual school was, made him long for the trees and warmth of his home state again. He'd seen the skyscrapers, and he'd gotten the business degree—and with his brief stint making extra money as waiter and bartender with his roommate Mikey's family catering business around the city, he also brought back home a drive to get into hospitality.

Ten years later, he was still doing his part turning Atlanta into a global destination, and he could feel the city was getting close. With future World Cup games being announced and new TV shows filming for months on end around the city, Atlanta was becoming the talk of the South, drowning out conversations around Austin, no longer cheap, no longer quirky. Things like this he thought about during his coffee, when he looked at his watch and realized he'd lingered too long.

He was walking down the steps to the lower level, when Mark, one of the weekend bellmen, caught up to him waving his hand. "Hey Danny! There's someone looking for you at the front desk," he announced.

"Shit, were we expecting any site inspections today?" he frantically asked, grabbing his phone and scanning for notifications he might have missed.

"No, it's not for the hotel. It's a young lady here to see you specifically. She said she's a friend? Her name is Marjorie."

Danny took a deep exhale, but another panic set in. "Marjorie? I'll head over to her now. Is she still in the lobby?"

"She is. Such a sweet woman! Think she came from church, she's dressed real nice."

He laughed a little and followed Mark. "It seems she's always dressed for church."

As Danny headed toward the lobby, he saw a magnificent young woman in a peach sheath dress with white heels and a gold headscarf wrapped around her full, long waves. She still had sunglasses on, but he didn't need to try and guess who she was. What he didn't expect was that she wasn't alone—in her hand was a leash attached to an old black dog who sat patiently next to her with his mouth open, almost like a smile.

"Oh!" he let out, not quite thrilled at his choice of greeting. "I mean, good morning! What brings you all the way out here?"

"Good morning!" Marjorie returned with a laugh as she removed her glasses. "Well, I was at the Fetch Park in West Midtown with a friend when I figured, you know, let's drive on down to Peachtree Street and check it out, and see if you happened to be in. I ran into your aunt last weekend, and she said that you were here more often?"

"She was right, it's been nuts around here in the summer with everything we're trying to step up. Well, I'm honored you thought to stop by the hotel and happy you did because"—he got to his knees and held out his arms for Doc, who immediately trotted over to him—"this guy alone already is making my day! Hey buddy, your mama didn't tell me about you."

"This is Doc, my sweet boy who deserved a day on the town. I wouldn't have brought him if I didn't check that you guys were dog friendly."

"As we sure are," Danny said, still in his high dog voice. "But it's been a few weeks since we've had a dog around here. Let's grab him a treat at the desk, and some water? Afterwards I'd be happy to give you a grand tour of the hotel, if you'd like."

"That's so lovely of you, I'd like that a lot. We're in no rush, we used the valet to park."

"Which I will take care of for you."

"Oh, please don't!"

"I insist! It'll buy your silence anyhow, so that you don't let my aunt know you went around her back to meet up with me."

Marjorie scoffed. "Oh, our lunch date is still happening. This was my own little surprise. Besides, I've heard so much about The Georgian Terrace and I'm holding you accountable to keep up the hype. Where shall we go first?"

Danny turned to look up at the tall dome that loomed high above the atrium and then behind them at the concierge and entrance toward Livingston Restaurant and Bar, but in the opposite direction was the hall down which all the grand event spaces lay. "Best course of action is upstairs," he declared, "and then we can make our way back down the old staircase that'll take us back to the restaurant and the ballrooms." He knelt down again to give Doc a big rub under his snout before asking the old boy directly, "Now, who wants a treat?"

They got into the elevators and made their way to the fifth floor, with Danny leading the way down the hall toward the hotel's pristine original marble staircase overlooking the atrium.

"The rooms aren't much I admit," he began as he led his tour. "Clean, with basic amenities. The real charm lies in the public spaces, they're the true gems. For being built in 1911, the hotel has maintained a lot of its original features and integrity, albeit some minor upgrades as the decades went on."

They looked out over the lobby and took in the sunlit space below as Marjorie asked, "Is it the oldest hotel in Atlanta?"

"Correct. The Georgian Terrace was built to bring a refined appeal to the city as it expanded, being constructed on the cross section of busy Peachtree Street and Ponce de Leon Avenue. She's always been regarded as an elegant must-stay, and when The Fox was built across the street in 1927, all the stars had to stay here."

"Convenience and opulence," Marjorie observed as they walked down the curving stairs, slowly descending for the sake of Doc's slow pace and little paws.

"Ten floors, designed in Beaux-Arts, and at the time of its construction, cost five hundred thousand dollars to build. I've seen some incredibly stunning hotels, but for Atlanta at the turn of the century, she was, and still is, impressive."

"How did you end up in your role here? And I guess, by extension, in hospitality?"

"Here, I was invited to apply for an open position last year by the current director of sales and marketing. I knew her from when I was at a boutique hotel over in Alpharetta for a few years before that as the food and beverage director, and when she told me they were looking to fill the operations director position here, I hopped right away on the opportunity. My aunt's right, I love history and old things thanks to her being me and my siblings' main babysitter growing up—and I especially love all the history of Atlanta. It's home. And when I came back from college after being homesick, I knew I had to get into hospitality and travel to show others what a great place Atlanta was—and is becoming."

"I think that's pretty cool, considering you're doing something you love in one of the most fascinating landmarks of the city."

"I definitely count my blessings. It can be a lot sometimes, the back of house, but when I'm walking through the lobby and see just how in awe our guests are of the place, I feel so good and remember how I'm a part of its magic every day."

"That's what I am hoping for with my job. I'd love to add to the magic of Marietta the longer I'm here. Right now I still feel like an outsider."

"Where did you move from?"

"California, actually. I moved here in January for a marketing job but then they cut my department, and on a whim, I just felt like sticking it out since I already relocated."

"That's ballsy, I gotta say. I've never been to the West Coast, but it's on my bucket list. If I got let go and stranded in a completely unfamiliar place, I don't know if I could do the same. I went to school up in New York, and I thought about staying there, but there were too many good opportunities back here. It made more sense to me to take what I learned in school and let it transform my home for the better."

"I get that. And look where it's gotten you! You totally made a good decision."

They were now back on the main floor, and they strolled past the entrance into Livingston, the restaurant and bar, peeking in to get a glimpse of the now dwindling crowd as Miss Joella blew kisses, her performance coming to an end. "It's so lovely in there," said Marjorie, "and lively! Is that a mezzanine level I see?"

"Sure is, although it's mainly extra event space for weddings or smaller gatherings. The real draw, I think, is this way." Danny led the way through wide doors that took them into the largest venue of the hotel, the Grand Ballroom. Elegant, high ceilings greeted them with Corinthian columns scattered throughout and chandeliers illuminating from above, brightening the ballroom as their lights reflected from the high arch windows and French doors that led off to the outdoor terrace on Ponce de Leon. Danny caught a glimpse of himself in one of the reflecting glass panels of the doors, happy he made the right choice to wear his light gray suit today. And Marjorie, looking around in her elegant ensemble, was just radiant, even as she puckered her lips in a funny way and crouched over to kiss an aloof Doc on his head.

"Beautiful!" she exclaimed. "I'd love to twirl around if I could."

"You want to?" Danny asked, reaching out to take the leash from her, and looked around with a smile. "No one's looking!"

"Well then," she said, and letting the leash go took a few steps toward the center as she let her arms swing while spinning slowly around, in the moment pulling off her headscarf to let her hair freely fall and move gracefully about her, which made him smile. She came to a halt followed by a short laugh. "I'd love to attend a party here. Is this the same place where the *Gone with the Wind* premiere was?"

"The premiere was technically at the Loew's Theater," Danny said, "but yes, the gala after was here."

"Are you a big Old Hollywood fan too?"

"Film, music, fashion—if it's older than me, consider it love at first sight. Thirty-three feels old some days. But yeah, there's just something about the beautiful things of the past. People might argue the music and films were boring and simple but no—they were pioneers, revolutionary for their time. You can't beat classics. And don't get me started on the pre-code masterpieces." He turned toward the light flooding in from the terrace, taking note of how it fell on the gold applique in her dress and shimmered a little. "I'll show you another place back this way, let's go!"

Down the hallway they passed again through more doors that brought them to the Piedmont Foyer, and he heard Marjorie gasp. While the Grand Ballroom was carpeted and its lighting more bright, here there was a reserved refinery, with marble columns and more elaborate Beaux-Arts flourishes along the edges of the ceiling. The original mosaic floor was bare beneath them, with Marjorie in her heels and Doc with his uncut nails sounding off a soft pitter-patter as they made their way across the room. She turned to look at the richly painted Florentine panels on the right side.

"This," Danny began, "is my favorite space. While the ballrooms have to serve a more comfortable function with the new carpet and fluorescent lights, the Piedmont Foyer is practically unchanged from 1911. Look at these chandeliers! Aren't they gorgeous?"

He was looking up at the chandeliers and then turned to briefly glance at the panels where Marjorie remained fixated. "The smaller ballroom is through those doors, but I'll quickly show you the lower level where the meeting spaces are," he continued as he turned to walk down the marble steps that would take them below. "As you can see, the grand ballroom spaces that were built for the hotel weren't conducive to the modern needs for conferences and functional meeting spaces, so that's where the basement areas came into play. We recently renovated and built out the conference rooms down here back in the 2000s—"

Danny was almost at the bottom of the steps when he realized he was alone. He stopped and turned to look behind him. Somewhere above, he heard Doc shake as his ears flapped and his collar tag rustled. Climbing back up, he saw Doc staring at him with his smile and wagging his tail steadily.

Marjorie still paid no attention to Danny. Her back was turned to him as she continued looking up at the painted panels. It was like she was in a trance.

He slowly approached her and held out his hand, ready to tap her shoulder. "Marjorie," he said softly. "Are you OK?"

She flinched as he said her name, slowly turning to him and blinking. "Oh," she said. "Yes, I'm sorry. I was just taking this all in."

"It's alright, I just wanted to check. We can skip the downstairs area if you would like to just go straight to lunch on the terrace? It's not much down there to look at, compared to spots like this." As they began leaving the foyer, he said with a laugh, "I hope she has been holding up to the hype."

Looking at him with a smile, Marjorie nodded. "She has. I've seen some spectacular things so far."

Danny softly sighed with relief. But there was a strange feeling he couldn't shake off. Especially as only moments after she'd snapped back and looked at him, in her eyes was a dullness, as if still waking from a dream.

Chapter 11

The hot nights of June crept into Marjorie's dreams, and she would slowly wake into a heaviness of the air that lingered in the bedroom. That and the slow rotation of her ceiling fan made it difficult to fall back to sleep, but it didn't keep the dreams away. The dreams that often came at night, especially since moving to Marietta, would bring Simon to her, back to that day they sat in Dolores, the walks along Mission and Market Street. Those memories intertwined with the visions that only sleep could bring, and when she lay awake in bed with Doc on his side in the empty space next to her, she fixated on the moments she'd been close with Simon; the moment she grabbed his hand, the few blocks later when he slowly nudged her closer to him and she held onto his arm, resting her head on his shoulder as they waited for the crosswalk to turn.

She missed their dancing most of all. The kiss they shared at the end of the night was so fast—it was a rush of emotions and entanglement, and despite the feelings that were so overwhelming that even now in these summer nights she could feel them, she couldn't remember their details. But the dance—that was slow, unexpected, and paced to just the right amount of time for the tune to carry throughout the soda shop and for them to feel like it was forever. If she could only hear him laugh again, see that slight curve upward of his mouth's right corner as she brushed away his heavy strand of blonde hair out of his eyes when his head hung low to rest on hers—she wanted to kiss him then, right in the middle of the dance, and would always wish she had done so.

At least it was only in the nights that Marjorie was reminded of it. She was looking forward to the week ahead, with more wine on the porch with Benny or strolling around the Square with Alex and the other stylists on a crowded Saturday night. Summer was her favorite season, even before that August in '64. In the past and present, summer found her among radiant company, people in better moods and moving about toward their afternoon pastimes, ice cold drinks, or lazy destinations. No better word for it than *joy*, and she was grateful that for the summer to come, she would spend it in Marietta, which was already proving to be a true gem as the days grew longer and stayed warmer for all of those who called it home.

But first, the busy workdays. They didn't feel as long since it was still daylight when the salon closed, and since Addie had recently left for another opportunity at a bigger salon over at the Battery, there didn't seem to be as many clients. On this Wednesday in June, it felt particularly slow. The clean laundry was folded in the back room, the floor was all swept, and the confirmation calls for Thursday were already done. Jeff had stepped out for lunch, and as Nelson and Alex were busy with their current haircuts, Marjorie grew antsy, finally feeling more awake after a third cup of coffee. But her restless mood was subdued when in walked Luanne, hair back in a headband and ready for her monthly upkeep with Jeff.

"Another day, another darling look," she greeted Marjorie, setting on the reception counter a yellow box from Caroline's, the fresh citrus scent of the creamy Key Lime pie seeping from within. "I felt the salon could use something nice and sweet on a hot day like this. Is Mr. Jeff ready for me? I hope he doesn't mind that I'm very early."

"He's out at lunch but will be back shortly," said Marjorie. "And he will absolutely lose his mind over pie! You're too sweet, Luanne. You better have a slice while you're processing, you deserve it!"

"Oh, for how long I'll be in, I know I'll just eat the whole thing myself—better not tempt me."

Luanne waited patiently on the bench by the window when another client came in—eleven-year-old Logan Reddy and his mom, Angie. He was always such a happy and fast-talking young man and upon walking in held out his hand to high-five Marjorie, their usual greeting. "Happy summer, Logan!" she said, and waved to Angie, his mom who proudly smiled at her son's radiating presence. "Glad you're done?"

"Yup!" exclaimed Logan. "We leave this weekend for Universal Studios."

"Universal Studios?" Alex repeated enthusiastically, coming around the corner to her next client with a high five of her own. "Cool! Can I come?" Logan turned wide-eyed to his mom, who laughed.

"He'd love it if you did!" Angie said. "Whatever this is that you've been giving him has every boy at school talking. You'll have to be a guest of honor next time." It was true—the longer tousled front of Logan's naturally wavy hair and short sides was causing such a stir among the local middle schoolers, which in the last few days after school let out, Marjorie finally witnessed as a few boys with their moms had come in asking Alex to explain what "The Logan" cut was that they were trying so hard to emulate. Everyone at the salon joked about how they wished they'd been that cool at that age.

Alex led Logan and Angie to the chair as Marjorie checked out Alex's previous client, then sitting back down and glancing at her phone under the desk. There were two messages she left unread—the first from her bank about an overdraft on her debit card that she needed to fix, and the second an invite to a special poolside cocktail hour tomorrow evening at The Georgian Terrace, from Danny.

The visit to The Georgian Terrace was so spontaneous, and she had to blame Alex for it happening. But to be fair, she was already riding the high of finally getting a car to venture beyond Mariettta, as well as seeing Doc so rambunctious and having a great time at Fetch. It felt right to continue the happy day with adventures. And seeing Danny looking quite debonair and in his element, she was impressed, amused. It was nice that he'd been so accommodating that Sunday and gave a great tour of the hotel, which she would love to see again— especially if it were to bring her back to that party in 1932.

Two weeks later, she and Danny were still talking. Not every day, but enough to warrant casual one-offs about how their days were going or mentioning random Atlanta history or old film and music suggestions, and seeing when that luncheon with Roberta would be able to happen. They already settled for next Sunday on the Marietta Square, Doc being extended the invite, but then Danny followed up with this second invite, a message which Marjorie read over and contemplated whether or not she'd accept. Soon Jeff walked back in, and quickly she pushed her phone back under the desk.

"Luanne just got here a bit early," she warned Jeff, who nodded and waved to Luanne.

"All good!" he said. "You can seat her in ten."

"You got it," said Marjorie as he disappeared into the back room. Back to her phone. Did she dare reply yet? She didn't have any plans, but she didn't want to drive all the way down to Midtown. Still, *It'd be great to see you again*, said his last response.

Nelson's client was ready to check out, and after he was gone, Nelson himself came out to join her by the front, staring through the windows to watch the passing afternoon from the comfort of the air-conditioned salon. With the free time he had these last few days, he'd been clearing out Addie's old station, which was toward the back, but it seemed that he was in no rush at this moment. "Was that pie I saw Luanne bring in?" he asked Marjorie, taking off his glasses to wipe on his navy gingham shirt, his usual ritual after each client, as Marjorie had observed.

"Key Lime," she responded. "If that's all I have for lunch today, I'll die a happy lady."

"I concur. Thank God for Caroline's. But I hope that's not all you're eating today. You bring something else?"

"Nope. I was running too late to pack myself something at home but figured I'd just heat up one of the mac 'n' cheese bowls in the back."

Nelson let out a small groan. "You shouldn't miss out on a good meal and a beautiful day. It's terrible outside, but you seem to tolerate it better. Not one peep out of you since the humidity fell upon us—and you'd be the most annoyed, I would imagine, considering how dry the West Coast is."

"You would think that—but truthfully the humidity feels nice, the heaviness is like being hugged."

"If you say so, crazy girl. If you like it so much, go step out and get yourself something to eat. I'll watch the front, get Jeff to come up here."

"You sure? I appreciate that, Nelson. Want me to grab you anything?"

"Weren't we not just discussing how we'd die happy only eating pie? But I'm an old man. You're a growing girl."

"Twenty-nine is hardly growing anymore."

"Aren't you always complaining about how cold it is in here?" Marjorie conceded with a laugh, grabbing her phone and purse under the desk. "I'll promise to be back in twenty!" she reassured Nelson.

She found a seat by the fountain in the Square, pulling out of a brown bag a ham and cheese croissant she was excited to pair with a cream soda she picked up at the Pop Shop. Through her sunglasses she looked around at the blooming white crepe myrtles and squirrels scampering down from branches of the old oak trees onto the brick paths, then shifting her eyes to the diamond-like droplets of the flowing fountain. The rippling sound of its stream paired musically with the kids shouting at the playground on the north side and the laughter of teens that were gathered in the grass trying to film something with one of their phones stuck on a tripod. By the gazebo, the bubble couple was out, a man and woman whose big wands produced massive, sudsy orbs and had a decent sized crowd clapping around them and admiring their magic. So long as the bubbles didn't travel over to her bench and pop in her hair, Marjorie was in awe as well.

She was on the last few bites of her sandwich when a tall man and a small dog very slowly walked past, taking a seat one bench over. Maybe in his forties, he had a brown stubble on the cusp of growing into a full beard, and despite the hot day out, a gray sweatshirt over moss green cargo pants. His dog was shaggy, almost like a beige Scottie, but its ears were floppy and big, its fur slightly matted with dirt and its face very sleepy looking. The man had a duffel bag that he placed on the other side of his bench, pulling from it a bottle of water and pouring some out for the dog to lap a drink. Smiling at the slow and steady wag of its tail, Marjorie heard the man beginning to talk, seemingly to her. "This is Mikey, and he'd forget to drink if I didn't pour it for him." Then to Mikey, in a higher, slow voice, "Ain't that good, buddy boy."

"Even on a hot day like this?" asked Marjorie. "Dogs are so funny, aren't they?"

"Oh yes, but we only think they need us. Really, it's the other way around."

"I can't agree more. My best friend is an old mutt. I moved here only months ago, and if it weren't for him, I don't think I'd know anyone, really."

"Oh yeah? I'm not from around here too. Where you from?"

"California. What about yourself?"

"Lubbock, Texas. Same place as Buddy Holly. You know Buddy Holly?"

"Absolutely! That'll be the day. Peggy Sue."

"Peggy Sue! I had a crush on a girl named Peggy Stewart in high school and would think that song was about her. Sue and Stewart, close enough. But nope, just been me and little old Mikey. He was a buddy of another guy I met over at the Must Ministries housing, but the place he moved into not long after wouldn't let him take dogs. So, Mikey and I have been a team for just a few months now. Old as shit, slow as shit, but still a good boy."

Marjorie laughed and said, "I don't think you could ask for a better partner in crime. Old boys are the best."

"They sure are, ma'am. You enjoying your day, I hope?"

"I am, thank you! Just on my lunch break."

"Oh yeah? You work around here?"

"Yup, over at the salon down Church Street."

"Ooh, that's luck. I've been in need of a good haircut, trying to find work and such. How much do y'all charge for a guy's cut?"

"Just forty bucks."

"Damn, that's a little steep for what I can get nowadays. It must be a cool place, though, if they got friendly people like you there. Maybe one day I can pop in and treat myself to a good shave and cut." He started getting up and tugged gently at Mikey's leash, the old boy slowly standing up and looking toward the man, ready when he was. "We gotta get moving but enjoy your lunch! We'll see you around."

"See you!" Marjorie called out, realizing that only knowing Mikey's name, she didn't know the man's.

Back at Nelson's, a white pickup truck was just leaving the loading zone as Marjorie returned to the front, which was peppered with a few boxes of old tin lunch boxes, bobbleheads from various baseball teams, and cigarette trays. Nelson and Jeff were taking them toward the back hall when he pointed toward the blue bike from the wall, old but still in good shape. "You want that?" he asked Marjorie.

"Seriously?" She went over to examine the bike, a mixte frame style in light blue with a worn brown leather seat. She was used to Nelson and Lara Jean taking in heaps of antiques and collector's items from the locals who'd casually stop in and beckon to Nelson that they had something either for him or Lara Jean to keep after moving or clearing out grandparents' houses. This was a first for Nelson to ask her if she wanted any of it.

"I figured you can save time with this, since you're so close," Nelson explained, "and gas. Don't know why you would want to switch to driving here when the streets are terrible as is and parking is a nightmare. Anyhow, I don't have any use for a bike, and neither does Lara Jean. And I would ask everyone else, but I know none of them would appreciate it like you would."

Marjorie chuckled. "A bike doesn't have AC. But I guess I could give riding into town a shot. Does it need any work?"

"It's ready to go for the most part. Tubes are still good in the tires, but just need some air. You got a pump at home?"

"I can check at home, I think I got something." She wasn't sure.

"If you don't, I can bring one by tomorrow to take home. Make like the wind tonight! It's gonna be a beautiful evening."

Marjorie laughed and reminded him, "If I'd known I'd be getting a bike today, I wouldn't have taken my car."

Thankfully the bike fit in the back of her car—and the minute she pulled up to Dogwood Daze, she leapt out and briefly greeted Doc before heading into the backyard where the tin garden shed, to her delight, had an old pump after all. As Doc lingered over his human pumping air back into the tires, Marjorie was eager to get back the muscle memory of riding and test it out, but not on Morris. Still too many cars and still always going too fast. Instead, she walked the bike over to the cemetery and once through the gates, mounted the bike and slowly pedaled along the paths until she got her groove. Her legs ached a little as she pushed and pedaled along, it having been years since she last got on a bike, not since her old roommate let her have a go down the hill near their North Beach apartment, and she had nearly collided with a Muni bus turning to go up toward Coit Tower. *Never again*, she told herself—until this night. And it was worth it, getting back into the rhythm of the bike, adjusting her speed as she squeezed the brakes, all while taking in the splendors of the summer evening she rode through.

The twilight was slowly descending over the graves that faded into the shadows of the coming night, the air growing slightly cooler, and the echoes of cicadas chirping as they rose from their slumber in the ground. And then, giving her the most magical thrill, fireflies—a twinkle here and there, bright and quick before another took its place as they floated and disappeared in seconds between the ancient headstones. She'd never seen them before. In this darkness, summer was even more breathtaking than ever.

...

Thursday came, and through the day Marjorie counted down the hours until she could drive out to Midtown and meet with Danny. Feeling good after her little ride, she'd messaged him back to which he quickly replied, *Great! See you.* In another brocade dress and hair teased a little bit bigger, she was looking forward to the rooftop views of Atlanta, the festive crowds and live music, and the teasing thought of what Danny might wear that night.

Simon was there in her dreams, but wide awake, it was a comfort knowing that Danny wasn't far away.

When it was closing time, Marjorie was all but ready to head out when her phone started ringing. "Benny, what's up?" she answered.

"Hey, Margie," Benny responded through sniffles. "I'm sorry, girl, if this is last minute, but are you free tonight?"

"Aww God, Benny."

"The crying's that obvious, huh?"

"No! No, I'm absolutely around." She paused, but sighed and continued, "You wanna come over to the house? Doc would love to see you and he's such a good cuddler!"

"No, I wanna be out tonight. If I'm sitting around, even at yours, I don't think I'll stop thinking about things. You wanna find somewhere close so we can all just walk home after? Invite Alex too, if she's still there! I'm so sorry, I just can't, though. Tonight was rough, I heard a song at the bookstore today and it just got me all—"

"Girl, I totally understand. Songs can be the worst. Are you home? Let me get Doc settled and then we can all head back here for a bit. I'll ask Alex now."

She heard Benny sniffle some more. "Thanks, girl."

Chapter 12

That Friday had Marjorie feeling sluggish, but the magic of coffee would set her right again. She wondered how Alex would be this morning. Benny had today off, and the poor girl was probably sleeping off the whiskey sours from their night out at Duke's Juke. The bar that now occupied the old Sinclair Gas Station was Alex's recommendation for their meetup and jumping point from which to keep Benny distracted. Besides asking the live band to play Benny's favorite songs from The Strokes and Amy Winehouse as well as taking care of the tab, Marjorie wished there was more she could do for her. She was happy she chose a night out with her friend over The Georgian Terrace with Danny, especially when Benny surprised her early, a little after opening, with a coffee frappe from Caroline's.

"Oh, you didn't!" she cried, realizing that she brought one for Alex too.

"Of course I did!" Benny happily assured her. "I'd forgotten how fun Duke's could get. Drinks still strong as ever."

"Guessing you're not taking a beating like I am."

"Well, my sister stocks up on Liquid I.V.s in case, so physically alright. Still emotionally in shreds, but you know, better today. I really did appreciate the night out with you ladies."

"Glad I could have another night out on the town, it's been a minute for me."

"And I'm guessing the last time you had a night out you weren't dressed like that." Benny playfully eyed Marjorie up and down in her work frock: a dusty blue pencil skirt and fitted cotton blouse, complete with the headscarf she'd found at their last estate sale tied into a headband around her hair.

"You're not wrong about that," Marjorie said with a shrug. "I was still wearing jeans back then. *That's* history for me, Marjorie in her San Francisco era."

"I'd kill to see you in jeans again!"

"Girl, I'm flattered but I'm not your rebound girl."

"God help me if you were my type," she responded with a sigh. "But really, thanks girl, and sorry I took you away from your night in Midtown."

"Midtown isn't going anywhere, but you know what will be gone? Your misery, if I can help it. Or Alex—she's got your back too!"

"She's a trouper. Is she in today? Or called out?"

"Actually, she's in the back, just fixing herself up before someone gets in for his appointment." Benny's eyes widened as she mouthed *Stephen?* to Marjorie. "Uh-huh, in ten minutes!"

"Well, if I didn't park in your loading zone I would stick around to get a look at the fella. But I'll leave you ladies to it and catch you later. Oh! That's a beaut, Clark." She pointed to the blue bike propped up off to the side behind the reception desk. "That yours?"

"Yeah! Rode it from Dogwood. I was in no shape to be behind the wheel today. Nelson gave it to me."

"Shit, that's nice of him. I like that I get my employee discount, but a vintage bike would be dope too."

The frappes that Caroline made at the pie shop had a range of flavors, particularly unique in that they were the exact same as the pies she offered. The Brown Sugar Chess frapp that Benny dropped off for Marjorie was icy and refreshing, sweet, and magically just like the pie in coffee form—although she could have done without the hint of bourbon she tasted, making her wince a little. Still, she was grateful to Benny for the drink—and the good memories.

The door opened and in walked the comforting presence of Stephen, although he seemed a little more reserved in his greeting, nodding to Marjorie without his usual grand gestures or asking about her day—after a moment Marjorie saw why. Behind him followed a slim young lady, hair in a high ponytail and wearing a knitted olive crop top over low-rise jeans and raffia wedge sandals. She trotted behind, with her hand in Stephen's. "Hi!" she said, rather perky with a big smile at Marjorie that made her unsettled.

"Hey there," Marjorie returned, before saying to Stephen, "Alex's all set for you if you want to go have a seat."

"Thanks, Marjorie," Stephen said as he made his way over to Alex's station. She soon emerged from the back to join him, wearing a flowy skirt and a mauve T-shirt, her dark velvety hair freshly curled. As she and her client exchanged smiles, Stephen's girlfriend hung back to ask Marjorie, "Is it alright if I go over there?"

"Oh! You can if you'd like, but we have seats over here that are really comfortable." The woman went to an open chair by the window, her gaze still over toward Alex's chair. Only a few minutes went by when she stood again. "I'm just gonna see how he's doing," she said.

With the blow-dryers going and the jukebox picking up a Badfinger track, Marjorie couldn't hear what the girlfriend was saying to Alex, but she was talking to her, looking at her work in the mirror and gesturing to the stylist where on Stephen's head to go over again—the whole time, Alex looked on guard, and Stephen said nothing, silent but not tense. Marjorie turned her attention to Nelson's client who was just checking out, and before she could watch them again, Nelson came from the back and waved to her to meet him over at Addie's old station to the back right.

It was so weird seeing the bare red leather salon chair and clean station, devoid of curlers and Addie's preferred creams and pomades. Each station's mirror was supposed to resemble a vintage vanity set with the oval frames that flipped around, and in the case of Addie's particular station it was pushed out a few feet from the wall, where the already crumbling brick behind it had broken away significantly, lying in small heaps on the wooden floor.

"Good Lord," said Marjorie. "Did all this just happen now, or has it always been like this?"

"Well, moving things around didn't help," Nelson said. "But it's been a gradual erosion. Not because of how old these bricks are, actually, but because these particular lays aren't the original." He placed his hand over a brick that had already been halved, and after a tug it gave way. Right behind it, to Marjorie's surprise, was a dusty, but still bright mint tile. It gave her an instant rush, visions of the Hunt's clock ice cream cones on the wall and that taste of mint chocolate invading her memory.

"Is this from the old diner that was here in the fifties?" she asked Nelson, touching it herself, half expecting to look up and find herself there at the counter again in 1959.

"Sure is. The old backsplash they had just behind the counter seating. A nice and mostly forgotten detail of the place. It closed going into the 1970s and whatever business came after just plugged in these bricks. I'll need your help sweeping these since I'll be booked for the rest of the day, but I'll call my guy about patching it over the weekend. Although I gotta say, perhaps we should open it up and have the old backsplash on display? What would you prefer?"

It was a small but beautiful detail indeed, and as Marjorie slid her hand across the tile, she thought about the history, the memories—her own memories—being covered up, again long forgotten.

"Honestly, we should expose it."

Nelson nodded with a smile. "I agree. But regardless, this mess has to be cleaned up before the end of the day. We'll see about how to start the removal later. Thank you."

"Of course!" Marjorie swept the debris while keeping an eye out on the front, and over at Alex, making progress on Stephen's curls and still under the watchful yet beaming eye of his girlfriend, standing straight by the mirror and looking back at him. Once he was trimmed and set with a light application of curl cream to his head, he met Marjorie at the front desk to get checked out, and after a quick smile from him—and his girlfriend—Stephen was gone, and Alex was coming from the back room to debrief with Marjorie.

"Seriously," she began, "I think I'm gonna need to bum a smoke off Jeff after that. So fucking weird. No wonder Stephen talks the way he has about her. I'd try asking him things—hair wise, new projects—and she'd speak up for him! Like, before he could even respond."

"Damn, that is weird," Marjorie said. "Well, to me it seems like she was pretty intimidated by you."

Alex let out a snort. "Ha! I honestly thought so too. But Stephen's a catch! I don't blame her."

"I do—if she wasn't so overbearing and trusted her boyfriend, I'm sure she'd have nothing to worry about to begin with."

Jeff came around to the front, almost looking like he was gliding over as his shoulders playfully shook off the chill of the AC. "Boy, it's cold in here," he declared, trying to pull his arms to tuck into his teal V-neck for warmth. "Is it just me?"

"Just you," Alex said. "Say, you got an extra cigarette I could have?"

"You don't smoke," Jeff flatly replied.

"No, not lately, but my last guy's girlfriend got me feeling one."

"Oh yeah, I saw. Helicopter girlfriends are weirder than parents. Don't worry—that shit won't last."

"Hopefully it won't before his next appointment. They got out so fast, didn't even set up his next visit."

"That's when you dress up in your sexiest shit, work appropriate that is," said Jeff. "If she's back, you're gonna drive her insane, and if she's not, then he'll definitely realize he's been wasting his time with her."

"I second what Jeff says," Marjorie added. "I feel bad for him, must suck to stick with someone *that* overbearing."

As Jeff and Alex headed out to smoke in the alley, Marjorie saw her phone light up. On silent, the screen let her know that she'd missed a call and got a voicemail shortly after. It was Danny.

Hey! It's me, his deep, jovial voice spoke. *I know you're at work, but I wanted to leave you a message this way. Sometimes it's easier to speak than write it all out. Anyways, I don't want you to feel bad about missing yesterday—I'd like to come out your way to Marietta if you were free tonight? Just give me a call when you're off, we can figure something out. Again, don't worry about yesterday—there is hopefully tonight, if you're not sick of me.*

She hung up the phone and took a deep breath. So, he wasn't mad but sounded unphased, more hopeful even. When Alex came back in, she stopped her quickly to ask her to watch the front for a second as she left to call him back.

…

Later that night, Marjorie admired the neon glow of The Strand as she waited beneath the marquee for Danny. Moments later she spotted him strolling over to her. His hair was combed back with a bit of bounce, and he smiled widely as he went in for a hug, to Marjorie's surprise, briefly wrapping her in a hint of vanilla and bergamot with musk.

"Hi!" she greeted. "Thanks for meeting me over here, and just coming out this way."

"Of course! Going north on 75 is easy," he said. "And nice to just get out of the city for a bit. This has been one shitty week, I'll tell ya."

"God, now I really feel worse about yesterday!"

"Oh no! That wasn't it—it's just trying to coordinate with all the events and conventions we've been hosting this summer that have been particularly difficult. And also, I told you yesterday doesn't matter—we're still here tonight, aren't we?"

"We sure are. So, let's go upstairs this way." She pointed to a stairway just off to the side of the theater. "Since we didn't get to be on the roof yesterday, I figured it would make sense to check out the finest one here in Marietta."

"I can't wait, show me the way!"

Marjorie went first, and up a few floors they found themselves in the crowd of the town's only rooftop bar. Seats were scarce, but there was a small opening by the railing overlooking the Square by a high table being used as a holding station for other patrons' drinks. She raised her hand to Danny, who came out with a glass of red wine and his own favorite, an Old-Fashioned. As they got situated against the railing, he held out his glass for a toast. "Great spot," he said, taking a sip of his drink and looking around into the bustle of a Friday night in Marietta stories below them. "God, I needed this."

Marjorie chuckled as she took her own sip of the wine. "You know, after last night I was ready to stave off any alcohol for a long time, but wine isn't so bad."

"I can grab you a soda or water if you'd prefer just that? I forgot you'd been out already. Did your friend feel better afterwards?"

"No, no, my wine is good! More sweet than strong. And yes, Benny is doing better. She really needed it last night and so I appreciate you understanding why I had to bail. I was gonna come, though! I was dressed and everything."

"I don't doubt it. I'm happy you could be there for her. There's no rulebook for handling breakups or how long it takes, so do what you gotta do."

"It's been a while for her, but it was a long relationship. She hides it so well every time we hang out, but all it takes is one trigger—a song, in fact—to just bring someone to their knees." In that moment, Marjorie swore she could hear through the cacophony of chatter and shouts a song of her own that would wreck her, "Oh My Angel," and she held her breath. No, a false alarm.

"For being new here, glad you've already got yourself some good company. It was a minute before I could feel comfortable with people at school when I was up in New York, and for a while I didn't even like my roommate. He'd always bring other guys to hang in our room without asking me, and they all had things in common like coming from the Tri-State area and rooting for the Mets. Mike turned out to be one of my best friends, that bastard."

"Good things take time! You ever want to go back to New York?"

"I mean, my dad's originally from Long Island, and I go back occasionally for family and make time for my guys, last time was in September. But no, I'm done with that. It's good to be back home. I live not far from the Beltline, and that's been pretty cool seeing it come alive these last few years. You'd love it, I'm sure. Especially the history, how it was an old rail corridor before it became the trail."

"Repurposing the old for a new generation, I like it. Interesting that they didn't try reopening it as a train line, though. God knows Atlanta needs an upgrade. Wonder how that must have looked like back in the day—I probably wouldn't make it far to be honest, given how the South used to be."

"Aw, come on, you'd be welcomed with open arms on the train! Maybe not the front of it, but you know." Her snicker in response was infectious, and he smiled with relief.

"I love old things," she began after taking another sip of her wine. "The movies, the music. But often I think about if I did want to live in those times, and then I think about some of the shit my grandparents and aunts and uncles faced growing up in the sixties, even in progressive San Francisco. So no, the ugly stuff can stay behind, just give me all the antiques."

"Oh, things were shit back then, for sure. But that's what history is for, learning, not repeating."

"Except when it comes to outfits."

"Absolutely the outfits! And I'm not just talking about yours. Only Cary Grant could get this emo fucker to give up skinny jeans."

"No! That's something I'd pay to see."

"Scroll back to 2009 on my Facebook and you'll see it for free."

"Man, 2009. Now that is a year I'd love to revisit, honestly. Nostalgia's something, isn't it?"

"Facts. It's ironic too—the longing we have for times when we were young and yet moving forward."

The twilight was passing now, making its way out of Marietta with the last of the train cars that disappeared into the glimmers of an uncertain night. And Marjorie smiled and took a sip of her wine in agreement. A beautiful summer night held them both together on that rooftop which, like small memories, would be fleeting and then gone—until hours later, maybe even years, it would reemerge completely overwhelming.

After some silence Danny sighed and said, "Poor Aunt Roberta."

Marjorie giggled. "Why's that?"

"The lady has been dying to see you again and yet here we are coming up on what, two meetups?" She could feel him nudge her a little, and she looked back to him, holding his amused gaze.

"Only two more days," she said.

Marjorie, 1956

There was still about eighty-seven minutes left of *High Society*, but Marjorie was ready to leave. Who knew how much longer she had until she'd be back in 2023, and besides, she'd seen it before, at home, at other theaters in different times. It was fascinating, though, how little of the theater was changed from the merchant meetings held there. In the darkness, Marjorie looked around at the sea of faces present on this summer afternoon, mostly youngsters laughing among each other and occasionally peeking over to other groups they knew sitting in front or behind them. There was a loud *shhhh* and looking up, she discovered it had come from someone in the mezzanine—the segregated seating. Remembering the side door to the theater that Lara Jean had mentioned led upstairs, Marjorie felt a shiver run through her realizing what that really meant. In most of Marjorie's many travels, she was not as discriminated against in such times as she would have thought, but nonetheless it never made her feel any more at ease. She wondered if anyone noticed her here on the main floor, unannounced from the future and surrounded by the other moviegoers, but luckily all eyes were on Grace Kelly.

She ducked low and made her way to the aisle, then out of the theater and into the sunshine of that summer day. It was comforting to see the Marietta Square, but in this lifetime it felt more old, unkept; a wild contrast to the paved streets and colorful cars parked on its perimeter. Based on the sky, it might have been sometime in the late afternoon with the sun just west beyond the tall trees. Crossing the street, she steadily made her way up the paved path cutting through the Square that led straight to the fountain, still at the heart of town. It wasn't as grand, but still made of solid wrought iron and flowing gracefully as it gently sprayed a much-welcomed cool mist.

Around her the town was busy that Friday. School had been out for weeks, and she could see some little boys riding by on bikes while teens were getting ready to cruise for the weekend, driving by in their older Chevys and honking at some girls they knew crossing the street. To Marjorie's delight, the signs were grand above the businesses, bold and big, but welcoming every passerby to the town's variety of drugstores, jewelers, shoe stores, and restaurants. One sign in particular caught her eye, on the southeast corner in the spot where Marietta Mercantile would take over many years later. The windows of Saul's Department Store were lined up with tall mannequins dressed in the most popular fashions of the summertime, and it was as if they called out to Marjorie with their bright looks. She got up and made her way over to the storefront, making sure to look both ways to avoid getting run down by any one of the passing Bel Airs or Nomads. She paused in front of the windows, seeing the reflection of the parked cars behind her and beyond the Strand and the smaller movie theater beside it, which mostly played Western films. On display were cotton summer dresses and suits, but she wondered what might be in stock beyond. She walked in.

"Good afternoon!" a cropped-haired woman restocking a revolving jewelry case greeted her. Her gaze lingered in that familiar way that made Marjorie nervous, the way the waitress had looked at her at Hunt's. "How may I help you today, miss?"

"Hello," Marjorie politely said. "I'd just like to look around, please."

"Absolutely, miss. Let me know if you have any questions or need assistance."

Looking around the vast store with a sea of clothing racks and stacked shoe boxes on the far back wall, she wandered around the front where her eyes glowed at the sight of the many dresses. Bright plaid prints, shirtdresses in sorbet colors, and fun eyelet styles ran through her hands as she imagined wearing each one at the next live concert on the Square, but she had to remind herself of her true mission here. Still, she could at least admire and document the labels for later, to find these beauties online on eBay or Etsy.

Rather than waste time walking around the Square for answers, she turned back to the counter and approached the young woman. "Actually," Marjorie began, "this might be a very offhanded question, but do you have a local directory I could browse really quick?"

"A directory?" the woman repeated. "Yes, I do." She ducked and pulled out from under the counter a thick red leather book that she slid over to Marjorie.

"Thank you!" she said, and not wasting a minute, flipped toward the back to residents, the Gs. Her finger ran down the lists past the Gossets, Gourleys, Gowders, and one Grace before it went into Grady. Abigail and Richard Grace, on 315 North Hillcrest Drive.

"Yes!" Marjorie whispered. "Ma'am, is there a phone I can use around here?"

"I'm sorry, miss, but we don't have a phone for customers. Might I suggest across the street at the courthouse? There's pay phones in the lobby."

"Right, I understand." She looked at the number next to the Grace's name and repeated it under her breath. "Hmm, could I borrow a pen then?"

CH3-4127. She never had to use a rotary phone during her travels, but out of curiosity Marjorie had learned to dial the old alphanumeric codes, and she joked in her mind that it was all meant to lead to this moment. Armed with the number written on her hand and holding her breath, she crossed the street toward the majestic yet crumbling old courthouse that would be razed in just a few years to make way for the current Cobb County government buildings, which Marjorie found ugly. There was an open phone booth just to the right of the entrance and Marjorie ducked in to make her call.

Exhaling after the full rotation, she waited on the humming tone until someone picked up.

"Good afternoon, this is the Grace residence," a woman answered.

"Good afternoon, ma'am," Marjorie spoke in her sweetest tone. "I would like to speak to Simon Grace please, if he is available."

There was a long pause on the line before the woman on the phone responded. "I'm sorry, but there is no Simon Grace here."

"Oh, I beg your pardon. As in, not home?"

"No ma'am, no one by that name lives here."

"I see. Hmm." Marjorie scrambled quickly to collect her thoughts and ask the next question. "I apologize, but are there any Simon Graces in your family? Or might I ask any other Graces who live in town?"

"No, I believe you have the wrong number," the woman now impatiently said. "Good day." The line went dead.

Fuck. Marjorie stepped out of the booth, but now, she had no idea where to go next. Was this it? The end of the line? It had to be—there was only one Grace household listed. And yet, he was here. He should have been.

As she felt the shivers of her time in 1956 fizzling out, she frantically looked about the beautiful day she was about to lose, that same heightened panic that she hadn't felt in a long time—not since she was with Simon on Market Street and was sure it was all going to end. How much she hated that feeling— even worse now, returning to her time and back to square one. A name, and no more.

Chapter 13

Four men and two women gathered along the southside sidewalk not far from The Australian Bakery, and with this Sunday afternoon still as bright and warm as the morning that preceded it, the town's bluegrass band came together before her eyes. It was a sweet pluck of a familiar country tune in which they all joined in while one man sang and carried the song across the crowded Square. It was almost a week after the Fourth of July, but Old Glory still dotted the paths along the brick sidewalks of the Square, each flag fluttering softly in the wind. Having just left the History Museum for more gala work, Marjorie messaged Benny to meet her outside for Sun Glows when she was done at the bookstore. Benny was running late, but with a live performance before her, Marjorie didn't care.

Among the band was a familiar face, the man she'd met earlier that summer by the fountain with his old raggedy dog, Mikey. He sat between the two older ladies, strumming gently on his banjo and looking down with a smile. Mikey wasn't far away, sleeping under the chair of one of the other players by a plastic tub of water. The song was trailing off now and applause came from the other spectators that Marjorie hadn't realized had gathered around her. As the band members all took a quick sip of water or adjusted their instruments, the man looked Marjorie's way and she smiled. He seemed to remember her as he grinned and waved back. Then it was onto the final song, a stripped rendition of Johnny Cash's "Jackson."

The last applause faded, and the group began to pack up. Mikey's human took his banjo in one hand and his duffel bag and Mikey's leash in the other, saying quick goodbyes to the others before he walked off. Marjorie went over to him, and he smiled again, greeting her with "Well hello, lunch lady!"

"Hi!" said Marjorie. "I didn't know you were part of the band, you were all terrific. I've heard about you guys and been meaning to catch a session."

"I'm glad you got to see us this last time," he said rather solemnly. "We were told that we gotta move on. Our shows are too loud and now that they got a noise ordinance for the sidewalks around the park, we won't be allowed out here anymore."

Ah yes, Marjorie remembered. The ordinance was announced at the recent Marietta Merchants Association Assembly last month, the begrudging solution to put an end to the street corner preachers that in the summer only grew in numbers, and only got louder. "Oh! That's a shame! Do you guys have a new place to meet at?"

"No ma'am. Unless the kind folks at the bakery here could hire us and then there's some private employee loophole or something like that, but I don't know too much about that. And the bakery wouldn't be able to pay all of us for how often we meet up."

"That's a shame. It really felt like summer when I was listening. Has anyone reached out for a new location for you guys?"

"You'll have to talk to Sonny right there, he's been the one the city talks to." Sonny reminded Marjorie of Doc from *Snow White* and was nearly packed and talking to other members of the banjo band. "I gotta get Mikey back home and out of this heat. Shit, it's so bad!"

"I agree, let's get him home. He seems to not mind the loudness, which is good!"

"He's deaf in one ear, so he don't hear much."

"Oh, I see. He's such a sweet guy and a gentle companion, I'm sure. I'm Marjorie, by the way! I got Mikey's name last time, but I didn't catch yours."

The man seemed shy about giving his name, taking a pause before he said softly, "Christopher."

"It's nice to meet you, Christopher. I do hope that I can catch the band somewhere else around the Square someday."

"We sure hope so too, Miss Marjorie. We sure hope."

Benny was now crossing the street and called out to Marjorie, with Christopher nodding to Marjorie and smiling as he tugged at Mikey to wake up and follow along. They walked away as Benny came up to marvel at the crowd that was dispersing.

"Aww man, I missed the band?" Benny asked dejectedly. "Sorry I was late! Had to hang back and talk with my boss about the summer traffic with all the kids out of school. Dude, we're legit having gambling problems."

"Wait—gambling?" Marjorie asked. "Who is? Other staff?"

"No! The fucking kids! We usually get bigger crowds of them just hanging out in the front rooms by the window during summer and it's usually fine, we got cameras, but recently they actually started playing games, dice, cards—and we've caught them passing around cash to people who are winning."

"No they weren't!"

"That's what I said! The bookstore isn't trying to be a front for tween gambling. So, I was making signage to print in all the rooms about loitering."

"Hey, maybe you can bribe them to go elsewhere, if they've got all this money."

"True! Who would have thought. Shit, I guess a bookstore is genius, no one would think that would happen there. But after that revelation, I am in need of a Sun Glow."

Marjorie laughed in agreement. After the sad news of losing the banjo band she only now just got to enjoy, she definitely needed a drink.

...

The banjo dispute didn't go quietly into the good balmy night of that summer. In fact, it was the first issue for debate at that month's Merchants Association Assembly; that Friday was a sweltering afternoon outside and, instead of the usual coffee and donuts, sweet tea and lemonade were being poured with ice. Again, Marjorie was in attendance as proxy for Nelson, although it was the norm now to just have her go. She had some news this time, and she couldn't wait for her turn. Currently, Amanda from The Australian Bakery was speaking, expressing her concern about the sidewalk in front of the bakery no longer being a holding spot for the banjo players. Today, she brought a guest, the bandleader himself, Sonny.

"Perhaps we can acquire special permits to perform?" she was asking.

"I know it'll be a lot for us," added Sonny, "but since we're not performing right now, I've got plenty of time to sign as many papers as I need just for us to continue."

Officer Dennison, center stage, shook his head and rubbed the back of his silvery head. "Even for any permits, the noise is still above the allowance formally approved by the city."

"This is honestly so stupid," called out Ken, turning to Al for his agreement. "People play up on the bandstand all the time even when there's nothing going on, no permits either."

"But it's usually one or two people on guitars or drums," responded Officer Dennison. "And not loud enough to prohibit."

"It's not even a guarantee that the preaching kids will stop," added Art. "You just got rid of the megaphone problem, not the kids themselves." A spur of murmurs agreeing with him erupted softly.

Luanne rejoined Officer Dennison on the stage. "Hey guys, we know that this is not ideal, especially for you, Sonny," she said, "and we love the entertainment y'all bring to the Square each Sunday. Unfortunately, as the new ordinance states, any noise level above the reasoning of the regular noise of the immediate Square with the traffic and pedestrians cannot be permitted, and at that the most we'd allow to play would be just you and another member, but no more."

"Let's make the Square louder then!" suggested Al. "More foot traffic will fix everything. And more cars—just raise the noise, right?" Marjorie stifled an oncoming laugh.

"As if we need more dangerous cars whizzing through," responded Caroline, in the aisle in front of her. Marjorie, looking at Caroline, raised her hand, and Luanne, smiling, pointed to her.

"You said 'immediate Square'?" Marjorie asked. "Officer Dennison, when you say *immediate*, how big is this radius we are talking about? Perhaps a business not exactly on it might be able to be a new gathering spot?" More murmurs.

"The new notice did specifically say the immediate proximity to the sidewalks surrounding the Square park," Officer Dennison said. "Well, Sonny, perhaps you could reach out to another business off of the Square, I don't think you would be penalized to just move a few blocks away."

As Sonny was speaking, Marjorie tapped Caroline on the shoulder. "Would you be interested?" she whispered.

"In front of the pie shop?" Caroline said, sounding rather surprised.

"How fun would that be? A slice of pie and a few songs to go with it?"

Caroline thought, and then nodded. "We'll see," she whispered back.

They both turned forward as Sonny thanked everyone for their time and offering solutions. And then, it was Marjorie's turn.

"Alright everyone," she began, smiling and taking a deep breath. "Over this summer if you've stopped into Nelson's, you might have noticed a little bit more debris than usual toward the back. What we initially planned on doing for renovating and restoring a unique and forgotten part of the building's history has now turned into an expansion." She pulled out her tablet where she had ready a rough sketch of something she'd been working on for the past two weeks, a logo. "By the end of this year, Nelson's Salon is excited to announce we are going to be opening a limited soda fountain. Nelson's Salon and Soda on the Square!"

...

There was a home comfort to the hot, salty crispiness of the drumstick Marjorie took a bite into, holding the chicken over the greasy brown bag to catch the crumbs. The Big Chicken was strictly Marietta, but KFC was a taste shared by all. As she ate in the car, her taste buds took her back to the old KFC that was always on the way to her grandparents', off Clayton Road, still stuck in the eighties with frosted glass and weird geographical pastel art on the walls and false planter partitions between the booths. She could even taste the fake bacon bits she would sneak from the salad bar.

Despite drifting off in her memories, she still had to contend with leaning away toward the window so Doc, standing over her shoulder from the back seat and whimpering softly, couldn't try to steal a bite.

"Do you need some napkins?" asked Danny, sitting in the passenger seat and having just eaten his wing clean off the bone.

"Please!" said Marjorie, grabbing a few from him to wipe her hands. Looking for any excuse to hang out with Doc, so he professed, Danny got out of work as soon as he could that Wednesday evening and drove on over to Dogwood Daze, and having had barely any lunch earlier, he and Marjorie craved something quick but flavorful, so The Big Chicken it was. Here they were parked beneath the giant steel bird, its uplights casting a glow on the moving beak and rolling eyes, clucking silently as the humans below peppered in and out of the restaurant and filled up the outdoor seating. Doc turned his attention to Danny, as his own mama wasn't giving in, his snout close behind Danny's ear.

"Aww, buddy," said Danny sweetly, "I can't if your mom won't." Then turning to Marjorie, "You sure I can't just give him a small piece?"

She huffed. "Ok, but just the meat, no skin! The vet said his stomach is getting more sensitive as he gets older, so we can't go overboard since I gave him treats before he left." Doc happily took the big chunk from Danny's hands and licked his chops after scarfing it down without chewing, then moved over to Marjorie to lick her cheek. "Ahh, baby!" she let out.

"He's loving this!" Danny said. "A boys' night out. And mom."

"I'm basically the chaperone since I'm the one who drove us here."

"True. I need more one-on-one with this little guy—if you ever need a dogsitter, just holler!"

"Ha! I don't do much besides going out to the Square, and even most days I try to bring Doc."

"As much as I keep telling you that you'd love my side of town, I can see the charm of Marietta. There is always something going on here, isn't there? Live music, new restaurants, I'm impressed. I'm sure Fourth of July was something, which, I'm sorry I had to miss because of work."

"All good! We were only fifteen minutes into the fireworks before the rain came in and my neighbors had to disperse. It was a shame—I'd never been to a block party before, and it was nice to meet other neighbors besides Benny and her sister." She stuck her head close to the window and looked up into the skies, a soft purr of thunder being heard. "It looks like we might have a do-over of that tonight. I can't believe it—so much rain for the summer. It's always so dry in California, only rains during winter and spring."

"I'd love to experience that San Francisco fog right now."

"Good old Karl. It's probably so cold right now as the sun's setting over there. My space heater would be on full blast, and I'd probably be sitting right in front of it and loving life, listening to Nat King Cole on vinyl—he's always a cold weather kind of sound."

"I can't even think about being chilly when I'm sticky right now. But I'd love some Nat too—I always like him for the summer. Summer evenings at least, playing 'Smile' or 'For Sentimental Reasons' when I'm sitting out on my balcony, and I've finally gotten away from the hotel. And 'Lazy Hazy Days of Summer'? C'mon."

"You're right, I can see that. I'll have to listen to his record tonight and see for myself." Maybe the next time they hung out, she'd suggest they spend a day at Al's record shop.

"Billie Holiday too," Danny continued. "Or Julie London. They carry nicely into the warm evening air."

"I don't think I know anyone else who could even name me a song by Julie London."

"My aunt, man. She's to thank for all of it! There were days we would be in her family room going through all her records and dancing or playing Restaurant. She'd act like a diner, and I'd be a waiter carrying her special china to everyone, pretending the finest food was on them. I got to choose the music to play, and when the record skipped, she'd start booing like the band sucked."

"That's adorable! And that also explains a lot about you."

Danny smiled and shook his head. "Full circle. But going back to San Francisco—tell me about some other things you miss. I'm curious."

She crumpled up her bag filled with her scraps. "The way that Victorians blended with the new buildings. And the cool air that had a hint of eucalyptus in it. I loved walking straight from my apartment down to Columbus Avenue to grab a cappuccino and then go a block over into Chinatown for coconut cream buns at one of the thousands of bakeries. And if I went down the hill, I'd be right on Union Square and could do some shopping. I miss the interconnected little worlds that the city provided me with. And the best part was how old, well aged, each one felt. Pretty much unchanged. Downtown is where all the real change has happened, and I couldn't care less about it. But the neighborhoods, they stayed the same."

"Where do you think I'd like it the most?"

"Well, do you like boats?"

"Sure!"

"You like brunch?"

"When I'm not working one, yeah."

"And you have a lot of polo shirts."

"Yes, this is true."

"Then you're a Marina guy. Also known as the basic bitch of the city."

He was laughing again. "Fuck, you got me," he joked.

"I think you would really love North Beach like me. Obviously great Italian food, and the cable cars pass through it. But the history is unmatched. The Beats gathered at my favorite bar, Vesuvio."

"It all does sound amazing. Maybe next year I'll try to plan something. I could shadow a sister hotel for some ideas to see how the 'Frisco hospitality measures up to its Southern counterpart."

Marjorie dropped her smile. "'Frisco is the *worst*," she exclaimed. "Don't ever call it that around any Bay Area native."

Now Danny was laughing. "Yes ma'am," he agreed. "San Francisco it is."

They were driving back to Dogwood as the storm that Marjorie suspected earlier was hovering above finally poured down, first softly, then picking up its brutal pace as the rain began pounding against Marjorie's car making its way toward Morris Road. She pulled up to the curb behind Danny's parked car, where she could see on the porch the twinkle lights she'd strung up for the block party swinging violently against the strong wind of the storm.

"This drive back is gonna suck," Danny said, opening his door a little to see how much rain was outside, and quickly closing it. Doc was calm and lying down in the back, looking at the rain as he panted. Danny and Marjorie sat still for a while, just in awe of the storm that kept them close together.

"I'm so sorry about this weather," Marjorie finally said. "I should have checked the app earlier. Are you sure it's OK to drive in this? I feel terrible."

Danny shrugged. "It's not gonna be any different on the freeways, just as crazy whether it's pouring or not."

"Be careful, please." She was looking straight into his brown eyes that seemed to have a glow amidst the darkness. Suddenly leaning in, she gently wrapped her hand around his neck and kissed him softly. She slowly pulled away, but his own hand reached up under her chin, nudging her back to where she'd just left him wanting a second kiss, one that was deeper, longer, against her soft lips.

"You could just stay until the rain stops," she breathily suggested.

"If you'd like me to." She could feel him kiss the top of her head, and leaning back up she took Danny's hand in hers.

"I'd like it if you just stayed the night," she confessed. "And honestly, Doc doesn't think it'd be safe to be on the road so late."

"He's an old, wise man." Danny couldn't help his grin as he moved his other hand around her waist to pull her in a third time.

The thunder was fierce and all around metro Atlanta trees had fallen, crashing into brick buildings and cars left out on the streets. But neither Danny or Marjorie knew, or didn't care, wrapped in each other's arms among the twisted comforter in her old iron bed the next morning.

"Glad you stayed," she whispered, nuzzling her face into his shoulder.

"Thank you for having me," he sleepily said, kissing the top of her head again. "Or I should thank Doc. He called it." He winked at her and poked his head up to look out the window, the sky once again bright after a howling, dark night. He fell back onto his pillow and brought his hand up to her arm as he traced her soft skin, intertwining his fingers with her loose curls that fell across her bare chest. "Think 75 is gonna be a shit show?"

"Is someone looking for an excuse to call in?"

"Oh? Is someone looking to kick me out?" His words held the opposite effect as Marjorie slowly moved up and leaned across him, hovering over her guest with a big smile and running her hand through his dark, tousled hair.

"I wouldn't want you to be anywhere else right now," she declared, bending down to kiss him. In a moment before getting carried away a third time, they both started laughing as Doc, only sleeping minutes before on the floor, had snuck up on the bed and prodded his wet, cold snout in between their faces, his tail curiously thumping against the headboard.

"And he seconds that motion," Danny mused, pulling the dog gently to him as Doc happily collapsed into his arms. "I swear, if we didn't have that awards dinner tonight for the film festival, I would call in. But my God." He looked up again at Marjorie, still rubbing the belly of Doc in his arms, the corner of his mouth slightly raised in that smile that used to seem mischievous to Marjorie, but now felt like a plea as he admired her. "I'd love to come back again, if you'd have me."

It'd been years since Marjorie really took an interest in any guy to grant such a wish. But something about Danny made her feel more than just satisfied in that way—she felt at home. It'd only been six months of being in Marietta, but still there were times where she didn't feel quite settled in. Someone staying with her for once here at Dogwood, that made the difference. And of course, Danny wasn't just someone.

"I'd like that," she replied. She crawled back to him and adjusted herself into his side to lie together a few minutes more before he'd leave, closing her eyes, taking in the warm musk and vanilla of his cologne. It was all nice, all made sense. But secretly, she felt guilty. No, Danny wasn't just someone, but she resented thinking about anyone like that, other than Simon.

...

Marjorie was expecting a full Pie Night. Benny, her sister Morgan, and Alex had all come on various nights individually, but never all together like tonight. And even more exciting, Danny would be joining.

The special for the evening would be the season's new Strawberry Cream and the comforting S'mores pies, a good variety for all to enjoy, especially when paired with bottles of wine. It was expected to stay clear all through the night, and with the string of lights over the porch ceiling having survived the July storms, all would be magical.

She waited in line at Caroline's, looking over her shoulder a few times to make sure her bike was still resting against the planter outside. Ahead of her, the same young woman who had helped her that first visit was taking orders, catching Marjorie's eye as she gave her a quick wave. Inside the shop, it was a busy Tuesday after work, and it sure was a beautiful day for pie. Marjorie could only imagine how much cozier Caroline would make this place feel when it came to the coming fall and winter.

As if sensing she was on Marjorie's mind, Caroline herself came from the back to restock some scented candles on the counter next to the pie display, and called out to Marjorie, "Happy August first!"

"A beautiful August!" greeted Marjorie. She joked to herself that had she not paid the rent today, Caroline's greeting would have been much different. "Just grabbing my usual fare for Pie Night."

"Another one already? And how are those going?"

"They've been successful! I'm expecting a pretty full porch tonight."

"Such a fun idea. Perhaps I'll keep this place open late for that, and have you be our host?"

"You're so sweet! I'm so busy as is with Lara Jean and Nelson for work and the gala, and now especially with the soda shop expansion at the salon. You should still do the late opening, though! The next full moon is at the end of the month. It might be on a Sunday too—see if Sonny and the gang will stay late for it!"

"I won't rush them into anything new just yet! They're still trying to figure out their seating with the rocky brickwork. I probably should have called the city to come look at those tree roots before I took on anything new for the shop, much less a banjo band."

"Oh, but they are so grateful to have the space, I'm sure! Roots or not."

"They've been quite lovely, actually. Always cleaning up the front chairs and bringing the plates in for me, and I don't even pay them! I think I should at this point. But you were definitely right—pie and music, an excellent draw, and I'm glad you suggested it. It adds another layer of liveliness to this place."

Caroline then went over to the cashier and said something to her, pointing at Marjorie. Before she disappeared into the back, she called out to her tenant one last time. "It'll be a clear one tonight! Enjoy."

Moments later, Marjorie emerged from Caroline's with a bag in hand, still beaming at the generous business neighbor discount Caroline put on her order. There was now one less thing to do before the night, and a little bit of savings to put toward some better cabernet and some more treats for Doc. Maybe bourbon for Danny?

She smiled thinking about it. It'd be a good excuse to have him stay again and not be on the roads, just to be safe. And as he had left that morning after the storm, he'd kissed her over and over again, and she was sure he would have loved to stay many nights after. As Marjorie felt warm again, no thanks to the August heat, it seemed to her that tonight might be just that.

Walking her bike toward the path on the other side of the tracks, she heard the ding of the railroad crossing sound for the coming train. She tried collecting her thoughts even as the approaching horns roared and finally rolled through, but it was no use. Watching each car whizz by, she began noticing that chill again—she quickly looked around, but nothing had changed, yet.

The horn sounded again and she looked ahead. The train cars seemed to slow, and she could see the other side of the tracks, still familiar, but decades behind—cars that weren't there seconds ago were now waiting on the other side for the train to pass, an Oldsmobile and a red '84 BMW M6. *How odd*, Marjorie thought, that in a sense she had traveled but not—was this a weird glitch?

And just then, she saw him. That blonde hair, a little grown out with streaks of gray, the long face and familiar blue eyes emerging from the BMW as the driver's side car door swung open and Simon, an older Simon, got out and stood there—looking straight at her through the cars.

As quickly as the rest of the train passed, so did this small minute in an insignificant time years ago. The red BMW, and its driver, were gone.

Simon, 1964

"What's home like?" Marjorie was asking Simon as they were leaving St. Francis Fountain.

"You mean Marietta?"

"Yeah, is it really tiny?"

"I wouldn't say tiny, it's been growing since the last few years. Before the war, Mama would tell me it was much smaller and quieter, but with the Bell Bomber Plant being built so many folks moved to work there and stuck around when it became Lockheed Aeronautics. It still can feel like a sleepy little town with the big Square and old brick buildings, but now there's a drive-in, some great ice cream spots, and attractions along the big four-lane that goes all the way up to Illinois and down to Florida. I got my license and I remember speeding down that thing with some friends. After that, Mama took my car away for a month—it's growing, but it's still a small town, and word can reach anyone what you're up to."

Marjorie nodded, taking a second before she followed up with, "It's pretty racist, I'm guessing?"

Everyone in California seemed to have their suspicions of Simon, being from the South. But as much as the assumptions made him uncomfortable, he could understand why, given the news, the laws, the protests. Changes he was all for, in fact, and was excited to let Marjorie know.

"Well, not really. Everything's been integrated since the summer, and from what my family tells me, it's been going on without much controversy. I'm glad it's all done away with the separate spaces. There's a few in my circle not too pleased with the upheaval in the South, but a lot of the folks I know are just trying to stay out of trouble and worry about themselves. I know home isn't perfect. Coming to California and seeing how we get so much wrong, it's really why I haven't run off yet."

Marjorie shrugged at his confession, followed by a smile that seemed like relief. "Well, I'm glad you're not scared off by us crazy progressives. I'm probably the first Asian person you've ever talked to, right?"

"No ma'am. There's a few in town and it just so happens that on the plane over I was right next to a fine Chinese gentleman on his way home from a business trip in Atlanta. He was excited to bring his son the Crackers pennant he got at a baseball game."

"Cute! Well, it's not quite the easiest getaway back home anyhow. You must miss your car. Can't quite exactly speed down these hills now, can you?"

"I actually love walking around here. How far is this bus stop now?"

"Not too far. Honestly, you don't need to come if you don't want to come all that way to the other end of the city."

"A promise is a promise. I intend to walk you home. Who knows what strange characters you might encounter."

"I've been doing seven years just fine, thank you! If anything, I'd be watching out for you."

They were arm in arm heading down 24th before turning up on Mission to where the bus stop was in front of a music shop. Simon was loving this feeling, her warmth against his own bare skin as he held his sweater in his hands. Still was so crazy to think that she could be in a knit sweater on this hot day, but the heat she radiated now was anything but uncomfortable to his touch. His heart was racing with her so close to him and the scent of jasmine in her hair. He would stay here for as long as he could, rather than find shade. But someone was walking out of the music shop and a burst of cold air hit the back of his neck. He turned around and had an idea.

"How often does this bus come?" Simon asked Marjorie.

"It's a pretty frequent line, about every ten minutes," she said. He looked back again at the shop and started walking toward its entrance.

"C'mon, let's go in really quick," he suggested. He'd spotted something near the front of the shop and his hunch was right—an upright piano lay open and inviting anyone to give it a whirl, and that's exactly what Simon was itching to do.

"What are you doing?" Marjorie asked him.

"A musician has to start somewhere," Simon said, taking a seat and pausing before he began pressing at the keys, getting a feel of the melody and rhythm he wanted to play with. First something fast, Jerry Lee Lewis-like. But with the misstep of his middle finger and thumb, he was shamed to a halt. "Well, shit," he mumbled and turned to Marjorie, who was giggling.

"No need to impress me," she said. "What's your favorite song you learned to play, ever? Doesn't have to be rock 'n' roll."

His thoughts raced through all the years, the melodies, the genres that their elderly music teacher Miss Gartrell had hunched over his shoulders for as he'd sit straight and stiff while fingers pricked, then glided, across the keys. Naturally, his hands found a position, and he began to play softer, slower, at ease. And soon Offenbach's "Barcarolle" came to life in the quiet of that little corner shop.

He glanced over to Marjorie, a sense of calm on her face and her mouth slightly turned at the corners. He was still playing when she finally said, "That's very beautiful."

The next bus was only in two minutes, and they were lucky to get empty seats for themselves to enjoy the views of Mission Street passing by. Still arm in arm, they both looked out onto the traffic and the buildings getting taller by the time they reached where Mission and Van Ness met. As it grew crowded with each stop, Simon was getting restless and hot, but Marjorie seemed unbothered as she continued watching the city scenes, and he wasn't about to ruin her happiness with complaints. He'd suffer in silence. Even if he had no idea how he'd manage to get back to Valencia from North Beach. Her trust in him, of all things, kept him going.

"So?" Marjorie then asked, turning to look at her companion.

"So what?" Simon responded, gently pulling her in closer from the window to his side.

"So, when can I expect your first album?"

"Hmm, that I'm afraid will take some more time."

"Well, I have a feeling it'll be a masterpiece. At least to me. I can see that sentimental sounds speak to you. You should lean into it and see what you produce."

He felt his face grow hot. "You haven't even heard me sing, just play."

She shrugged. "Maybe you don't have to sing, if you're not ready. Like Santo and Johnny, they only play. And who can forget their songs?"

He nodded, and he began humming "Sleepwalk." She grinned and gently laid her head down on his shoulder. "You could do just that and I'd have the record on repeat."

The bus came to South of Market Street, where the buildings were more dense and the Victorians that made up most of the Mission District made way for brick warehouses with fire escapes. Approaching 6th Street, Marjorie sat up and held her hand out to pull the cable to stop. "Let's get off now and walk from here," she declared, already getting up. Simon scooted out of his seat and let her lead the way down the steps of the bus and into the still-bright afternoon. Simon had only come here a few times, but today he took more notice of the sprawl of movie theaters and department stores with their big signs hanging out over the sidewalks of the city's bloodline. People darted across Market Street and above them, wires glided the white and green streetcars up and down from the water. At the end of the line, he could see the massive overpass by the Embarcadero eclipsing the clock tower of the Ferry Building, invisible behind the concrete but still sounding as loudly just as it was chiming three o'clock.

"And then where do we go from here?" Simon asked Marjorie, who was still guiding him up Market and rushing past the men and women in their finery as they strolled along to shop. But suddenly she stopped in the middle of the crowd. She was grabbing her arms, still holding her coat, and she started looking around, almost in a panic—and then back to Simon.

"What's wrong?" he asked, bringing her close to him while he surveyed the passing crowd for whatever was threatening her.

She didn't answer him, but in their embrace, he could feel her cling to him tightly. A few seconds felt like forever, before her body relaxed and she looked up at him. "Are you feeling OK, Marjorie?" he asked her again.

"I just—" she began, then exhaling before she went on. "I felt cold and then I thought—I thought something was happening. But it didn't." He couldn't understand.

"Do you get fits?" He thought of his cousin Annie, a sweet and bright fourteen-year-old, who stopped family gatherings due to her sudden seizure outbreaks that might have her writhing on the floor.

"No, not that. It's not even anxiety but—" she stopped again. "You saw *Breakfast at Tiffany's*, right?"

"I sure did."

"Well, then you remember her whole thing about the Mean Reds? It was like that. For a second, I was scared that everything was changing and something was coming but I wasn't sure what or when. Most of all, I just didn't want to lose you."

Even if he couldn't understand the worries she'd felt in that quick moment, all he wanted to do was keep holding her close. "I'm still here, darling," he told her. "I'm looking after you."

The crowds kept coming, and people were visibly annoyed at their pause in the middle of the sidewalk, some even aggressively brushing past Simon's shoulder. But in spite of San Francisco moving around them, all that mattered to Simon was shielding this precious girl from it all, to stop the moving seconds and remain frozen there with her, as best as he could.

Chapter 14

September was just another month of summer. But the heat had grown unbearable to Marjorie, and she did start longing for the coziness of fall with cool mornings, cinnamon in her coffee, and unpacking her favorite sweaters. There was still the murmur of the late-rising cicadas singing on the soft breezes, and the trees kept a radiant emerald glow to them—but Marjorie could see they were beat, looking tired from being lush for so long.

Her gift had given her a quick, painful glimpse of why she would never forget this first summer in Marietta. Her search was still on, but oddly she felt distracted by all the good times on the porch and warm nights around the Square, especially the times she'd spent with Danny. But what else could she do? Her time at the Museum was just spotty timelines and archived photos, the microfiches of nearly eighty decades that exhausted her—and nothing of Simon Grace. The longer it took for her to look, the harder life seemed to tug at her to move forward.

This month also meant that official expansion for Nelson's would start, now that the permit to expand and operate was approved, and that the Museum gala was just around the corner. November first seemed so far away, yet it felt so close. Gala aside, Marjorie was anxious for that date—it was also her thirtieth birthday. For years she'd been looking forward to this one, this start of a new decade in her own short life, but now that it approached, there were no plans. Nothing big. Well, there was one big thing: Eileen. Her older sister would be visiting Georgia to celebrate with her. They talked every day, at least through messages, and Eileen had promised her little sister she'd be there on her thirtieth, whether it meant dinner in town or just cake and wine on the front porch. Marjorie would take it for any time together, to catch up about her parents, and how big her niece and nephew were getting. A gift in itself.

Marjorie tried not overthinking it while setting her table for tonight's dinner, excited for a comforting meal of bratwurst sausages and lumpia that when paired with any one of the family staples growing up—rice, Mafran, or soy sauce—would make everything right. The only Asian supermarkets were on opposite ends of town closer to Kennesaw or Smyrna, but to her surprise, the big market down the road in the Latinx neighborhood carried most of the same items that her own mom would pick from 99 Ranch back in California. No matter where life took her, traces of home miraculously followed.

She was lowering the heat on the pot of rice when her phone rang. Marjorie was sure it'd be Lara Jean, but Eileen's face appeared with her name across the screen.

"Hola!" Marjorie greeted her sister, their signature salutation that came from an inside joke in high school that neither sister remembered. "I was just making dinner."

"Hola, nice!" said Eileen. "What time is it again over there? I still can't remember off the top of my head."

"Close to seven. What have you and the littles been up to?"

"Got it. Well, we're about to head over to Charlie's parents' for the usual Sunday dinner, and since the weather isn't too bad I think they're gonna barbecue, so that'll be nice. Cameron and Claire will get to play outside. But before we head out, I wanted to just to make sure you're gonna be up in a little bit?"

"Oh? Why can't you just tell me now? Everything OK?"

"Yeah! We're fine. We're taking off soon, though, so I don't know if now is—"

"Well, now that I've been ambushed, I'd like to know what's wrong now rather than later. Geez, Eileen!"

"Alright, sorry!" She took a pause. "Well, it's about your birthday. It doesn't make sense that I should go all the way out there. Charlie's been asked to work double since some guys will be out of office that week—"

"What about Mommy and Daddy? Weren't they gonna help watch Cameron and Claire anyway?"

"Marge, regardless, I don't think I should waste the money."

"So, you mean you don't even have a plane ticket yet."

"You knew it was gonna be fifty-fifty—"

"No!" Marjorie interrupted. "You always assured me that we were still on to celebrate, you even told me back in May that you'd find the cheapest flights to make it work!"

"You don't even have anything planned, you would have sent me links and photos of places we'd go like you always do when we'd plan things."

"Yes, I had lots planned, like drinks on the Square—"

"Marge, it's your thirtieth, and all you wanna do is just dinner in that small town? You used to dream big about this birthday! A night out in the city, in San Francisco! You should be going all out back here—"

"So that's it. It always still has to be about not being there."

"You know it's always gonna be about that. We wouldn't even be arguing about this if you didn't move thousands of miles away."

Marjorie was starting to regret picking up the phone. Her rice was probably burnt, the brats were going cold on the table. And she didn't want to see Eileen any longer in November, even if she were still to come after all the shouting.

"OK, well I gotta go," Eileen began again.

"Don't call later," Marjorie snapped back. "Just have a good barbecue. I gotta reheat my food."

"Oh, come on, you can't expect it to be easy to just fly out there—"

"You know I did. And only because you had promised that you would. Yes, I know that it's shitty that I left in the first place and stayed, but you know why I needed to be here—"

"And Marge, you know it's the dumbest thing to do. What you can find there, you can probably find online if you just searched hard enough. Simon's probably dead. And if he was alive, it's not like you'd live happily ever after with some old man."

It felt like a slap in Marjorie's face. Eileen was the only person whom she'd trusted to share her gift and could comfortably talk about her travels with. Even if she was humoring her all these years, she couldn't fake her reaction when Marjorie had shown her the St. Francis Fountain receipt and recounted how she got it in full detail. But her trust also came from a protectiveness over her younger sister that Marjorie was grateful for, and she often forgot that's where some of her recent resentment came from. But at this moment, she couldn't care less. It hurt to hear her say the one truth she feared the most.

It took her a few seconds before she could respond, "You're such a bitch sometimes. Thanks for already making this birthday memorable." And hung up.

Eileen was sending her messages, probably as Charlie drove their car to his parents', but Marjorie refused to look down at her phone, blowing up all through dinner. Whatever Eileen was sending her, she had to protect her peace. She'd already gone through the emotions of reading the similar vitriol that her sister had sent her when they were bad off and on over these last few months, for being selfish, immature, and breaking up their family. What she sent now was probably already sent before, already felt and hurt just the same.

And it hurt because Marjorie agreed with each word.

Doc had awoken from his slumber by the fireplace the minute that Marjorie's voice grew louder, rubbing up by her leg and sitting down on her foot during the rest of the phone call, licking her leg. He still sat by with his head on her lap as she tried to eat. But she wasn't hungry anymore. She knelt down and broke apart her last sausage in bits to feed her caring old boy, and started crying.

...

The fight with Eileen still ran through her mind into the beginning of the new week, but thankfully she had a busy Tuesday to keep her occupied. The bike ride back to Dogwood was usually a quick ten minutes, but for a day like this Marjorie wished it went on longer. Rolling along felt so peaceful to her, calming and almost like she was floating through an endless sea, away from any rocky shores. The road was usually empty, and sometimes she really couldn't tell which time she was in, past or present. As she cycled along, she took in the dark green trees swaying in the soft breeze one last time before, in the coming weeks, they would transition to deep shades of gold and reds. She did miss Doc, though, and it was great to see him so quickly. He trotted slowly to her after a big stretch from a long day of napping, and she figured a walk with him was just as good as being on the bike.

Taking a long silk scarf about her neck to layer against the cool evening air, Marjorie led Doc toward the cemetery and surveyed the quiet of the headstones scattered along their usual path. Turning left up the hill, they were moving along the older side where she'd grown familiar with certain markers and citizens of Marietta's past, names she could finally place to the stories she learned about from her time at the Museum. There was the Founder's Lot, a cluster of faded marble tombs behind an iron fence that belonged to William Harris and his family, the oldest graves. Alexander Clay, the city's only congressman, was closer to Atlanta Street, but always his tall kiosk could be seen from every inch of the cemetery. Smaller graves were scattered around with little lamb statues, young children taken too soon, and at the top of the cemetery was a plot of various stones that marked each buried enslaved citizen predating the Civil War, the Slave Lot.

Marjorie's favorite story was the grave they were just passing now, just beneath the tall cedars at the center of the park—the grave of John O. Kemp from 1903, or rather, the grave of his right leg, which he'd lost in a train accident. John Kemp himself, ironically, met his death elsewhere years later, which resulted in his final resting place being an unmarked grave in Acworth. Marjorie didn't believe it when Lara Jean relayed this tale until she saw the grave herself, a simple stone monument etched with only a boot on it.

Though warm as it still remained out, the days were getting shorter, and the sky fell into a sleepy shade of periwinkle as Marjorie and Doc made their way down toward the gates on Atlanta Street. Along the dirt path, over bumps of cedar pods and twigs, she suddenly felt that familiar sharp coldness again, and looked around. It wasn't that she was surprised by another travel, but only that it was happening now, in the middle of a cemetery, which she'd always assumed had no capabilities for such. At least, they never had in her past experiences.

The cemetery looked surprisingly the same to her as it did in the twenty-first century. By the looks of some of the more ornate headstones in the distance and youthful trees, this was probably the 1900s. Looking forward, she nearly jumped back. Only feet away from her there was someone standing in front of a grave.

It wasn't just any grave, it was one she would pass so often and found quite beautiful. It belonged to Mary Annie Gartrell, and her monument was perhaps one of the most ornate in the cemetery, a towering marble tribute on which an angel stood, looking down with a sheaf of laurel in her hands. At the base of the marble statue was a small woman, cloaked in all black, her face invisible behind the shroud that covered her head. As frightening as this looked, especially since the sky was dark and more gray than it had been only moments ago, Marjorie wasn't scared. She felt a sadness growing in her as she moved closer, but slowly, to the mourning figure. As she was facing her, Marjorie was sure the woman saw her. Her head did move up slowly, giving a nod before turning back to the monument.

"Good evening," Marjorie softly called.

"Good evening," a voice spoke from behind the shroud. It was a gentle, mature voice, rinsed with age and grief but still holding onto an air of formality. Marjorie was sure that was that regarding their exchange, as she didn't want to bother her in such an intimate place. But the woman kept on. "Visiting someone as well?"

"Just passing through," Marjorie replied, pausing to look up at the angel. "It is a beautiful memorial."

"As she would love it," the Lady in Black said. "My sister was a rather frivolous woman. But rightfully so. She loved life's beauty, and yet here she lies, taken too soon from it. I felt it suited her just fine. For the angel that she truly was."

"I'm very sorry for your loss."

"Thank you, ma'am. It's already been nearly fifteen years and yet, that feeling forever haunts you. A person can try to continue on living, but somehow, no matter what I do, nothing brings me more peace than when I come here." She exhaled deeply, lifting the veil to reveal an older woman with deep laugh lines and soft blue eyes. She smiled at Marjorie.

"She's always looking out for you then," Marjorie said. "And I'm sure she's happy every time you're here. My sister—" she stopped, not having expected to bring Eileen up. "My sister and I live far apart, and so often I do wish she were closer. It causes a lot of arguments lately."

The Lady sighed. "Sounds like a silly thing to waste your words on. Distance alone should be a reason to write words of love, not hate."

"No, you're absolutely right. But she's too hurt that I chose to not be near her, and I understand. As much as I would love just to talk to her about life, she always has to remind me I left."

"And does she know that you understand?"

"Yes, and I don't know what else to do."

"Can you not go home?"

"No, I can't now."

They stood side by side, both looking up to the angel that watched over them. A few minutes of silence passed before the Lady spoke again. "Love, my dear. All you can do is focus on the love you both have. If you must stay, then do so, but don't forget to always tell your sister you love her. At the least. If she is wise, then she wouldn't want to waste her breath on anything sour all the same."

Marjorie nodded. "Yes, ma'am," she acknowledged.

The Lady walked forward and looked up, directly under the gaze of the angel. "Sometimes, if you're quiet, I feel like her music still carries through these graves. She inspired me to follow in her footsteps too. Until I can follow her into those gates of heaven, I keep on playing my piano, spreading the love of the songs that she loved in life. Tell me, can you hear anything?"

Marjorie closed her eyes, ears tuning into the soft wind sailing through the pines nearby and the familiar concerto of cicadas following along. There was a faint, exaggerated whistle that seemed to dip and raise to give off a distant melody. It was most definitely a familiar tune, carrying on in the air and beckoning to her into another vivid memory—of Simon, sitting upright and concentrating at the keys of the piano where he'd sat in that shop and moved his fingers gently but effortlessly—in the air was "Barcarolle," and she nearly gasped at how close it now sounded.

She opened her eyes again to tell the Lady in Black her answer. But she was gone, and so were the gray skies, the red cedars—and alone with Doc, she was back.

She got home quickly and picked up her phone to dial Eileen.

"Hola," Eileen softly said upon answering.

"Hola," Marjorie returned. "Are you busy?"

"No. Just about to wrap up my work for the day. What's wrong?"

"Nothing. I just miss you. I love you and wanted to tell you I'm sorry for being annoyed at what you said about Simon. You're right, and you know I know that I'm a selfish and stupid person who shouldn't have done any of this. I don't know why I got mad, and I shouldn't be, because you're right. And you're right about my birthday. You need to save money regardless. I have to learn to live with the consequences of being alone out here. But I miss you and Mommy and Daddy and Charlie and the littles, I really do! I wish this was just all closer."

Eileen let go of a long, deep sigh. "Sis, it's OK. I'm sorry too. We're both hopeless romantics, and with what you have, what you can *do*, I think you should try and find him. Give yourself a peace of mind. I do want you home is all. I miss you. I'm just sad that you're gonna be missing some big moments, like Cameron and Claire's birthdays, all the big family outings and parties. Everyone was at Auntie Liz's a few weeks ago, and she was talking about how much she missed going thrifting with you!"

"I won't miss all of them! I promise that when I'm more settled and saved up a bit I'll be back as much as I can."

"What about Doc? He's too old and big to bring, who would look after him?"

"I've got friends in mind."

"See? You're moving on. You already have a circle of friends and a life, and I'm not a part of it."

"You absolutely still are. I miss you so much and wish you could be here. I want to show you everything here! I've discovered so much about this place, this life that was his—I honestly feel like I am getting closer to him."

"Do you really think so?"

"Mm-hmm. Tonight I think I got a sign. I've been getting more recently. If I give up now, it'll always haunt me."

Another sigh from Eileen. "Marge, I love you so much and want you to be happy. I'm glad you are happy doing this. I just wish I could help you. I wish I could be there for you. In case you find anything that might make you sad or upset."

Marjorie knew what she meant. "If he's dead, it's still closure all the same."

She heard a chuckle. "That'd be the worst thirtieth birthday present ever."

"Oh my God, Eileen!" But now Marjorie was laughing too.

"I kid! But hey, about your thirtieth—I'll see if it's still possible and I will find some cheap flights. I want to meet Doc! He's adorable."

"No, honestly save your money! Just video call me that day, and that'll be good."

"You sure? OK. I love you, Marge."
"I love you too, Eileen. You're really the best sis ever."

After hanging up, Marjorie went out to the porch and sat on the wicker rocker, Doc following behind her and lying down at her feet, one of which she used to rub his back. *Love,* she reminded herself, *always focus on the love*. The Lady in Black had appeared at the right time and said in only so many words the right things that made everything seem more clear.

Flipping through her records inside, she brought one back out with her Crosley and dropped the needle onto her vinyl of Offenbach. It should seem that hearing it in the wind had been a dream in itself, but, as with most of this magic she would never be able to explain, she was certain it wasn't.

Marjorie, 2012

October, 2023. A cool morning was finally here in Marietta, and it was magical, just as it was eleven years earlier to the day.

Ever since running into the woman with her dog at Bextor's in the summer, Marjorie began her own pilgrimage on Sundays to Lewis Park. Sometimes Doc came with her, but as the weather grew more windy, he wasn't bothered to leave his spot on her big armchair by the fireplace where it was always warm enough to sleep the day away. When Doc did come, Lewis Park was the perfect place for him to be left to his own amusement should her gift take over. It was a spacious enclosure for dogs of all sizes to freely roam and socialize. October was halfway gone, and summer only a memory now, completely eviscerated as the surrounding groves of trees turned into sharp canopies of red and orange, a few leaves starting to fall and clutter where Marjorie stood, wrapped in a wool coat the color of terra-cotta with a silk blue scarf draped around her neck. It was a beautiful, cool morning as she walked toward Bextor's for the coffee and back again, crossing the street just in time to see another train passing behind the bistro that sent a strong wind through the nearby trees, shivering off golden leaves to the ground below.

Every train that now passed Marjorie brought her back to August. She still couldn't shake that startling moment when she last saw Simon, if only for a few seconds in another time. But he'd stepped out of the car, looked straight at her, and his gaze was as if he were relieved to have found her again. It was a cruel thing, this gift of hers, to sporadically bring them together and tear them apart and tease their close reunion like that. And then, there was Danny. They were enjoying their unspoken exclusivity over these last few months, and Danny especially was sweet and sincere; she felt it often in his tender kisses, how his head lingered close to hers in their embraces or when he'd softly rub her back when sitting together on the porch or inside watching a movie. Still, Simon was somewhere, and she still had to know.

Back at Lewis Park, her usual morning routine would start with walking the perimeter outside of the dog enclosure, slowly pacing herself as she looked inside at the few, sometimes many, dogs and their owners. The air was crisp now and she caught a whiff of the cinnamon from her oat milk latte, along with another sweetness in the air, almost like chamomile. Then, she would move on to the hillside at the back of the park, walking upward where she'd sit down beneath the trees lining Radium Street. It was even more breathtaking to see these trees that were at first bright green now flushed red, and she would usually sit a good while before going back down. If nothing by then, so be it. She'd come back another Sunday.

But at last, this was the moment she'd always been searching for. And it happened on this clear October morning that would soon bring tears to her eyes.

She'd only been sitting for about fifteen minutes beneath the shade of the trees when that familiar chill came over her and she looked down below. She could tell it was another time by the cars that were no longer parked in the lot, and a few trees in the distance that now looked smaller, younger. Getting up, she walked up to a car and checked its plate. A 2012 tag. She turned her attention to the bottom of the hill down at the dog park, a few barks heard from within as she saw about four other dogs running around with their humans not too far from them. She narrowed her eyes to focus on each one, and then she saw him. It had only taken a span of five months, eighteen different Sundays, and four travels to find Doc in 2012.

She made her way to the fence with a smile, hand still tight around the cooling coffee cup, as her eyes followed her young dog prancing back and forth, engaging in a chase with an Afghan hound. But this was not her Doc, not yet at least. This Doc was just a puppy, barely a year old and darker in color, his coat a glossy black and his small ears more stiff and pointed, with a brassier caramel snout that she knew would turn powdery in the coming years. He was panting heavily whenever he'd pause with a swift, playful bow, kicking up the dirt with his tiny front paws. Marjorie couldn't help smiling wide as she saw him so lively in his youth, as she had expected he would be. When he ran by her, she whistled coyly and he stopped again, turning and wagging his slender black tail as he trotted over to stare at her.

"Doc!" she heard a man say, and she looked up to see an older gentleman in jeans and a green windbreaker slowly jogging up. He sort of reminded Marjorie of her own grandpa, thin gray hair atop a puffy face that was very jolly-looking and had drooping cheeks like he was a bulldog himself. "Doc," he repeated, "What's the matter, buddy?" He looked up to Marjorie and nodded. "Good morning," he greeted warmly. "He's not bothering you, I hope? He's a very friendly boy!"

"Oh no! He's so sweet," Marjorie replied. "We were just becoming friends. How old is he?"

"He's about a year," the man said, leaning down to give Doc a good scratch right behind his ears. "A friend of mine found him as a puppy wandering on the street a few days after the Fourth of July in Acworth last year. He's a big softie, not much of a guard dog, which is why I originally took him. But you can't beat a dog like Doc. Sharp and energetic. Sometimes I can't keep up! But this place is good for him, and I can just sit and watch him have fun."

"It's a great park for sure," Marjorie replied. "I'm new to the area and always heard about this place. Was checking it out for my own dog to see if it'd be a good fit."

"Oh, it's fantastic! Your dog would do just fine here, and he or she would already have a friend in my boy."

"I'm sure he would."

A phone soon started to ring, and Doc's own human, still smiling, frantically searched his windbreaker for it. "Excuse me," he said as he found the phone and picked it up, turning before Marjorie could hear him answer, "Wyatt speaking."

Doc Holliday and Wyatt Earp. She smiled as she finally understood his namesake.

Wyatt was still on the phone as Doc stood looking at Marjorie, his tail wagging. She knelt down and held her hand up to the fence, which Doc slowly approached and sniffed first the air between them, then her hand against the chain. His snout lingered for a good minute before he stuck his tongue out and profusely licked at the fence and her hand behind it.

"Hi, baby," she whispered to him. "I'll be seeing you soon, my love."

His human, Wyatt, had hung up and was coming back over. "Aww bud, you're such a good boy!" he exclaimed. "He's such a ladies' man. I don't know what I'd do without him. It's just me since most of my family are up in Michigan. This boy is the best family you could have." He bent down and gave Doc a bear hug and kiss on the head. "As I said, he'd love to be your dog's friend. We hope to see you around!"

Marjorie nodded. "I'd love that. It was lovely to meet you both! I'm sure I'll see you around soon." She could feel a sharp chill again. She turned toward the hillside and began walking, looking back once more. Doc was still there, standing alone as Wyatt was walking back toward the bench, on his phone. The dog kept his gaze on Marjorie, his tail still wagging. As if he knew.

She blew him a little kiss, and walked forward, wiping away tears as she thought about him at home, fast asleep on that saggy chair by the fireplace in the old house that made their future together.

Simon, 1964

They made it up Market Street in silence. Marjorie smiled at Simon and held his hand tightly, but now kept quiet as she looked around at the crowds of people waiting in line for the cable car gliding down the hill, flowing in and out of the round grand entrance of Woolworth's just steps away. She tugged his hand to follow her as they went left up Powell toward Union Square. "I think I want to sit for a quick second," she told him.

"Alright," Simon replied. "Are you feeling hungry or need a drink? We're close to where my roommate is working, and he can get us some food at his restaurant."

"No, it's not my appetite. I just want us to get fresh air and out of these crowds for right now. And then we can continue on." Her grip relaxed as they walked side by side, passing hotels and travel agencies and tailor shops, reminding Simon of why downtown was the place he came to the least. But as they stopped at the light on the corner of Geary and Powell, he smiled at the sight of a small flower stall shaded beneath a red striped awning and bursting in vibrant roses, marigolds, carnations, and ferns from baskets. He turned to Marjorie, and she seemed to have been mesmerized by their color. The light turned green, and they started forward, but not before Simon reached out and plucked a single stem of a pink lily that he handed over to his girl.

"Simon!" Marjorie exclaimed, taking the flower. "Aren't you a bad boy."

"If it makes you feel better, it's worth taking a thousand more."

She held it to her face as she sniffed its sweet scent. They made it across the street and now walked up the steps toward Union Square. It was a busy Friday, with most benches lining the rose hedges already taken up by elderly gentlemen smoking, but they found shade under the wide palms on the west side and adjusted themselves comfortably. Marjorie leaned back, holding the lily on her lap, and took a big breath. "This will do," she said, looking around and then up at the Nike statue that jutted into the sky from the center of the park. "Just a few minutes, I promise."

Simon shrugged and told her, "Take all your time. I actually never come out this way, it always feels too crowded and touristy. But sitting here now, it's rather nice."

"Watching the crowds is better than being a part of it. Once in a while, it's nice to just remove yourself from things in motion." She sighed. "I don't want to go home. Wish we could stay here all day. This is heaven—and I thought I'd already been there."

"What do you mean?"

"Like—tomorrow. And the weekend, next week. Back at work. You know, I was excited when I first moved here for everything to come. I thought I made it, the big city girl with the incredible job, both things I finally got and was promised so much. I've been there three years, and it doesn't feel as thrilling anymore. It's been stressful, honestly, trying to hustle and be innovative and disrupt or whatever buzzwords they throw out. Sometimes I feel like I'm just going in circles."

Simon had no idea what *disruptive* or *buzzwords* even meant. But he took Marjorie's hand again and responded, "You can't be too hard on yourself. It sounds like you're trying to do so many impossible things at once."

"I am. And I wish I could just leave it all for tomorrow and never go."

The afternoon rush remained constant as shoppers passed between I. Magnin and City of Paris department stores, and tourists gathered around the base of the Nike statue to snap photos of her piercing the skyline. The big TWA billboard just beyond caught Simon's attention—it was the airline he took to get to San Francisco. He also feared tomorrow—returning to Georgia and settling into the quiet casualness of the life his mother already expected. It wasn't quite tomorrow but inevitable nonetheless.

A shaggy-haired young man in a striped shirt and denim jacket with his hands full of flyers approached them. He waved and crouched down to Marjorie and Simon as he began, "Hiya folks! A beautiful day like this is missing some of the best stuff Mother Nature's given us to enjoy. We're spreading the word on ways you can help make marijuana legal. Care to learn more?"

Simon uneasily laughed while Marjorie glanced at the flyer from the man. "Not right now, thank you, but we'll try and stop by this meeting on the ninth? Lincoln Community Center, that's south of Golden Gate Park, right?"

"That's right! We already got forty thousand San Franciscans smoking, but we can always use more folks to spread the good news. Have any of you tried grass before?"

"No sir," Simon admitted.

"Of course!" replied Marjorie.

"Aw man, it's great! Studies show all positive results, no dangers at all like the Capitol and surgeon general would want you to believe. It might not solve all the world's problems, but it's a first step. We sweat the stupid shit here in America, and we just gotta let it go and light up."

"Amen," said Marjorie. "Well, good luck, we'll try to make that meeting!"

"Thanks, sis," the young man responded, giving her a slight pat on the back before he went to an older woman scattering feed to pigeons. Simon looked at Marjorie in amusement.

"I didn't take you for a girl who smoked marijuana," he said, and she shrugged.

"Sure, I have. Smells terrible, honestly, but feels great." A bell sounded over the city from a clock tower, perhaps from The St. Francis Hotel, signaling four o'clock.

"I declare, Miss Marjorie, there is still so much I don't know about you—but I'd gladly love to learn."

"Good and bad?" She brushed his knee with the lily.

"You already say vulgar words and smoke pot. Nothing else should shock me."

"Oh, it's all been a work in progress. I'm surprised I haven't scared you away by now."

Another bell rang, now coming off from the cable car making its way up the hill on Powell as Marjorie adjusted herself to lie down on his lap and looked up at him, and his heart started racing as their eyes met.

"I normally don't get this comfortable with people I just met," she confessed. "And usually on days like this when I'm—I'm out by myself—I don't talk a lot to anyone."

"I wasn't even my most polite, I think," said Simon. "It's a wonder you didn't shoo me away." He handed her the stolen lily that she had left in the grass.

"I'm just at peace right now with you," she continued. "You make me forget about the terrible week to come. It's the best."

"What is it again that you do? Is it really that stressful?"

"I'm in marketing. Basically, I help with the branding and creating all the marketing materials for my company. And sometimes I do illustration, but they expect so much more with images, and somehow my job has turned into a graphic designer. They're too cheap to get another person and frankly, they don't understand how much goes into both roles."

"Hmm. Well, once you've gotten married, that'll put your mind at ease, I'm sure. Not worrying about those things or working for anyone again."

She sat up and shrugged. "I don't know if I wanna get married."

"Really?"

"Really. I've always been comfortable about taking care of myself. Marriage, if it is in the cards for me, wouldn't change that."

Maybe it was different out here on the West Coast, but seldom did young ladies in Simon's town gladly declare not setting their sights on marriage. Not that he was in any rush either. But his heart did sink a little. And Marjorie seemed to have sensed this, reaching out for his hand.

"Maybe the right person isn't here yet," she said. Then she seemed to chuckle to herself, following up with, "Maybe they've already passed."

"That would be a shame!" Simon exclaimed.

"I'm sorry, I'm just rambling and talking aloud all over the place. Guess those Mean Reds really are messing with me. But every time I look at you, it's like they instantly go away."

He returned her gaze, the deep brown eyes that seemed sad, yet at peace, meeting his own. "Much better than pot, I think," he chuckled.

"I should say so!" Her gaze lingered a few seconds more. "You're sweet, Simon. I'm definitely going to brag about meeting you when you're famous."

Simon blushed, but it gave him an idea. He searched his pockets and found the folded receipt from St. Francis. With his pen, he thought for a second before scribbling over it,

Yours Now,
Simon Grace
8.21.1964

"As proof," he explained, passing it to her. He'd always liked the ring of this stage name, and seeing it printed out, it felt right. Using the family name might have stirred too much talk or scrutiny back home if these musical notions of his ever became anything of value.

"Simon Grace. That's a lovely name. It'll be a tale I repeat often and fondly." Once more she glanced up to the Union Square skyline, where the light began to soften and dim through the buildings as the sun moved farther down west. The crowds continued to pile from the hotels and out of cabs to signify the start of a Friday night on the town.

"Let's keep going," Marjorie decided. "I'm ready."

Chapter 15

Marjorie turned thirty, and the first thing that happened that day was a knock on the door.

Doc still slept soundly on his side with his feet kicking into her back, and she was grateful he didn't bother to wake up and go off barking. She got out of bed and slipped on her sweater to meet whomever it was on the porch, but upon opening the door she only found a yellow box on the front mat and a bouquet of pink roses wrapped in newspaper. On top of the box was an envelope with a birthday card:

Happiest Birthday my dear! Here's to hoping you get all the dances tonight at the prom,

-   Caroline

Cute and sweet, just like the whole Raspberry Cream pie that lay inside the box. Breakfast, perhaps? She went back upstairs to check on Doc and fell back into bed. It was her day, and she wasn't going to rush herself on this day off, especially into this new decade—with other times and years, she could move fairly freely between them, but on her own timeline, she wasn't quite ready to move forward. The clock on her nightstand said 9:26 a.m., and she closed her eyes while gently placing her hand around Doc's outstretched paw. He was awake and looked over at her with his sleepy eyes, but he made no sudden moves to leave this cozy, heavenly spot they shared. On the edge of the bed, she could feel her phone vibrating with all the messages from friends and family reaching out to wish her well. Still, she kept her eyes closed. The birdsong had quieted down in these last weeks and only the wind and a distant leaf blower could be heard on this bright morning. Some time passed after she'd drifted back to sleep when she was aroused by the scent of cinnamon in the air coming from somewhere, and she only clung onto her comforter more tightly. But she couldn't spend her thirtieth in bed all day, as wonderful as it felt.

She slowly rose, and after kissing Doc once more on the head, got out and began her beauty routine for the new decade, showering and throwing on a satin robe and her freshly blow-dried hair in rollers before heading downstairs to get some coffee brewing. She opened the box and hesitated once more before deciding to cut a slice for breakfast. Best decision. She was at the counter eating her slice when her phone rang. It was Danny.

"Good morning!" she greeted him, licking the pink filling from her thumb.

"Good morning," he said. "And Happy Birthday. I know it's still early, but I do hope you're having a beautiful start."

"Well, with a call from you, I certainly am."

"Nah, I'm sure Doc would lick you in the face with his rotten breath, and that'd be a better birthday greeting."

"You're not wrong about that. Are we still on for drinks with Alex and Benny before the gala?"

"Absolutely. I can't wait to see you tonight in your birthday best. You're probably gonna look like a tulip in one of your big dresses."

"Wow, now I'm really excited to get dolled up." She couldn't help but smile at being called a tulip.

"I meant it in a lovely way!" Danny continued. "Tulips are gorgeous flowers. Would you like me to bring you a bouquet tonight?"

"You coming out with us is plenty enough of a gift. But thank you!"

"I'm looking forward to tonight. Happy Birthday again, Marge."

"Thank you. I can't wait to see you."

It wasn't long before Benny came over, bringing with her a dress on a hanger and her curling iron stuffed into a big makeup bag with all her other beauty products. There was also a small present under her arm that went unnoticed until Benny gave it to Marjorie on the porch after she made herself an Irish coffee. She watched Marjorie closely with the mug still to her lips as her friend's eyes widened when opening her little box to reveal two gifts: a lily-embossed leather copy of Longfellow's *Evangeline* from 1927 and a heart-shaped pearl on a gold chain.

"Aww, Benny!" she exclaimed. "Both of these are lovely, and this necklace is beautiful! I don't believe I have any pearls in my jewelry. This is a great start."

"Y'all know how we love our pearls down here," said Benny with a laugh. "As much as we love clutching them. Found both book and pearl at Westside, the pearl behind a glass case so you know it's legit and high quality."

"I'll be wearing it tonight. It's gonna look so great with the dress!"

"When are you putting yours on? I wanna see if I can try and steam yours in the bathroom real quick if that's cool?"

"I don't have a steamer?"

"Your shower. Just closing the door and letting the hot water steam set the clothing is just as effective."

Marjorie shrugged. "Do what you gotta do. You got time! Alex might be coming dressed already since she's heading over straight from the salon, even though it won't be for a while before we hit the town. You sure that stopping by the gala is OK? It might be a bit boring."

"Hey girl, it's your birthday! It's gonna be boring only if we make it. It's nothing that a quick stop over at Duke's Juke can't fix."

"Oh boy. As long as someone's getting the drinks. It ain't the birthday girl!"

It would be a while before the girls would head toward Marietta for drinks and then the gala at six, but the birthday celebrations carried on in other forms. The weather was exceptionally warm for this first day of November, perfect for sitting out on the porch, and until Alex joined them closer to four o'clock, it was Irish coffees and listening to all of Marjorie's favorite get-ready tunes like MGMT and Marina and the Diamonds, which took her back to her early days in San Francisco. As Alex caught up on a hot cup of her own and painted her nails on the floor of the porch, they each went over the memories of their best and worst moments in their twenties, Benny seemingly naming off the most debaucheries, which took place during and post UGA days, and that resulted in the relationship that she declared while shaking her head to be "the most beautiful tragedy of my young life."

"At least you got some adventure from your tragedy and the previous trials and errors," said Alex. "Before my shitty ex, the guys we did meet during cosmetology school were out at the Kennesaw Bahama Breeze, and really forgettable. But I do tend to meet the best ones when I'm working. The first place I apprenticed at, there was Kyle who gave me his number on a five-dollar bill—his tip. Not the smartest move, that was telling of him from the start. But still, he was honestly one of the better guys I've been with." A smile came over her face. "God, I wonder how good Stephen is."

Benny slouched over and took a big sip from her mug. "At least you got someone to think about. You and Marge. I've got shit. And I'm pretty sure there's not gonna be one lesbian tonight at the event. At least not one who's single or under forty!"

They moved inside to finish getting ready, Marjorie admiring her peach tulle dress in the mirror as she finished setting her teased hair with a few ringlets pinned at the back of her head; she couldn't have pictured a more fitting way to celebrate. Alex donned a deep blue wiggle dress with black polka dots that contrasted her dark red hair beautifully, while Benny was very playful in a satin green drop-waist maxi with loose blonde curls brushed out and parted on the side—far from her normal look, very Katherine Hepburn. A few selfies were taken by the front entryway mirror, and then they were off for the magical evening ahead as the Uber pulled up and whisked them off to the Square. At the seafood restaurant where Sun Glows were no longer in season, they sat at the bar and grabbed a few gin martinis while waiting for Danny, who soon walked in and flashed Marjorie the most excited smile as his eyes met hers across the restaurant. He wore the gray suit she'd seen him wear when he'd been at The Georgian Terrace, an excellent choice that everyone could see when they were sat beside each other at the bar.

"Well, I was right," he said as he leaned in to kiss her on the cheek. "You're a tulip."

"Oh, fuck off," Marjorie said as she laughed. "I'm guessing traffic was a shit show?"

"The usual. Gonna hate driving back, but I gotta make sure I'm back and up early for the big wedding The Terrace has tomorrow." He then whispered closely to her, "I wish I could stay tonight and properly celebrate."

She gently squeezed his hand. "Just a dance from you is celebrating enough. I'm glad you came out this way for this."

Suddenly, Alex reached around to tap Danny on the shoulder. "Hey Don Draper, you're covering this right?" she shouted with a wink.

"Sure thing," he nodded back at her, holding up his glass. "Just say when we need to leave, I can toss this back." Reaching over to the middle, he hovered his drink for a toast as he shouted, "Cheers to a new decade, Marge! Happy Birthday."

Walking side by side with Danny, he and Marjorie weren't far off from resembling a Ken and Barbie set from the sixties. On the way to the Museum, they caught up with Al and Ken, both in dark tuxedos but each one donning a contrast of red and gray scarves around their necks. "Miss Marjorie! We figured you'd be making your way to the gala in nothing less than lovely as that," remarked Ken, reaching his hand out to give her a twirl. "I see you've got an entourage too! Very Jayne Mansfield."

A train passed in the distance as they all walked together toward the old depot now event hall that was located right next to the Museum. Inside, Safiya beamed at the door as she gave them all their wristlets and drink tickets, she herself decked in a lavender wrap dress. As she stepped in, Marjorie gasped at how lovely the work of the Museum's small but resourceful event committee had come through for the gala and taken them back in time with the festive theme. It did feel like a prom in the 1950s, with plenty of crepe streamers twisted above them in mint green and gold with twinkle lights dripping against the brick walls. The DJ looked like a young Elvis with his own hair slicked back and a white tux jacket with black slacks, spinning the Rat Pack crooners for the opening hour as guests were grabbing cocktails. By the bar, Art and his wife, Tess, were toasting their glasses of red wine, and nearby, Stephen, hired by Lara Jean as the photographer for the evening, took a candid shot. The flash quickly went off, catching Alex's attention as her eyes got wide.

"Wait, he's here?" Alex asked Marjorie.

"Uh-huh. I suggested him as our event photographer."

"Was this before you asked me to come to this?"

"Yes, way before I even thought I was gonna show up. But look at you! I wouldn't be surprised if he asked to take more than one photo of you tonight." She looked over to Stephen and waved her hand to get his attention, and catching her signal he smiled and pointed his camera their way. As they quickly posed, Marjorie felt Danny's hand gently slide around her waist as he leaned in for the photo.

Luanne, blonde hair piled high up and wearing a ruffled collar brocade pink dress, waltzed through the dance floor toward the bar where everyone was getting their first drink. "My, my, aren't you the cutest prom queen," she teased Marjorie as she toasted her glass.

"Luanne, the place looks so magical!" Marjorie exclaimed. "The team really came through for this. I hope Lara Jean isn't still caught up in any more work. I haven't seen her yet!"

"Oh no, everything is all good to go! But Lara Jean went home after we decorated and haven't seen them since."

The music faded and the DJ spoke, welcoming the guests and announcing that to kick off the dance floor he'd be starting slow, a song by The Ray Charles Singers. A few people grabbed partners and made their way to the floor as the song started, with Stephen circling around them for a few quick shots. He then turned toward the bar where he set his camera down and looked over to Alex. "Would you like to dance?" he asked her, Alex nearly speechless as he whisked her back to the dance floor.

Benny and Marjorie exchanged smiles as Alex looked back at them with a silent scream. As Benny looked out into the crowd, that sadness in her eyes came back, and Marjorie knew what she wanted to do. "Care to dance?" she asked her friend.

Her surprise request instantly seemed to erase any somber thoughts, and she took Marjorie's hand. "For the birthday girl, gladly," she responded, and they both walked out to the floor, moving past Alex, who placed her hand on her heart as she saw her friends. Marjorie looked back at Danny, who was near their drinks and gave her a wink. As she and Benny settled into the movements, Benny's eyes looked almost teary again, but with a gleam. "Thanks, Marge," she said to her. "You sure you didn't want to dance with Danny?"

"It's not often you get to dance with your bestie," Marjorie told her. "Sorry, this isn't really exciting or for a younger crowd, but I don't know. That's not what I need right now."

"Honestly, neither do I. This is chill, and getting the hottest girl in the room to ask you to dance? Can't beat that."

"Damn straight." Marjorie chuckled. She glanced toward the entrance, and it just so happened that there was Lara Jean and Nelson, walking through arm in arm, Lara Jean radiating a glow with her dark hair swept up and exposing where the sleeves of the mint tulle dress draped off her shoulders. She looked very much like her mother's picture, which was one of the photos chosen to be blown up and displayed, and Marjorie saw Lara Jean walk over for Nelson to snap a picture of her right next to the festive old photo. She turned to the poster and touched her mother's arm, before taking Nelson's hand to head to the dance floor for the last few seconds of the song. She met Marjorie's eyes and waved to her, Nelson looking back and nodding as well before he pulled his wife in for a kiss on the top of her head. Everyone was happy, and it was only just the first hour of the evening.

Soon an upbeat early Beatles song took over and the girls headed back to the bar, where Danny had found himself in conversation with Al and Ken but not before getting them all fresh new rounds to sip. He turned back to Marjorie and took her hand. "You gals have fun?" he playfully asked her.

"Oh yeah, she was loving it," Marjorie said, taking a drink before seeing Caroline walk by and reaching out to try and wave her down. "Miss Caroline!" she called. "The pie! It was fantastic and so sweet of you."

Caroline grinned and took Marjorie's outstretched hand. "Everyone needs to wake up to a good pie on special days," she told her. "Well! We're off to catch a few dances ourselves." She turned to her husband, Cameron, whom Marjorie had never seen before, an older man with a long face and head of rather thick wavy brown hair. "Don't you forget what I said, missy! Get all the dances. I'll be seeing you out there."

"Yes ma'am," Marjorie nodded. She didn't dance too often, mostly taking in the room and walking around to see who else she recognized from around the Square and the merchant meetings. Danny didn't hover, leaving her to freely roam as he stayed by Alex or Benny, even slow dancing at one point with each of them when Bobby Vinton or The Temptations came on. But he hadn't asked Marjorie yet. Not that she was looking for a dance. As she found herself again at the bar waiting for a glass of wine halfway through the evening, she thought about what they might dance to. Whatever it may be, it would be a nice thought, but it wouldn't be Bertha Tillman, or St. Francis Fountain. There would never be another moment like that one she shared with Simon—

Then she heard it. It wasn't in her head, and this was still in the present, in the middle of the dance floor where she froze as "Oh My Angel" began to float across the room. She looked toward the DJ where she saw Danny walking toward her, smiling again as he held out his hand.

"May I have this dance?" he asked her. She looked at his outstretched hand and took it slowly, coming into his arms but feeling rather stiff as they swayed to the song.

"This song," she said, not sure what else to say.

"I know," Danny replied warmly. "I'd never heard it until you, and when I looked it up, I thought it was honestly one of the most beautiful songs. It'll always remind me of how we met. Our song."

This declaration stopped Marjorie. "No," she spat, staring at him for a brief second, then away as his confused eyes met hers. "No, this isn't it. It's not *yours*."

"I—OK, it's not. But if it wasn't for that record then we would have never—"

"Yes, met. But this isn't anything special. The song isn't yours, and you have no idea what it means to me. This is nothing. I don't know why you would think this was it." She slowly began stepping back, hearing how she sounded and began again, more softly. "I'm sorry. Danny, it's just that we shouldn't be—"

"Shouldn't be what?"

"Anything." She took a deep breath and put her hands to her face in disgust, embarrassment, to rub away the tears she knew would soon be falling. "I'm sorry, Danny, so, so sorry. I think we might have— no, *I* might have made a mistake. I wasn't ready, and now I'm realizing—"

"This was a mistake?" He stood still on the dance floor, his eyes still fixed on her with alarm. "I know we haven't really talked seriously about us, but to me, it's been a special last few months being with you. I was just trying to make you happy with the song."

"I appreciate that so much, but I don't deserve it. I've got a lot to still figure out being here, and this is the last thing I should be starting. It's all my fault, I shouldn't have brought you out, shouldn't have kept this going and just not gotten involved. I—"

The tears finally fell as the song came to an end. All memories of it, endearing and bittersweet, were suddenly tainted by this one moment here and now—and alone. She turned away and walked off to get a napkin by the bar, and she could feel Danny right behind her.

"Marjorie, please," he said to her. "I'm really sorry. I just wanted to make you happy, anything I could do to make this a memorable birthday—"

"I got that!" she snapped. "But you're wasting your time on me, Danny. Time is never good to me—" Turning around to look at Danny, in his face she could only see Simon, his blue eyes and floppy hair falling over his forehead with the smile he had when he chuckled at their dancing in that soda fountain decades ago.

"I'm sorry," she said. "Danny, please don't be mad. I know you are, I'm awful. But I can't help that right now—it's not right."

He shook his head and shrugged. "I'm sorry too. I didn't mean to ruin tonight. But I overstepped." Looking around for the exit, he began to turn. "I should probably get back to Midtown. I really do hope your birthday night gets better. Tell the girls I said goodbye, please."

Before he left, he paused and went toward her one more time, gently hugging her.

Frantically, Marjorie walked through the dance floor and back toward the bar where she found Alex and Stephen talking in a corner, Alex's face almost flushed as she was nodding to something he was telling her. She looked up and saw Marjorie, hugging Stephen before walking away and meeting her friend.

"What's the matter?" Marjorie asked Alex.

"Nothing is what's the matter," Alex said. "Nothing is going to happen with him and whatsername. He was explaining that it's been great to get to know each other, but he's been with her for so long and just—he's at peace with whatever it is, this dynamic they got. It's fucking weird, if you ask me. But he said he didn't feel like he should end things. Not yet at least."

"Not yet?" Marjorie was confused. "So, it's like he admits it's not the best thing for them—"

"But he says he makes her so happy. What the fuck, Marge." Just then Benny found them, her smile dropping as she saw both their flustered faces.

"Guys alright?" she asked them. "Is it time to go?"

Looking around, Marjorie nodded. "Please. Let's go find something to eat."

"OK! Let's go find Danny—"

"He left. We had an argument, and he left early."

"Oh, Marge," Alex said.

"It's fine. Maybe I freaked out when I shouldn't have. But let's get going. Where should we go?"

Benny smiled knowingly, turning to Alex who nodded as if she knew too.

...

The Waffle House off Whitlock Avenue was unusually crowded, so it seemed that counter spots were the theme of the night. Marjorie was fine with staring blankly out to the grills that were covered nonstop with grease and eggs frying side by side with chunked and smothered hash browns. She wasn't hungry, but she didn't want to go home just yet. Some start to being thirty.

Benny was not pleased at Marjorie's only order of chocolate chip waffles. "Please," she tried again, pushing her plate over, "take some of my hash browns—"

"No, I'm good," Marjorie insisted. "I didn't drink too much anyway. Thanks though."

"Of course." She took a few bites before starting again with, "You sure you're OK though?"

"Yes. I'll be fine."

On Marjorie's other side, Alex drank her coffee and sighed. "Christ, first Stephen, then Danny. Benny, you might be having the best night of all, actually. All dudes really are fucked."

"As much as I'd like to concur," Marjorie replied, "it wasn't anything Danny did. I just—I don't know, I don't really know, actually. One minute we were dancing, but then I was telling him he shouldn't have wasted his night coming up here."

"He must have said something."

"No, nothing he did."

"Then what?" Benny asked.

"It was—it was the song." She paused and began again. "He was trying to be sweet, but I couldn't. Not to that song. Too many memories."

"An ex," Alex said.

"No, not really. But it was something wonderful. I can't quite describe it—and he just took me by surprise."

Both Alex and Benny nodded, keeping their gaze on the birthday girl as she looked to each of them with a small smile. "I fucked it up. Simple as that." She sighed.

Benny shrugged. "Simple as that, it wasn't right," she assured her friend. "If you weren't feeling it, you were honest. And you know how I feel about being honest! I don't see how you could have done otherwise."

If only it all had been right. The stunning dress she wore, the beautiful night aglow in the lights of the gala, the song she loved dearly floating across the floor. Everything for this birthday had been destined to be perfect. Even Danny. But Marjorie wasn't feeling thirty—she couldn't feel a day over twenty-five, not while Simon still remained lost.

The girls wouldn't understand. She couldn't explain the tears she began feeling again, pushing them back as she sipped on some coffee of her own.

Marjorie, 1948

December, 2023. Chilly Georgia Decembers usually weren't the exception, but with the steep temperature drops of this Christmastime everyone was prepared for a little snowfall. Marjorie eagerly awaited a morning when she'd look out the window and see flurries, kicking off a cozy holiday ahead in her new hometown before she went back to California on the twenty-second. But as November moved into December and the last of the autumn leaves fell from Morris Road up to Kennesaw Mountain in the wake of the winter winds' sharp chill, there was still no sight of snow after all. Yet in spite of none, Marjorie still stayed bundled in the mornings under the warm covers with Doc, sleepy but awake enough to imagine thick powdery drifts building up against the frail, creaky windows of Dogwood Daze.

At least a little overcast sky and lingering clusters of red leaves in the treetops rounded the holidays in Marietta, already decked with the year-round lights on the buildings and gazebo where Santa would greet children every Saturday that month. A few new embellishments like big red ribbons across the bandstand and hanging orb lights from the canopies made the town feel truly like a magical snow globe. As Marjorie walked the streets with Doc, dressed in his own thick sweater, she took in these mesmerizing sights of the Square that would become fixtures for these new Christmas memories. And the window dressings were her favorite—the Pop Shop with colorful sodas adorning an old cardboard fireplace mantel with a pink tree next to it decked in retro toys like Yo-Yos as ornaments, Westside Antiques showcasing old red and plaid suitcases outside an old glass window with a snow sled propped up against it, and the towering Christmas tree made of only green books that was glowing with twinkle lights down its sides in the bay window of the bookstore—Benny's pride and joy on full display for the town to see. It was at Ken's own Marietta Mercantile that she enjoyed the window display the most—a little Christmas village collected and curated over the years by Ken and Al together. A labor of love, a beautiful little tradition they shared together, and the sight of it warmed Marjorie's heart as much as it made it ache. She viewed all these traditions alone, thinking that maybe in another time and place she might have made them with Simon.

It was on one of these frosty evenings that Marjorie and Doc were strolling around the Square, just coming up on Westside Antiques, when Roberta Hamilton was emerging from the entrance. She had on a red puffer coat and a white beanie with a fluffy pom-pom on top that jiggled as she bounced over to Marjorie.

"My darling! Merry Christmas!" Roberta greeted her. "Oh, you're so toasty in this coat! I'm gonna add one to my Christmas list. And look at your little fella! Doc, sir, you're just as dapper as your mama. Doing some Christmas shopping tonight?"

"Sort of, Miss Roberta," said Marjorie. "Since I'm going back home, a bulk of my shopping is mostly online or gonna be back in California, but it doesn't hurt to look around and get inspiration in town."

"I'm so glad to hear that. I'm sure your family will love having you back for the holidays. I'll just be with Daniel and his family—his older brother has a big cabin near Blue Ridge, and we'll be hunkered down out there. Daniel himself, my sweet boy, will be making it a road trip for the both of us! As long as I buy the snacks, I don't think he'll mind me singing carols for the whole drive."

Marjorie chuckled a little. "It sounds like it'll be a beautiful time together. How's Danny been? It sounds like he's been busy since Thanksgiving."

"Nonstop, I tell you. I am happy to see he's passionate about his work but apart from the time he spends with you, I don't think he's had much leisurely time outside of all the holiday racket at The Terrace."

Marjorie and Danny hadn't seen each other since her birthday. Still, she was glad to see Roberta; even before knowing her nephew, Marjorie always felt a kinship to this kind, enthusiastic woman who had given her a reason to remain in Marietta—and from how Roberta had greeted and now left her, with a rather tight bear hug, she was relieved that Danny didn't mention anything to his aunt.

The following Sunday, a week before flying back to the West Coast, Marjorie sat by the fountain on the Square with two cups of peppermint hot cocoa from Caroline's, waiting for Alex. Marjorie had an extra ticket from Lara Jean for helping volunteer that weekend during the Museum's last big event of the year, the Marietta Holiday Pilgrimage. A few dozen historic homes were open to the public to enjoy at their most festive, and while most of them were usually clustered in the same neighborhood, this year they were more or less scattered across the town. A few were strung out along Kennesaw Avenue, once referred to glamorously as the "Peachtree Street" of Marietta, with an array of grand Antebellum and Victorian styles. Marjorie couldn't wait to venture from home to home and was even more grateful that Alex was available to hang out and enjoy their elegance together with her.

She saw Alex walking from the Square's north side and waved her down with one of the cups in her hand. "Oh, thank God!" exclaimed Alex as she hugged Marjorie and took the hot cocoa from her. Cupping her hands around the drink, she took a slow sip, careful not to burn her lips, but let out a content little grunt. "You know how to kick off festivities," she told Marjorie.

"I might as well sweeten the deal, literally," said Marjorie as they began to walk down toward the Museum. "I appreciate you hanging out with me for this anyhow! I know looking at old houses isn't as exciting as a *Nightmare Before Christmas* pop-up bar."

"Nah, been there and done that, and I enjoy a good festive old house as much as the next old lady, especially the one I work with." She winked at Marjorie and took another sip.

Looking down at her vintage fur collared coat draped with a bright plaid scarf, Marjorie shrugged in agreement. "You got me. But I mean, it's Christmas! It's a very visually stimulating holiday and what's better than ogling over a cozy home or two decked out for the holidays?"

"It'd be more ideal if it was my house, but with today's inflation I don't think I'll ever be able to call an old Victorian off of the Square mine."

"Nope, you're absolutely right. But for forty-five dollars a ticket a person can dream, right? And in our case, we're doing it for free!"

They headed over to where the buses that ferried between homes began their routes by the cross street near the Museum. Jumping onto the yellow school bus, they were greeted by Luanne herself who passed out candy canes to each person. Grabbing a seat toward the middle, Alex and Marjorie both unwrapped their canes and dropped them into their hot cocoa cups for an extra kick. Before the bus took off Luanne turned around to raise her hands for everyone's attention, ready to make a quick announcement.

"Welcome, y'all!" she called out. "Are we ready for a very Marietta Christmas tour today?" Cheers and applause followed, and Luanne's smile grew. "That's the holiday spirit! It's going to be a beautiful chilly day to step into these cozy spaces of grandeur and classic Christmas cheer. Before we head out to see these grand dames of The Gem City, we got a quick word from one of our biggest sponsors of this year's Pilgrimage, Robert Chaffee representing Northfield Properties!"

Marjorie and Alex turned to each other and rolled their eyes as a tall man in a long gray coat and red scarf stood next to Luanne and began obnoxiously ringing a cowbell. As he talked, Marjorie and Alex paid him no attention, instead Alex whispering to Marjorie, "Like anyone believes they care about the community."

"Trying to save face, but it'll only be a matter of time before they tear down something else around the Square for some stupid mixed office space or pickleball court. It's too suspicious how quiet they've been about Nelson's expansion."

Chaffee finished his little speech, and after one more irksome ring of his cowbell, the bus drove off from the parking lot and up North Marietta Parkway where it looped around onto Kennesaw Avenue. They passed a few of the other home tours like the coral facade of the Archibald Howell house, where a line was already gathered from the sidewalk up to its wide looming columns, which framed a large wreath hanging from the front balcony. As impressive as the 1843 home looked, Marjorie was eager to begin their tour at Oakton, the house that had always seemed a mystery to her.

She'd always pass the green house on the hill on drives to the nearest Costco. Far up and shrouded by trees, she felt a tickling in her stomach as the bus pulled over at its gates. Everyone got off and followed the curved incline toward the home, where the farther they went up the quieter the traffic from the street behind them grew until it was only the sound of voices from the masses and the sleigh bells on the front door wreath chiming with each open and closure. Now in view, Marjorie saw the grandeur of this ancient homestead clear as the icy gray sky above—it wasn't a tall house, but it was stately, with a massive gable drenched in faded jade green paint looming over four sets of ornate columns wrapped in fresh evergreen, and bay windows on each side rounding out the front of the house that looked down over a small boxwood garden surrounding a single fountain. Walking up to the big front porch where wide windows with dark green shutters had been draped in holly wreaths, Marjorie took a big breath in anticipation of the Christmas charm to be revealed once inside.

The small cluster of attendees that included herself and Alex waited on the porch until the entry docent opened the wide oak door into an enclosed foyer that was a feast for the eyes. There was no grand staircase, but a large room that had doors on either side, and as the docent waved her arm for them to follow through the door on the right, their group came upon a simple but long dining room where more holly was swathed across the table and windows and dim lights cast a warm and cozy glow against the pale blue walls and paintings in gold frames. They went in farther to the grand parlor situated behind the foyer as Marjorie turned left and then, like it was Christmas morning, gasped at the sight of the tall Christmas tree itself. It was nestled beside the fireplace and trimmed in dried orange slices and cranberries threaded on blue velvet ribbon to match the walls. A darling sight, classic and yet rustic, more primitive to align with the age of the house.

It thrilled Marjorie to start this tour on a high note with Oakton, and turning to Alex, she nudged at her elbow with excitement. "God, don't you wish you could live here!" she whispered to her.

"Was hoping for lots of dark wood paneling in here," said Alex. "More Poe and less Dickens. But still giving that old world charm. We just have to be making six figures and over sixty to throw our hat in the ring for a place like this!" As their group settled into the parlor and around the grand tree, the present docent stepped forward and smiled patiently for the murmurs to quiet.

"Welcome, y'all!" he called out to the group. "It's only the beginning of much to see in this beautiful home, but as you look around and admire this room, note that it's one of many sitting rooms you will find throughout Oakton Manor. In the room beyond to my right is another that would be a private one for the main bedroom next to it facing the back of the house. But yes, this would be considered the main hub of the Goodman family and their visitors to come and gather, especially during Christmas. As my fellow docents have mentioned, the Goodman family, upon their purchase of Oakton from the Wilders in the 1920s, made Oakton a household name around Marietta thanks to their grand parties in the summer and winter for family friends and fellow townspeople alike. You might know the family best as being the founders of our beloved local paper, the *Marietta Daily Journal*, but for today, we only think of them as hospitable ghosts letting us glimpse back into what might have been a lively and cheerful Christmas weekend here in their home."

As the docent continued, Marjorie's wandering eyes landed on the loose curtains in the front window, a darker shade of green with stripes slouching over the coral settee below. She slowly made her way over to the window and leaned over the bench, looking down onto the now foggy hill and the people emerging through its dim haze from the buses below. Suddenly, that chill came over her, despite the roaring fireplace and the thick rugs that lay about the old home and kept it toasty. She knew another kind of magic was about to happen.

The soft and muffled flow of music fell upon her ears as if coming from a nearby radio. Marjorie turned slowly around, noticing first that the tree in the corner was shorter, tinsel dripping from its branches and adorned in illuminated Shiny Brite ornaments Marjorie had seen many a time in original boxes at the antique stores on the Square. The walls were now papered in a faint green floral and adorned with portraits in big dark wood frames, dotted by smaller black-and-white photographs on a side table. Listening to the music, she heard Judy Garland's voice softly crooning "Have Yourself a Merry Little Christmas" across the warm air in thanks to the fire that popped and crackled. The central sitting room was empty and the door to the foyer was closed, but looking back out onto the hill outside Marjorie came face-to-face with headlights making their way up the curved driveway. A red 1940s Buick pulled up right before the porch, and on the other side of the door to the foyer she heard footsteps as someone walked out and down to the car, one of the servants waving as they ran down to greet them.

Marjorie saw this as the best time to get out of the house unnoticed, and carefully opened the door toward the entrance. A panic struck her as she walked onto the porch and saw that the guests in the Buick were now emerging from the back. Quickly she ducked between a few rockers, but the woman and two children who emerged were too eager to make their way up the steps to notice her, greeted by a woman in a floor-length red dress who emerged from through the door.

"Merry Christmas, little darlings!" their hostess exclaimed. She looked in her forties and kept her dark hair neatly up on her head with the waves softening her round face. She hugged the little girl and boy who abruptly went inside after their embrace, and moved over to their mother, Marjorie presumed, who was wearing a dark gray wool coat and fur cap bejeweled with what looked like a pearl brooch. "Susan, how lovely you look tonight."

"Thank you, Dorothy," Susan said, hugging her. "Well, certainly not as spectacular as yourself! As you should be. We've been invited to six different parties this month already, but you know yours is the one we looked forward to the most. Oh! I almost forgot the gifts!"

"I'll have Bradley bring them to the tree. You go on and get warmed up and drink some punch! I added less cinnamon and a pinch of aniseed for that kick you always like."

Marjorie watched the two women as they continued their conversation up the steps and through the foyer, trailing off as the radio overtook the voices of those gathered inside before Bradley, the man who had greeted the car, followed behind with the gifts and gently closed the door. Marjorie stood and slowly peeked through the tall window behind her that looked into the parlor, gradually becoming full with the guests that piled in from the dining room and the little group of children making a beeline for the array of colorful gifts beneath the tree. As Marjorie observed the joyful party from outside, she smiled, longing for when she'd be back home with her own family. Then she saw someone approach the window, and she bounced back. If she'd been seen, she quickly thought about what she might say—*carol singer*, she reasoned. It seemed believable that a caroler could have gotten separated from their big group in the neighborhood, right?

The window was opened a crack, maybe for fresh air, but the sound of the festivities seeped through, followed by a rush of pine and smoke scents for Marjorie to enjoy. She heard familiar voices on the other side, and looking over, saw the two ladies from earlier. They each had a drink in hand watching over the children by the tree. "I do hope that Robert isn't too big for that Santa suit," Dorothy said with a chuckle. "If we don't get the presents open soon, I hope to God it's not because he's struggling upstairs!"

"They can wait awhile," responded Susan. "Patience is always good practice."

"This country practiced patience for the first five years of this decade, waiting for an end to that war. This is Christmas, and if Robert isn't down here soon, I'll dress up as the man with the bag myself, I swear!" This made Susan laugh.

"Oh, such pleasant times are always to be had here in grand old Oakton. Every year is a true delight, Dorothy, I don't know how we would have gotten through those years without you and Robert's support, or—" Suddenly she stopped, and Marjorie could see Susan dab her face with a handkerchief.

"I'm sorry. Christmastime—Hugh's favorite holiday. With every year we've celebrated it hasn't felt completely right. I know you and William try so hard for us, and I truly love you both—everything you've done, Hugh would be so happy to see this for the children." Dorothy leaned in, putting her arm around her friend and rubbing her gently.

"Of course he would want to see you and them smiling and happy. It's the best we silly Goodmans can do for the people we love." All eyes were now toward the gleeful scrambling of the children around the tree, still shouting at each other and shaking the blocks of presents. Catching Susan's eye was one little boy, the one who'd ran into the house from the car and was now trying to sneak off with two small, stacked boxes.

"Dear me!" she exclaimed. "Simon! You go back to the tree and place those gifts right where you plucked them from, young man."

Marjorie's eyes darted straight from Susan to the child—a golden-haired boy of about nine, looking sad as he slowly marched back to the gathering, his little face glossing with tears over the familiar blue eyes that Marjorie instantly recognized.

And then, she felt warm, realizing that she was back in the parlor again by the window away from the crowd that still stood around the docent, now ushering them on into the next sitting room. Alex turned to find Marjorie and, seeing her by the window, said, "Man, I can only imagine the parties they would throw here during Christmas."

Marjorie was still speechless. Only seconds ago she didn't have to imagine, seconds ago wishing that she could have stayed just a little longer to make absolutely sure it was him she'd seen. But in her heart, she was sure of it.

Chapter 16

At least in California, it was green in winter. The hills that greeted her back in the Bay Area were lush and rolled through the suburbs of Walnut Creek like a fairy-tale place, with mist dancing over the grass and dark oak trees brushed against cloudy skies. It reminded her of the places favorite Austen heroines might walk, and now she reveled in the chance to have one of her own. With Christmas and New Year's done, these last few days before she went back to Georgia seemed to drag as her mind became muddled with those moments in the past. When she returned to Marietta, it'd be like going back into a dark maze—the end was in sight for her search but made only more complicated by the uncertainty of where to go next.

On this particular walk through the hills near their parents' home, Marjorie slowed down as her niece and nephew hurried along to catch up with their dad. Eileen looked back and stopped, seeing that her sister was distracted.

"You good?" she asked Marjorie.

"I'm fine."

"OK, well, the littles are basically gonna be a mile away, we gotta hurry. C'mon, spill."

They fastened their pace, trudging up the coming hill where they'd already lost Eileen's family beyond the horizon. Despite months of biking, Marjorie was surprised at how out of breath she'd gotten. "Shit way to begin 2024," she joked.

"You and me both," agreed Eileen. "But truthfully, it's good that Charlie is so outdoorsy and keeps the kids active. All about balance."

"Damn right, 'cause who knows how they'd turn out if their dad just binged *Virgin River* and downed Flamin' Hot Cheetos with his wine, like their mom."

"OK, we've been all about veggie chips these last four years, thank you." Eileen exhaled loudly to catch her breath again. "Wait, so what are you gonna do next?"

"What do you mean?"

"I know Simon's been on your mind. How do you think you'll find him or his family now?"

Now Marjorie exhaled. "Well, the Oakton house is the start. Gotta go back and find out more about the Goodman family. Who their friends and associates were, what events they attended. The Museum has so much in the archives, and I wish I'd paid more attention." She paused to catch her breath some more.

"Eileen, it was just so good to see him. His existence is real—he's not a ghost or someone I'm imagining. The house and then the train tracks have been fucking with my head. It's frustrating. Like—how could he be there, but not?"

The wind that sailed across the grass met the sisters and set their hair blowing back with its gust, nearly knocking off the scarf wrapped around Marjorie's head. Eileen screamed as wisps of her long hair flew back into her face, Marjorie laughing as she helped to push them away.

"Jesus," Eileen exclaimed. "Well, I'm ready to turn back around, yeah?" Still wrestling with the lone strand on her cheek, she pulled her little sister in for a hug. "I'm gonna miss you again," she told her. "I just wish I could make you happy and that'd be enough. But now you got me invested with this! I want to find him as much as you do. At least we know he did go back to Georgia. You said it looked like the eighties? Maybe revisit the later archives again. Music shows, perhaps?"

Marjorie shook her head. "But he was in a suit. And I don't know, something about his whole composure didn't say musical or creative. Maybe he did become an architect after all."

"But the record."

"I know. But maybe something in the sixties or seventies changed. It's confusing."

Both sisters looked ahead where the kids and Charlie were making their way at the end of the hill into a ravine of thick oaks. Eileen sighed and rested her head on her sister's.

"But you're closer, remember that," she reminded her. "Closer to him now than you were last spring, and even than five—well, now six—years ago."

"Yes," Marjorie agreed. "Closer, that's all I want."

…

Walking her bike up to the curb, Marjorie saw Jeff off to the side of the salon, having his usual smoke in the morning right before opening. But he was looking down at the ground, lighting what looked like a second cigarette as his left foot stomped on a butt. Marjorie slowly pulled past and gently greeted him.

"Morning, Marge!" he returned, trying to fan away the smoke. "Good to see ya. Have a good trip back home?"

"Oh yeah, loved it, but too short of a stay. Was your Christmas nice?"

"Mm-hmm. Just a bunch of us stayed over at my folks in Cartersville. Scott's family went up to Indiana, so he stayed with me." Jeff looked down again, his fist tense around the lighter.

"Are you alright?" Marjorie followed up. He sighed and took another smoke.

"Not really. Kinda bummed today. I found out something sad. Remember Christine? Christine Roger, always got an Anna Wintour bob and parked in the loading zone because of her walker?"

"Yeah, it's been a while since she's come back."

"Well, she died."

"Oh my God. I mean, well, that makes sense."

"Yup. Been four months and almost forgot about her. Her daughter left us a voicemail yesterday, and since I was the first one in today thought I'd check the messages. Took the wind out of my fucking sails."

"I'm so sorry, Jeff."

"It's fine. These things happen. But you do start thinking about other clients who just trailed off. Some move away without telling, or others just pass. Their family I'm sure would agree that notifying their hairstylist is the last thing on their list, if we're even on it." He took another quick smoke, this time his exhale followed by a stifled sniffle. "Stupid tears, man. But Christine was so fucking funny. She always was down to try new colors, I think the last time I saw her she got violet in her hair."

Marjorie chuckled at a memory of her own. "The first time I met her she was checking out and before she left told me she needed to go find her husband—and then she followed up with, 'Or somebody's husband.'" They both laughed.

"Sweet, unhinged Christine," Jeff sighed.

Seeing everyone else trickle in that morning made Marjorie smile, just as much as it made her homesick for the familiarity of her old life in California. But a new year now began with a new place to call home and new leads on Simon from the remnants of Goodman family archives she couldn't wait to ask Lara Jean about. Nelson wasn't in yet, given that he had a fairly open morning. But then, even as it neared eleven fifteen and he was already late for his first appointment, everyone grew worried. No returned calls or responses to Marjorie's messages. Finally, he walked in. Bundled in a brown wool coat and a thick green scarf around his neck, he nodded briefly to Marjorie and Jeff as he headed straight toward the back room. "You wanna see if he's OK?" Jeff asked her.

"You think we should?" said Marjorie. But soon enough out came Nelson, grinning and already spitting out apologies to his client, who laughed and shook his hand.

Now that everything on the schedule was settled, Marjorie tried getting her focus back on the usual tasks of answering calls, restocking products that came in, sweeping the hair when Jeff was busy shampooing. But as busy as she tried to be, Marjorie still felt anxious. She thought of the email she sent to Lara Jean about the Goodmans, the photos and documents she'd already picked through for her gala work last year, and all the potential clues she'd missed.

Alex came by after her third client, finishing ahead of schedule as she leaned over the desk to look at the computer screen. "Nice, no one for another hour," she said. "How's it feel to be back in the groove here?"

Marjorie shrugged. "It's all muscle memory by now," she told Alex. "Good to be back. But too fucking cold! I wish it were summer already."

"That's all you, girl. Rather bundle up than sweat. Winter without the holidays is peaceful and cozy, cozier I think than fall sometimes. Great for snuggling up with Doc, who I'm sure would absolutely agree."

"You're not wrong about that, he's the saving grace of being cold. Wish I could be with him right now but gotta make that money. Although I think I heard him whimpering last night, he's probably missing Benny and her sister after being with them for so long."

"Aw, sweet guy. This day feels like it's going by fast and then you'll be back at Dogwood before you know it."

The day did go fast, but not without some upheaval. In the last hour, Art Martin had wandered in, greeting Marjorie with his usual pleasantries before sitting patiently in the waiting area—he didn't have an appointment, but he wasn't looking to make one either. He sat in silence until the door opened again—it was Ken. Marjorie would have written his entrance off as coincidental had not Caroline come in after. All the while, Nelson would glance over and nod, more flustered with each new appearance. Suddenly, it felt as if Lara Jean walked in to save the day, even though it seemed that based on Nelson's temperament, the damage was done.

Lara Jean arrived as Caroline was leaning against the reception desk listening to Marjorie talk about her Christmas in California, smiling and walking her way over to listen in. "My nephew definitely is not a nut person," Marjorie was saying. "They're basically vegetables to him. But it was a good surprise how much he really liked the chocolate-dipped brittle. Only a few days ago when I was on the phone with my sister after I got back, I heard him shout in the background asking auntie to send him more!"

This gave Caroline a good chuckle. "Guess chocolate did the trick. Might not be good for other things like the veggies to be dipped in it, though. Stick to cheese with the broccoli—but who knows!"

"Hope your sister wasn't too mad you gave the little ones sugar," added Lara Jean. "Overall it sounds like you had a lovely time back with family."

"I did! But I did miss Marietta. Sharing all my videos and pictures to relatives got them wanting to plan their visits for later this year!"

"Well, make sure you tell them spring or fall—we're going to get a scorching summer again and that would surely keep them away after one visit."

"Speaking of spring, Lara Jean," Caroline chimed in, standing upright and turning to Lara Jean, "is it true?"

Lara Jean let out a heavy sigh. "Can it wait until Nelson has finished?"

"We've been waiting all day, Miss Lara Jean!" Ken called out to her. "We've gotta know the truth. If it is, that's just outright dirty."

"Couldn't have said it better," followed Art. "And if it is, how long do you think *my* store has!"

Nelson's last client was finished and cut through the tension as she walked up to the desk and checked out, with Marjorie returning to her usual warm manner. As soon as the client left, Nelson appeared, with the other stylists following behind as he waved his arms to corral everyone outside. "Please, for the love of God, let us finish closing up and then I'll talk outside," he scruffily said. Marjorie stayed behind to help count the register and sweep the front, and when she stepped outside, she saw Luanne had joined the inquiring mob, much to Nelson's dismay at one more person to explain whatever was happening. Bundled up again, Nelson locked the door and turned to everyone lined along the sidewalk, including the stylists and Marjorie.

"Alright, Nelson," began Art. "What's officially going to happen?"

Before addressing Art, Nelson took a good look at everyone and began, "Well, as most you folks might have heard, Northfield did not take too kindly to our announcement for expansion after all."

"They said OK in October!" Ken exclaimed.

"Yes, they did, Ken, but they also said in December that after some consideration they felt it reasonable to hike up our rent forty percent starting this month."

Jeff gasped. "Wait, why didn't you tell us? And did you pay it?"

"I thought I could negotiate, but they're steadfast on this increase. We've been given an extension until end of next month, in addition to the lease in February."

"What horseshit!" muttered Art. "This was exactly what you and I had been speculating about, Nelson, and now it's finally here. Once the rent increases start then we'll all be priced out—then they can bring in their stupid pop-ups or whatever from Midtown."

"Regardless of their intentions, there is still time," added Lara Jean. "And, thanks to inquiries with Luanne at the City Hall, loopholes."

"What loopholes?" Nelson asked, just as surprised. "Is that what you were looking for at City Hall this morning?" His wife turned to him with a smirk so confident, it got Nelson to relax his shoulders.

"Why, yes darling," Lara Jean continued. "I even found the original documents recognizing the covenant. If Northfield wants to increase the rent by that much, they're going to have to prove this building—and by extension the whole block they own—is *not* a historic entity. In Marietta, signed into action September fourteenth, 1990, any structures deemed of historic significance to the town may enjoy the privileges of a fixed lease for pre-existing businesses that have been at the property for more than ten years."

"Well, thank God for that!" exclaimed Caroline. "I'm sure there's a lot in the archives then about the building? Hunt's Diner alone is mentioned so often by locals."

"Memories aren't good enough unfortunately," continued Lara Jean. "Everyone knows Nelson and Art's building is old, but we have to find something 'historic' tied to it. Honestly, what I have at the Museum is a heap of bills and deeds from before the eighties. So many businesses moved in and shuttered at once in that time period that any archives related are just a mess." Her eyes subtly looked over to Marjorie, who nodded, already agreeing to the task she knew she was asking of her.

"Well, we better find something fast," Art declared. "I knew those sons of bitches were being too quiet on a venture like the soda shop." Taking another deep breath, Nelson turned to Lara Jean and pulled her in as he placed his arm around her waist.

"If anyone is gonna beat them at their game, it'll be the town itself," he added. "The Museum will find just what we need. Just gotta find it in a month."

As everyone dispersed, Lara Jean followed Marjorie over to where she had locked her bike and said cheerfully, "Sounds like we face another challenge, my dear."

"Well, compared to a rather vague and sentimental theme," returned Marjorie, "at least our search is narrowed on one place only. What sort of papers will we be sifting through?"

"Honestly, who knows. A lot of items regarding Church Street before the eighties are in boxes abandoned to the back room of the salon when Nelson took it over. Thankfully I didn't throw any of it out! But we've got a long road ahead of us and such a short time."

"Always happy to help, and more than ever for Nelson." Before kicking off the stand and heading out, she turned again to Lara Jean. "Would it be any trouble if I were to look through the archives again on a personal project as well? Of course the salon takes precedence, but there was something about one of the homes from the Pilgrimage that caught my eye, and I just wanted to know more about Oakton and the family who lived there."

"The Goodmans? Oh darling, there's absolutely plenty on them I can easily pull up for you. You are always welcome to have at it. But I'll do you one even better. The Goodmans don't live in Marietta anymore, but I do know that Natalie Duncan, a great-niece, is on the Museum board and will be in town in a few weeks for our next meeting—shall we all grab lunch?"

Marjorie's stomach fluttered at the excitement. "That would be lovely, Lara Jean!" she answered. "If she wouldn't mind?"

"Of course not, she's a Goodman through and through. These old Marietta families are humble folk, but do they love to tell tales."

Chapter 17

Lara Jean had always been kind to Marjorie, but certainly this was too much. Did the Goodmans even ask or wonder why this random girl wanted to speak to them? For whatever reasons, the great-niece of Robert Goodman seemed pleased about the meeting with Marjorie. But no one stayed in Oakton year-round, and Marjorie had to act fast before the niece left town for Asheville again, where she'd been for the past eighteen years.

That January cold wasn't as harsh as last year's, but the tease of warmer mornings already had Marjorie in the mood for spring again. Everything in Marietta just felt, well, quiet. But the hope for a visit with a Goodman descendant, that was sunshine enough. Sunday the twenty-first couldn't come faster, and as she counted down the days there were still slow hours at the salon and independent digging through history archives for Nelson. So far, the stacks of old and faded paperwork throughout the years proved nothing of value to the historical society that would be in the salon's favor. Receipts, *Marietta Daily Journal* clippings, all highlighted significant commerce except anything official. If this were any other person, they would be sick of research. But the task had fallen upon Marjorie, and there couldn't be a more dedicated, and gifted, woman for it.

Then the weekend of the twenty-first came, and it was off to a delicious start. The salon finished early and as Marjorie pulled up to the curb on her bike, she could see Doc looking through the window at something on the doorstep. Another yellow box from Caroline, enclosed with a note,

A single slice of a chocolate strawberry fusion greeted her nose and her eyes widened upon seeing the white chocolate drizzle and pink rosettes piped along the crust. Too bad she was still feeling full from her late lunch or else she'd dive straight in. But on to other matters—it was hair wash night, and after a long week her big waves were starting to loosen and grease. Unraveling herself from her thick houndstooth coat and greeting Doc, she set the mail and pie down on the kitchen counter before she heard a knock on the door. Benny stood on the porch, bundled in a gray down jacket and rubbing her red wool mittens together as a smile came over her face.

"Look who's back from Tybee!" exclaimed Benny. "I saw you ride by and thought I'd drop in."

"Aw, glad you did!" Marjorie assured her. "Bet you miss the warmer shores by now. Come in! I was about to take Doc on his walk if you wanted to join and tell me more about your trip."

"Sure! But first, I wanted to give you this." As she stepped into the foyer, she held out something wrapped in brown paper. Opening it, Marjorie was delighted to see a beautiful abalone shell hair comb with dots of pink coral, definitely vintage.

"Jesus, Benny! This is stunning! I love it."

"You damn right better love it! This wasn't from just any junk shop by the beach. Family and I had a few trips into Savannah, and this was actually on display in a beautiful café and antique shop called The Paris Market, which you would have loved." Marjorie ran her thumb over the comb before she fastened it into her hair behind the ear.

"It's so unique," she said, going in for a hug. "I wonder what Savannah belle cherished it before it found its way here. And you already got me something for Christmas! Thanks, girl, you're too much."

"You can't expect me to see something I know is *perfect* for you and not snag it. I also got some goodies for my boy Doc, where's he at?"

Doc hadn't made his usual jolt over to the front upon hearing Benny's voice. She followed Marjorie toward the kitchen. "Huh, he was down on his chair by the fire, maybe he's peeing in the back." Marjorie stepped out the back door and looked to the shed, but no Doc. As she came back into the kitchen, her eyes locked with the yellow box from Caroline's Pies—only it wasn't on the counter but knocked down with the top torn and the chocolate pie slice completely gone.

"Shit," she said under her breath. She hurried past Benny toward the dim hallway that led to the laundry room, finding Doc on his side against the door, panting heavily, his paw stretching out for her as he started to convulse and cough. "Baby!" she nearly shrieked. "Oh my God, Benny, we gotta go."

...

Her childhood dog, Carl, got away from death perhaps a dozen times in his fifteen years of life, having downed all sorts of toxic things like garlic bread and Starbucks Caramel Frappuccinos, but as Marjorie recalled, he was never affected or showed any signs of distress. Not like Doc now, her sweet old boy tight in her arms and across her lap in the back seat as Benny drove them to the vet clinic out on Roswell Road. With no time to waste they got out and into the building where in minutes Doc was taken away to be examined. She struggled to fill out the basic forms while tears continued to form and swell up her eyes. Benny gently rubbed her back and even offered to take over the paperwork, but Marjorie shook it off.

"I'm such a fucking idiot," she moaned softly. "It's not the first time he's tried eating things on the counter. I don't know why I didn't push it in farther. Fucking hate myself."

"I'm sure he's eaten plenty of bad shit in his life," said Benny. "He's such a strong old guy. And we got him here right away. You can't beat yourself up on it, Marge. It happens so often."

"But it shouldn't have happened at all." Marjorie sighed deeply and wiped her eyes on her scarf. Twenty minutes went by, feeling slow and not reassuring. But soon enough Dr. Tillman, Doc's vet, appeared before her, her composure relaxed.

"Hey, Marjorie," Dr. Tillman greeted her calmly and warmly. "He's gonna be fine. But we fear the overstimulation of his heart rate and seizures might have ruptured his pancreas. But all treatable, he's on IV fluids and we were able to pump out most of the chocolate. It seemed very concentrated and dark, the most dangerous kind of cocoa. But as I said, most has been removed and currently just hydrating him and steadying his heart rate."

"But you said he might have ruptured his pancreas?" Marjorie asked.

"Yes, but that's why I'd like to keep him overnight and do an endoscopy to make sure that isn't the case. For any ulcers or other complications with his gastronomical tract, we might have to do surgery."

Marjorie sighed and nodded. "Do what you'll need to do, doctor."

"Thank you, Marjorie. I do want to remind you that Doc is very old, and if it comes to surgery, the anesthesia might not be favorable for him in the long run."

Dr. Tillman disappeared again, and the waiting commenced. Benny stayed next to Marjorie, even DoorDashing some Starbucks for them while they sat with no new update. Checking her phone for the time, Marjorie decided to call Lara Jean. In a subdued voice she greeted her and said, "I am terribly sorry, but I don't think I can meet with Natalie tomorrow. I'm here now at the vet because Doc is really sick."

"Oh no, dear!" said Lara Jean. "I'm so sorry to hear that. Is there anything you need from me or Nelson? I hope he's OK?"

"I think he will be, but the vet just has to do some tests to make sure nothing else is affected. He got into some chocolate."

"Oh, sweetheart. I do hope everything is alright. Don't worry about tomorrow with Natalie. I'll talk to her. It's not like Goodman history is going anywhere."

Still, it was a blow to Marjorie, not knowing when her next opportunity to speak with any remaining Goodman could be. But Lara Jean was right—Doc was now. There was nothing she'd be missing meeting with the family's past.

Dr. Tillman came back out. "So it looks like no ulcers are there from what we saw," she told Marjorie. "But still this was a traumatic incident. Doc's heart rate is coming down and his breathing is slowly stabilizing again. We'll still keep him overnight to make sure everything is fine by tomorrow. But he's gonna be OK."

Marjorie let out a big sigh, but the tears were still forming. "Can I please see him one more time before I leave? Can I stay until you close?"

"Stay as long as you'd like. We love Doc, and he's being well looked after."

She followed Dr. Tillman to a back room where Doc was being monitored in a padded kennel, the door open, with one of his paws slowly reaching out as the old dog sensed his human was near. He had a blanket over him and an IV connected into his other paw—even with his slow panting, he mustered all the joy in his body to wag his tail upon sniffing and licking Marjorie's outstretched hand.

"Baby," Marjorie spoke gently to him, kissing his snout. "God, you're so stupid. But so am I. I am so sorry. I love you. I'm praying. I'll always love you, as long as we stay here together."

She and Benny stayed until a little past closing at nine, but even pulling up to the curb of Dogwood Daze, Marjorie felt uneasy being back home, and alone. She got inside and made sure to charge her phone in case overnight staff tried calling. Benny started up a fire in the living room and put on the kettle as Marjorie changed into comfier clothes. When she was finally downstairs, she gave her friend another big hug. "Thank you," she said to Benny. "I don't know how I would have gotten through tonight without you." She could hear Benny's own sniffle as she finally pulled away.

"You're a sweet girl, Marge," Benny told her. "With all your smiles and pretty dresses, I know there's so much unrest that you keep to yourself. You're alone here in Georgia, and it's hard to feel supported. Just remember, girl, I'm here for you! Anything you need, or need to talk about ever, shout out."

"You're right, I need to remember that. You've been too generous with me."

Once Benny left, she poured some hot water from the kettle into a big mug and made her favorite orange spice tea with a dash of cream. She carefully held the mug in her grasp as she sat by the fire, trying to read *Evangeline* but finding herself staring over to the empty, sagging armchair that was Doc's preferred spot. How heavy her heart felt then, how she wished he were there and they could both fall asleep peacefully in the glow of that fire he loved so much. She nearly did, warm and cozy and almost drifting off to her dreams when she felt her phone vibrating in between the pages of the book where she had left off. But it wasn't Dr. Tillman.

"Hi," Marjorie answered.

"Hey," Danny's warm, deep voice responded. "I'm sorry to call late, but I wanted to check up on you and Doc. How is he?"

Benny must have messaged him. "He's stable, but he's staying overnight at the vet to be monitored for any changes. But he should be OK by tomorrow."

"Thank God. Chocolate, was it?"

"One of Caroline's creations. I can't believe I let this happen."

"It was a mistake any of us could have made. You're such a good mom to him. If anything, Doc probably is happy and thought you left a big treat out for him. Nearly killed him but I don't think he's gonna hyperfixate on that."

Marjorie laughed a little. "Thank you so much, Danny. I appreciate you reaching out."

"Absolutely." He paused a few seconds before following with, "Is there anything you or him need? Would—would you like me to stop by?"

She felt her heart grow heavy again, but instead of the weight of sadness, it was a desire—but the guilt rushed in. "No," she answered. "We'll be alright."

"OK. But please don't hesitate to reach out. I hope your time back with your family was nice."

"It was lovely, thank you. I ran into your aunt a while back, and she told me you were all going to be at your brother's?"

"She told me she'd seen you. And yes, we were! It always feels like Christmas when we go up to his place. Wish it had snowed, though. Would have been perfect."

"Well, let's hope next Christmas will be more generous." She paused. "It's great to hear your voice, Danny."

"And yours, Marjorie. If you ever need—"

"I know. I promise I will."

"Alright. Stay warm tonight. And when Doc comes home tell him his buddy Daniel misses him. I'm sending a pup package from the hotel to you tomorrow when I get in."

"He would love it!" She heard him chuckle before he spoke one last time.

"Sweet dreams, Marjorie."

"Thank you, Danny. Good night."

Simon, 1964

The fog was approaching. The farther along up the hill from Grant Avenue they went, the more it seemed as if they were coming into the clouds. A beautifully clear day was long gone. Simon walked alongside Marjorie, his hand in hers, the other making sure her coat wasn't slipping from her shoulders as she had only just draped it across.

There was still plenty of light but diffused by the fog it felt closer to evening. To Simon, time seemed to stop, and that was what he was wishing for at this moment, trudging up this hill together with no end in sight. If by her side for eternity, he wanted nothing more.

They got to the top of the hill, and both turned around. Simon pulled her in close as they admired the thin skyline of downtown below. "Some view," he said.

"Sure is," responded Marjorie. "A nice way to end the day."

"Who says it's over?"

"Well, seeing as my home is that way." She tilted her head back slightly to point north, then let out a heavy sigh as she let it rest against him. "Gosh, we're already in North Beach! It felt too quick."

Simon had to agree. With all their talk about big next steps and Marjorie describing feeling high to him and pointing out all the major landmarks they hit going through Chinatown, like the oldest bakery in the city and peeking into Sam Wo to see if the world's rudest waiter was working, it all felt like it had passed in mere minutes. Night had an hour to go before falling over the bay, but he felt panicked that the day was practically over if she declared it so. "Well, now this gives me more of an excuse to come out this way," he told her.

They continued walking up Grant, Marjorie still in his arms as they slowed their pace, mostly now passing apartments and a bar that looked like it belonged on the main street just a few blocks over.

"Simon," she began. "I hope today hasn't ruined any of your plans."

He smiled, leaning into her as he replied, "I had nothing going on for today. And I'm glad it was so or else I wouldn't have spent it all with you."

"No, I didn't mean today. I was talking about school, sticking it out in the city. I was actually thinking about how stupid of me it was to say silly things like *quit* when this is a really big part of your life."

"What silly things? You've done nothing wrong but be honest, and I appreciate your input. I only just met you but getting to know you for what little time it's been has really put things in perspective. You're so certain of everything. So free. If not my girl, then a muse."

She blushed. "You'd like me to be your girl?"

"Wouldn't you like that?"

"You barely know me."

"True, but if it wasn't any of the Lord's doing, then I'll be damned. I haven't been this happy being here since, well, coming off the plane I guess."

She squeezed his hand, slowing down as they were just coming up on her building. It was a burgundy stucco complex with a wide stoop that led up to a door dimly lit by a single light over the entrance. "If that's true, I take it back.

I'm glad I could provide some perspective." She looked up to the building, pulling her coat closer around her shoulders.

"Simon," she said again, pressing herself once more into his arms. "You've put my own worries at ease, thank you so much for that. I haven't been this happy here either—and I've been here my whole life!"

He leaned his face closer to hers. "Something tells me I'll be here the rest of my life too."

"What about your family?"

"I'll tell them things out here are just as I hoped. Everything is perfect. God, it's been a perfect day! Well, except for..." He stopped himself as he laughed at the hair that again fell across his eyes, stiffly blowing upward to brush it away. She couldn't help her smile, and once more she reached out to push it aside, but while she was slowly running her hand through the rest of his hair, he felt compelled to grab her by the waist to him, kissing her gently. She didn't pull away but held Simon close as his hands slipped farther down her backside, which now was pushed against the wall of her building. Her red lips, whose touch he'd imagined before, were soft and full, exciting him and forcing him to catch his breath between each kiss as he couldn't believe this dream coming true right before his eyes. Her hands slid around him, and he lifted her slightly as he began kissing down to her neck, smelling traces of jasmine and the lily she still held in her hand.

"Marjorie," he gasped, moving his head up and resting it against her own. He felt her stomach rise and fall against his body, her hands still clasped around his neck, one of them tugging at his cardigan.

"I wish I didn't have to go," she whispered.

"Darling, I'd do anything you'd ask me to. Ask me to stay, please." Her tug softened, and she slowly moved back to look up at him.

"No," she said, her voice shaking. "I can't tonight. I wish you could, I truly do. But I can't." She stayed there, resting her head on his chest and he kissed the top of it, not wanting to press her any more than she wanted to be.

"This summer I really thought I made a bad choice, coming out here," Simon began again. "But you—it's proven me wrong. This day was the best part of moving here—meeting you, on such a beautiful day. We can have so many more."

Marjorie looked up to him and slowly kissed him again. "I'm so happy I met you too, Simon."

"Let's meet again, perhaps tomorrow?"

"No, I can't promise tomorrow."

"Anytime then, if not tomorrow. We've got plenty of time now that we've found each other. There is so much I'd love for you to show me in this wonderful city."

She pulled away again, this time moving up the steps of her building. She took a strange, panicked look around them before saying, "I've got to go now, Simon. But thank you again, for everything."

Simon looked up at her with a wide smile, tipping an imaginary hat and bowing as he kissed her hand. "Good night, Marjorie," he said. He turned around, still smiling, but only made it a few feet before he realized he'd forgotten the obvious. "Wait!" he nearly cried out. "What if I called you tomorrow instead?"

He turned to face the steps, and no one, except for the single lily left on the dark steps, was there.

Chapter 18

For the first few days being back at home, Doc would lie down and sleep most of the day on his big bed that Marjorie placed right in front of the fireplace. He was slower than usual when he did move, either to burrow on his bed or take a few steps over to drink from his water bowl, but he was well. With wet food mixed with rice, per Dr. Tillman's orders, he'd be better in no time. Just being close to his human seemed to be proving that.

With Lara Jean knowing, Marjorie figured it wouldn't be long before the word got out. Nelson had messaged her that if she needed, Doc could come into the salon and rest by her. Benny's sister, Morgan, worked from home and had been looking after Doc, but when Marjorie came into the salon that Thursday and saw the big checkered green dog bed with a basket of goodies by the reception desk, she felt tears again in her eyes. Inside the basket was a soft blue robe for dogs and handmade rope toys from an Acworth artist, complete with a "Get Well" card signed by Art, Al and Ken, and Caroline—who snuck in an abundance of home-baked dog-safe biscuits to atone for the role she had played.

Doc was now going to be full time at Nelson's, and his first day went with ease as he mostly slept during the busy hours and was loved by all. She hated bringing her car again and looking for parking on the Square, but for her boy it was all worth it. A week since bringing him in, Marjorie now slouched over at reception resting her head on her hand as she watched her peaceful old man. He was dreaming and kicking his back paws in little jolts, as if he might be sprinting, maybe in Lewis Park. Did he ever dream of his old owner, Wyatt?

The door opened and she turned around. It was Stephen Martin, a gray beanie over his curls and a leather bomber on to keep out the February chills. "Hey Marjorie!" he said, taking off the beanie to fluff out his curls. "Happy New Year! How have you guys been?"

"Aw good to see you, Stephen!" Marjorie returned. "We've been good, living the dream. Been a minute since I've seen you!"

"Sure has been a few months! But it felt like the last few just went quick! I don't have an appointment, but I would like to see Nelson's next availability for Friday, please?"

Marjorie raised a brow. "Not with Alex?" she asked him.

He exhaled and replied, "I don't think it'd be a good idea. She'd hate to see me."

"She'd honestly hate you tiptoeing behind her back to see someone else. Just talk to her. Or else you're better off finding a new salon."

"It's been too long. It'd be so awkward to try and talk after all this time."

"No, trust me. You just gotta message her—or at least continue booking with her." She was nervous to disclose that, in fact, Alex had another cancellation and was free right now. "Actively trying to avoid her is just gonna make things worse."

"Are you sure?"

"As long as you came in without your girlfriend, to be honest, it'll be fine. She won't cause any drama at work."

Stephen slyly smiled. "I wouldn't either. And I wouldn't bring her in. We broke up."

"Oh?"

"Yeah. It's been a long winter." Looking over to Alex's station, he continued, "But don't think that would change anything."

"But you desperately need a cut, otherwise you wouldn't be walking in and willing to see anyone else. C'mon, it's not gonna be as bad as you think!"

"If I can trust you. I'll be back next week then. For Alex."

After Stephen was gone, it didn't take long for Alex to come out from the back room. "And so the prodigal son returns," she scoffed.

Marjorie thought quickly before she said, "He wanted to know if you were free next Friday."

"I literally could have taken him right now."

"Don't you want to be more mentally prepared, especially since it's been a few months? Well, he'll be back at around two that day." Alex leaned over to look at the schedule on the computer.

"Fine," she continued. "But swear to God if she's coming too—"

"She won't. He told me they broke up."

"Ohh, did they? So now he thinks everything is gonna be fine and we're like before. Like I'll be here with open arms. Fuck that."

Marjorie narrowed her eyes. "You're gonna wear a dress, aren't you."

"In the thirty-degree weather? Absolutely." Alex walked off toward the back, but not before flashing her friend a mischievous smile.

...

With outside being so dry and cold, Marjorie was glad to be warm indoors sifting through hoards of papers from the archives, never mind the Goodman files. There were old receipts, newspaper ads, city permits, and photos of the row of buildings along Church Street, with any one of these items being the Golden Ticket to designate the Marietta landmark loophole. The key was explicit ties to a significant event on the Square or legacy figures like the founding families or government officials—none of which Marjorie had any luck so far in finding. At best, most papers collectively referred to the businesses as the "Church Street brickyard," but that meant nothing. Lara Jean helped too, the both of them sitting in her office with a space heater blasting in the corner. "Think happy thoughts, and be positive," Lara Jean mused. "Just be the warmth you're looking for, and Lord knows we'll find some fire in these piles."

Marjorie grunted. "I'm so nervous. We've got this week and next and then if there's nothing here, I don't know what else to do from here." She turned her face away from the pile of papers in front of her and looked out the window to the dark, cold day. "I feel like we're close, but there's still so much to go through."

"We'll find it," assured the older woman. "The task at hand is much easier than last year's gala. And, there's two of us! I've been truly grateful for you, Marjorie, and Nelson surely appreciates it as well."

"It's not distracting me from my work at the salon, if he was worried. I'm not the best receptionist but I owe him for the opportunity."

"It's not that—the Museum really can be a lot for just a small group of us. He wishes he could spare you more, knowing how relieved I've been feeling since you came along."

"Anything I can always do to help. You and your husband have been nothing less than generous to me. I really do feel like I've lived here my whole life." The words came out so naturally and sincerely— she wasn't even thinking about her time travels to make her realize how dear Marietta really was to her, what the town could be losing if they lost Nelson's.

She got out of the Museum just before the sunset, and as it wasn't yet dark, something made her want to walk toward the Square, where the twinkling orbs in the trees still hung and the fountain was shut off to prevent the water from freezing in the weeks to come. As she watched the dormant fountain, she felt someone walking past. How pleased she was to see it was Christopher, accompanied as always by little Mikey who, cute as could be, was wearing a gray turtleneck.

"Good evening, gentlemen!" greeted Marjorie. "How have you two been?"

"We're not too bad, Miss Marjorie," said Christopher, grinning as he tipped his worn Braves baseball cap. "The band broke up about an hour ago but thought we'd get some steps in before heading home. It's good exercise for the both of us."

"Well, I'm glad you're both bundled up for tonight's walk, Mikey's rather stylish with his sweater!"

"Yep, a Christmas present from Miss Caroline. Those pies of hers are a gift themselves, I told her just to give me a slice now and then instead of any presents for me. Sure nice of her to let us keep meeting and playing there, even indoors! The world always needs music, especially in these times."

"Agreed. When it's warmer for me, I'll be back around to listen. Springtime couldn't come any slower!"

"Come anytime you feel like it. We won't be in your way, but it was good to see you!"

"Always a joy. I'll even walk with you both to the other side of the Square, I'm in no rush."

From the fountain they turned toward the northeast side of the Square, where at the traffic light Christopher and Mikey continued past The Strand, Christopher waving once more to Marjorie. She was ready to turn around when she looked up at the cross street from the opposite side: Archer Street. She stared blankly at the name when it suddenly hit her that she'd seen Archer in passing with the archives. The Archer family was a legacy line. And then she realized where she recently came across the name—it was on a document for the Church Street buildings.

...

The next day as morning made its way to noon, Lara Jean appeared at Nelson's with a wide grin and a stack of paper in her hands.

"My God," she declared to Marjorie. "How did we not catch this before? You were absolutely right! When you messaged me last night about seeing the name Archer, I just couldn't sleep. So, I went through the files you had yesterday, and there it was!" The top paper of her stack was a permit stamped with approval by the city for expanding the space for Schweitzer's Jewelry, the business that leased from 1969 to 1978. It was insignificant as a business and unremarkable a document as any permits went, except for the name printed under LANDLORD: S. ARCHER.

"I just didn't put two and two together," Marjorie replied. "Looking after so many documents for so long, I'm just glad I didn't let it escape my mind. So, this is it? The Archers once owned the building, even if it wasn't during like, the 1800s?"

"Legacy family is instant classification. Even though it was the seventies and eighties, the Archers were still pretty prominent then. I was a child, so I don't remember much about them, but they did own as many buildings around the Square and, of course, Nelson's happened to be one of them! I think the previous landlord Mr. Lawson took over in the mid-nineties before Northfield came along, so it was a good while that Simon Archer had influence with his hold."

"Simon Archer? The S. Archer here?"

"Mm-hmm. He took over the property management at the time and his father, Hugh Archer, had cosigned on a lot of businesses in the decades before, practically keeping Marietta commerce alive and giving way to most of the familiar businesses we know around town today."

Hugh Archer. Suddenly, Marjorie jolted out of her seat—*Hugh would be so happy to see this for the children.* The somber voice of Simon's mother echoed in her head as she then asked Lara Jean, "Could I see more about the Archer family? Would it be any trouble if I came back with you to the Museum on my lunch?"

"If Nelson can spare you on lunch, you're happy to go through everything. It'll help me further build the case for the building! Oh, I'm so relieved!"

But Nelson's was the last thing on Marjorie's mind. The next two hours of phone calls and ringing up clients was a blur until two, when she dashed over to the Museum and anxiously took the elevator to the archives floor. Lara Jean waited, having prepared photos and articles and even personal belongings of the Archer family out on the table where only months before she'd been searching through items for the gala. She didn't know where to start.

"There is so much," she said.

"Plenty," Lara Jean said. "So much on the history of the Archers and their ventures perfectly ties all the threads together to Church Street. Here! Have a look at the first Archers. The first to come here in 1834 from England by way of Baltimore, Henry Archer and his brother Francis, in these tintypes here."

Henry and Francis Archer faced opposite each other in a folding frame, stoic yet handsome mutton-chopped men with light hair, and eyes that Marjorie knew she'd seen before. Then a photo of Francis and his wife, Susannah, with their four children, followed by photos of each passing generation until she nearly dropped to her knees on seeing the photograph of Hugh Archer and his family from 1943; a tall and gentle-looking man in a lieutenant's uniform in front of a grand Victorian home, with the familiar sight of Mrs. Susan Archer, in a floral cotton dress and wide-brimmed sun hat by his side, and their two children, Annette and Simon.

Her Simon. So here he was, nearly six years since she first met and lost him for what she was sure was forever—now freely displayed before her eyes was his whole life and history. The child that he was, smiling with missing front teeth and standing awkwardly next to his older sister in what was probably the last family photo together before Mr. Archer's deployment, was such a comforting sight, a feverish rush of bewilderment and relief overcoming her as Marjorie frantically looked through the rest of the photos. There was a copy of his senior photograph from Marietta High School, youthful with short slicked-back hair and grinning that smile that until now she only could see in her memories, onto another from years later, suited up and standing next to his mother and sister, who was dressed all in white beneath an arched trellis of magnolias—her wedding day.

"Simon Archer," Marjorie said softly to herself. Why he had not given his proper last name, she could not understand. "He was very handsome. Must have been a lot for him to take on with his father gone."

"He did pretty well for himself, I'd say. And it makes complete sense that our salvation lies with him. So much of Marietta as we know it today was because of him. He was a part of committees that pushed for preservation and beautification of the town, including the Square as you see it today. He even funded a music program for the high school and scholarships for Kennesaw State when he returned and took over property management from his brother-in-law, who was doing a terrible job."

"You said when he returned? From where?"

"He was in California for a brief time, initially for grad school to study architecture, but he never completed school. Then he was summoned back to his mother's deathbed in 1971 and then the rest, as you can see, is history. Although I don't know why there wasn't much about the Church Street brickyard in what we already had." Lara Jean came over and pulled out a news clipping from 1982 of the *Marietta Daily Journal* reporting on recent city initiatives, and just under the article's main photo was a smaller photograph of Simon, debonair in a suit and looking much older as the caption below read:

ABOVE: Simon Archer, 43, stands in front of the old Brumby factory he eyes for renovations. Archer, whose family were one of the first to settle in Cobb County, recently completed an overhaul of his Church Street properties and welcomed two new businesses to the Marietta Square upon completion.

But those blue eyes, in spite of the years that had passed, were still kind, lively. He looked just as he did that day standing outside the red BMW on the other side of the train tracks last summer.

"This little clipping right here says it all," Lara Jean continued, followed by a big sigh. "Thank you so much, Marjorie. I'm so glad you caught on to the name! I can't wait to tell Nelson later tonight. He only knows that I have some updates, but keeping him in the dark until I can tell him the good news after work."

"He will be so happy," Marjorie agreed. Her eyes now traced a few stacks of papers up to a framed photo from the opening day of the new Marietta Square renovations in 1993. Simon was among the few lined up at the ribbon cutting, off to the side alone but looking so pleased at the changes unfolding before him. At the bottom were the signatures of everyone in the photo, including his own, *S. Archer*. The same curve of the *S* from the old 45 record, the St. Francis receipt.

She couldn't put off any longer the moment she feared. "What happened to Simon Archer?"

Lara Jean took a second to think before answering, "Simon's doing alright. We don't hear much from him these days in his retirement, but from what Luanne's told us he's settling in nicely at his home in the Winnwood Community."

"He's still alive?"

"He is. If you ask Luanne, you could probably meet the man himself! She's his niece."

Chapter 19

The February Merchants Association meetup was held a week earlier to share the good news about Nelson's luck in pushing back on the Northfield leasing hike. Standing on the stage of The Strand with his wife, Nelson said nothing but smiled as Lara Jean spoke on his behalf and presented all the evidence of the Church Street building as a historic entity. It gave the local businesses all hope against the sinister commercial exploits that were trying their best to uproot the heart and soul of their beloved way of life in this town.

Everyone rejoiced at the news; Marjorie herself was in attendance, but her mind was far from the excitement. Painfully she sat through the whole meeting until the end, when, scanning the dispersing crowd, she found Luanne.

"Miss Luanne!" she called out, nearly running through the crowd to Luanne, who was bundled in a pink tweed overcoat.

"Miss Marjorie!" she warmly replied. "Well! Wasn't this a meeting! You and Lara Jean are a fine pair of sleuths. I'm sure y'all are relieved and eager to continue work on the soda shop."

"Oh, we've got our next few weeks surely cut out for us. But I wanted to talk to you more about your family. I didn't know you were an Archer."

"Oh hush, I'm a terrible representation of them. Only on my mother's side. If there's any more you'd want to find out you're better off with Lara Jean or my poor uncle."

"I actually did want to talk to you about your uncle, Simon. Are you free after work?"

"Hmm. No, nothing going on. This was the main highlight of the day! But I'm happy to meet up if you'd like to grab a coffee at Caroline's. What did you want to know about my uncle?"

"Oh, honestly, everything? I mean, from the rabbit hole I got into about your family, well, all the legacy families, I found it all so fascinating and I just wanted to know more."

"Let's chat more then after you're off work. Caroline's at seven? I'm an open book!"

Again, Marjorie painfully passed the hours of the workday until she left and walked up the street toward Caroline's, dropping Doc off at the bookstore to stay with Benny while she met with Luanne. Luanne had found them a table by the window, and she sat upright looking down at her phone until Marjorie approached her.

"Ugh, my bad! Still some emails I have to get to," Luanne explained. "I'm almost done. Get yourself a drink and maybe some pie and then I'm all yours!"

The pie ordered and the coffee poured, Marjorie stirred her cup anxiously until Luanne shut the screen off and placed her phone back in the pocket of her pink coat draped over her chair. "So," she began, "Uncle Simon. He's a dear man. In great shape too! I think it was all the business that kept him spry and sharp until now."

"Lara Jean mentioned that he took over things in the seventies from your father?" Marjorie said.

"It's true. I loved my dad, but with every family we all had our share of problems. Dad was not a natural businessman, or even a family kind of guy. He and my mom met in college at UGA, and he always wished he stuck with football instead of taking over the family business. It made my grandmama so happy, but he wasn't cut out for it. My mom and him got divorced right before my uncle came back and my grandmama died. I was still very young and tried to not focus on all the changes, and for that I thank Uncle Simon. He set everything right and, truthfully, filled in a great hole that my dad left. I mean, that's just personal. Historically, Uncle Simon not having a statue in town is a complete tragedy."

"He sounds like a very dedicated person."

"Absolutely. He loves Marietta, which is so funny because he left it for a while. He was out west and I guess just wanted to see the world and explore. But he did come back, and for the better, because he really shaped Marietta as a place you never would want to leave. Ironic, right?"

"Where did he go out west?"

"San Francisco. Then he moved down to LA. He was in school originally but dropped out and tried doing stuff with music. I don't think he ever recorded or sang but he did produce and write some tunes, I think. Nothing big. If so, he would have told me!"

Marjorie joined in Luanne's laughter, and then, slowly, she pulled from her purse the 45 record and pushed it toward Luanne.

"It's funny you said that. I think he was a great singer," Marjorie said.

Examining the record, Luanne's eyes widened. "Oh my!" she exclaimed. "That's his signature alright. Is this a song he wrote?"

"No, not an original song. But he sings on here and I thought you'd like to give it back to him. I found this at Westside Antiques not long ago, but all I could get from the owner was that she most likely got it from an estate sale."

"Well, that's true. My uncle and my mom and I lived together for a while in the family home not far from here, a beautiful Victorian we called Grace Hill. A few years ago he decided to sell the home when my family and I wanted to move to something bigger. He's over now in the Winnwood Retirement Community, keeping busy, but I visit him as much as I can. Just as long as he's still close to town, he seems happy with the downsize. We did have an estate sale, which explains how it ended up at the booth in Westside. Hmm." Luanne looked puzzled as she ran her finger over the initials S.G. "You sure this is my uncle? It should be S.A. for Archer."

"It's for Grace. Simon Grace. Maybe it was a pen name for his songwriting? I only just recognized the handwriting from all the archives at the museum."

"It sure is his handwriting! I can't wait to embarrass him and bring this over." She looked back up to Marjorie. "Would you like to give it to him yourself?"

Marjorie held her breath at the suggestion. "When?" was all she could say.

"Well, maybe at the end of the month? I'm a bit tied up with things at City Hall, but I could arrange for you to go alone."

"Oh! No, I'd feel less awkward if you were to come with me."

"Very well. I'll look at my calendar, and then you just let me know what day you can go. Sundays and Mondays, right?"

"That's correct."

"Then I guess it's up to me then. I won't keep you waiting! In fact, I think you and him would get along swimmingly."

December 31, 2023

Simon,

It's strange to think that you might never read this, and for obvious reasons. They always talk about the right people, wrong time—I don't know if you really were right for me, but the timing—that for sure was wrong. In the decades that followed I wondered what you did with your life, and it drove me to places I never thought I'd be, in a life I never envisioned for myself. I should be in California again, in our favorite city sitting at a desk in a big open office with views of the skyscrapers that I don't know if you ever stuck around to see. I miss that view sometimes. That was my life. That should have been my life continued. But here I am, in Marietta, in a world that was once your own.

I should be in California—but I wish so badly it was back in California with you. We never should have met at all, but fate, time, and a warm day brought us to that spot in Dolores where everything changed. I could have moved on and back through the years without any lasting impressions on the past, but it's evident by your recording that was not the case. You remembered me. You sang that song. Our song. Our silly little tune we danced to by ourselves stupidly in the middle of tiny St. Francis Fountain. I guess love is stupid, though. Yes, I am in love with you now, as I was then, although I didn't admit it because it would be impossible to love someone of another time, but while I was there—and while fate had sent me back to you in those few hours we shared together—I wish I had told you then since everything, like time, was not in my favor, and cruelly, we could not have that time at all.

A part of me is always going to be stuck in 1964 with you. And as I live in Marietta, your home, now my home, I try so hard to use this crazy gift of mine to someday, hopefully, take me back to you. And if only just for those seconds, I may get to let you know I loved you.

Marjorie

Simon, 2024

As he got older, Simon began to realize that spring was the best season. These summers were getting too hot, and the winters were cold and lonely. He loved the festivities at Winnwood during the holidays, with the dinners and live carolers and the porches decked in fresh green holly, but Luanne and her family always seemed to be away more often with each passing year. They'd be visiting her husband's family out in Arizona, and while they were there in the desert sun, he was back here dreaming of the West Coast himself. It'd been fifty years since he'd left California, and his biggest regret was not seeing it one more time. Spring reminded him of it, warm and dreamy without the stickiness of the Southern humidity that always took him back to his youth. Spring was coming, but first the last frosts of March had to end.

He had on a light green sweater as he sipped his coffee and looked out at the budding green of the trees; it was Saint Patrick's Day after all, and he could sense something good was on its way. Even in his eighties, there was still a lot of luck left, like today. Luanne would be visiting this afternoon with someone who had found one of his old recordings in the antique mall on the Square. He'd forgotten about most of the demos he'd made, especially since all he ever really sang were covers. He was told that Laurel Canyon was gonna be the place to go, and they weren't wrong—but he just wasn't right for it. He was too sentimental, not really creative. After she'd disappeared, he was only ever interested in love songs that might have brought her back somehow into his life.

But life had other plans that he'd resigned himself to, and coming back home wasn't all that bad. Marietta was changing, and had he not returned, some of it would have been for worse. He was meant to be where he was now, especially for Luanne. For all the troubles she had in her youth, it made his heart full knowing she was happy now. She was family, the closest to a child he would ever have.

He waited patiently on the porch of his little apartment where he lined up geraniums in blue pots and pulled his brown rocker out into the sunshine. He had his phone on loud, but while he waited he opened up his Spotify and decided to listen to some tunes. He loved how easy it was now to have all the music of a lifetime ready at your fingertips. Everything from his youth, which he played now, whizzed by on shuffle, bringing up memories and especially those of LA. Ugh, he should have gone back west one more time.

Finally, the phone rang and he picked up. "Good morning, sweet Lu," he playfully greeted. "Are you here?"

"Yes! We're almost at your door," replied Luanne. "We brought some pie! Hope you're not full from breakfast."

"I had a feeling you'd be bringing treats, I've only had coffee. I'll be right over."

As he went back inside and walked over to the door, he got a sudden rush of nerves. Not bad, but a tingling that made him think about what luck was about to happen next when he got this record back. He never told Luanne about his demos, and maybe this was impending embarrassment. But it would be a beautiful visit, nonetheless. He smiled and opened the door, elated at the sight of his niece and her guest right beside her—

"Uncle!" exclaimed Luanne. "Are you alright? You're flushed!"

"Lu dear," he softly said, exhaling and going over to hug his niece. Maybe if he closed his eyes for a second, he'd adjust his sight. But a quick blink and turn to her guest, his eyes weren't playing tricks on him. Could he see ghosts? At this very second, could he have died and gone into the afterlife?

How was it now that, decades after he'd lost her, she was here before him again?

"No, no, I'm alright," he continued. "I—I am so sorry, I guess I just lost my thoughts for a second. Old people."

"Maybe you should have more than just coffee, geezer," Luanne joked. "Uncle, this is the young woman who found your music in town. She was so excited to personally bring it back and was hoping to learn more about your work in LA and even here on the Square. She's the one who's been helping with a lot at the Museum and with the gala I invited you to last year! Marjorie, this is my uncle, Simon. Uncle, Miss Marjorie Valdez."

He felt a lump in his throat as she spoke the name. Marjorie. How was this so? She was alive—and unchanged. Still so young, maybe a little older from when he first saw her on the grass in Dolores all those years ago, but just as stunning. She was in green, as they all were, but her floral dress beneath her camel coat dipped slightly off her shoulders in a square neckline and cinched sensually at her waist; her rich brown hair was longer, flowy and big, almost like Raquel Welch. It was as if she never left the sixties.

"Simon," she finally spoke, the same voice he never forgot and only echoed in his own memories. "It's so lovely to meet you."

"And you, ma'am." That's how he knew it really was her—how those words evoked the dotting of tears in her eyes that he now noticed. "Please, please come in, the both of you!"

He ushered the women into the small living room where, coincidentally, a vase of fresh lilies were at the center. She stared at the flowers and looked over to him, the stillness of her face warming into a small smile as she took a seat opposite him and next to his niece. Trying his best to be as calm and hospitable as he could, he sat up and leaned over to take the yellow box of pie from Luanne's arms. "Smells wonderful," he said, peeking in to see a Lemon Meringue.

"We can cut it up now if you'd like," Luanne suggested. "I actually might need to hop on a call soon, Uncle, but I'd figured I'd give you and Miss Marjorie some time to get to know each other and for her to ask away about you!"

"Certainly, Lu." He nervously turned to Marjorie. "And what was it exactly you wanted to hear me jaw on about, ma'am?"

A slight laugh came from her, and she replied, "I mean—I've just heard so much about you since moving to Marietta and was fascinated by you—you and the families here. There's just so much to learn about this place."

"There really is. Marietta hasn't really changed much from when I grew up here. But then, it's not the same either. I prefer it now, actually. Better food. Always something on the Square—I mean, there always have been gatherings and parades but not as often as this. The park now reminds me of certain places—Dolores Park, perhaps?"

He could see her draw in a breath before speaking again. "Yes! Dolores. I'm actually from San Francisco. To me it's the most beautiful place in the city. I heard you lived there for a while."

"I did. And it was my favorite place to be as well."

"My uncle always said he'd take me there," chimed Luanne. "The offer is still on the table."

"Well, whenever you can get away from your work, I'd fly you there myself!"

"Ugh, it just never seems to end. Now with Northfield about to throw a hissy fit about the salon, I don't think I'll be seeing the daylight for a long time. Nelson's Salon is getting ready to expand into a soda shop service, thanks to Marjorie. She helped find the documents to keep them there."

"I'm glad to hear it's been passed. It'll be nice to have a soda shop in that space again. Like Hunt's. You sound like you've been pretty busy since coming here, Miss Marjorie." This was not the day he thought he'd be having, never thinking this reunion would ever come. Simon couldn't look away from her, from how lovely she still looked. How was it this was not heaven at all? He couldn't be alive.

"It's been quite a year," she simply said.

A brief silence passed as he heard the cardinals call in the distance from the big magnolia tree just outside of his back porch. Turning to Luanne, he asked, "When do you need to take that call? If it's soon, Miss Marjorie and I can sit outside. Maybe if you'd like, ma'am, we could walk down to the garden."

"It's not for twenty minutes," Luanne replied. "But if you two wanted to go on out, please do! This place is gorgeous, Marjorie. I saw some azaleas are already starting to bloom. Sure is a lucky day, isn't it?"

Marjorie smiled and nodded to him, awkwardly standing and prompting Simon to follow as he showed her the way to the back. "Take your time," Luanne said, staying put on the couch and pulling out her phone.

Simon closed the door, and faced Marjorie, now just the two of them.

"Is this real?" were the only words he could find to say next.

Her smile seemed more natural now. "This is all real," she assured him, scanning his sorry, frail sight from toe to head, and held out her hand. He saw no ring. "Simon," she continued, "I've found you."

He could feel tears in his own eyes. He had many questions yet, but for now, he let the joy in, taking her hand in his. "How I've missed you, darling."

"You're probably wondering what the hell is going on."

"You're not wrong. I don't understand—what happened to you? How are you so—still so young?"

She took a deep breath. "I can tell you the truth, and as crazy as it sounds, it's all real."

"You are standing here before me, alive and just as beautiful as when I first saw you. It isn't crazy. It's a dream come true."

She slowly moved closer, taking him in her arms as she hugged him tightly. The jasmine wafted from her locks and all over again, if not for the brightness of the sun, it was as if they were back in the cold of North Beach that sunset sixty years ago. He wrapped his arms around her, never wanting to let go. "How did you find me?"

She backed away, looking around them and up to the big magnolia tree. "Let's keep walking, shall we? I feel strange being so near to Luanne as I explain everything."

Down the gravel path from his porch, they continued along toward the gardens. Arm in arm, Marjorie looked around them before turning again to Simon. "Where do I begin? I didn't even think you were still alive until just a few weeks ago. I came here trying to find closure but instead I found you."

"Well," Simon began. "I definitely cut back on cigarettes. And milkshakes."

"Well shit," she said softly, getting him to laugh. "I'm glad to see how healthy you are. What about the music? And California?"

"I thought you were letting me ask the questions first."

"True! I'm so sorry—you can't imagine how nervous and excited I am right now. But yes." She exhaled once more and began again, "Simon, I am thirty years old. When we met, I was twenty-five. I was born in 1993, but as early as eight years old I discovered I had the ability to go back in time."

Simon said nothing. 1993—he was fifty-four when she was born. It was ridiculous, but really simple to understand, and clarified so much.

"Are you able to go back and forth?" he then asked her.

"No. I can't control when it happens or how long I stay. I can be in one spot in the present and all of a sudden, it's the same place but ten, forty years ago? I usually don't try to make my presence known. Most times, I'm there for as little as a few minutes to maybe a few hours. But when we first met that summer of '64, that was the longest I had ever remained back in time. I don't know why I was there for so long. And I was so afraid to just disappear when I was with you."

"And you did. But that whole time together, knowing that you'd be gone at any moment—why didn't you just try to leave me?"

"I didn't want to leave you."

"But you disappeared all the same, and in such a sudden and cruel way. It was one of the happiest days of my life and made me realize everything I was doing out there—everything was going to be OK."

"I really wish I hadn't left when I did. I wanted to stay, I wanted you to stay with me. But I just told myself that maybe you wouldn't have remembered me. I thought that maybe every time I went back it was just all a hallucination or dream, that no one I met would truly remember me. But then, I came to Marietta, I found your record—"

"Which record was it you found?" He felt her arm tighten around his.

"Our song."

"Oh."

"That is why you chose to record it, didn't you?"

"It was. Even to this day, I still have dreams of us dancing there at the soda shop. Recording my rendition gave me some peace. It made me miss you less in that moment, strange enough. But the dreams still came."

They finally got to the garden, where a few pink azalea buds slowly popped through ahead of the coming spring. Off to the side of the garden was a mossy swinging bench where Marjorie and Simon went over to sit. "Why did you come to Marietta?" he continued. "To find me?"

"Of course. Well, originally a job brought me out this way, but then I got laid off and decided to come here. I wanted to find you and know what happened to you. It turned out you never became a musician, never did anything I thought you were going to do. But little did I know that you were here all along." She paused once more before asking him, "Are you happy with everything, Simon?"

Her brown eyes scanned his worn face, worried in their expression. *Anything I thought you were going to do.* It stung, thinking of the life she thought he had, but he sat straight and told her, "I am happy. I didn't become a musician, but I didn't *not* do anything about it. I tried. I quit school, as you encouraged me to. I left the city, moved down to LA, got in good with a few producers. I met David Crosby and Cass Elliot. It was a good time, even if I never made anything original. But I was meant to be here, back home in Marietta."

"Your family."

"Luanne was so young when her parents split, and my mama was fading fast. I would have never forgiven myself if she'd died alone without me there. After losing my father I had to make sure she knew she wouldn't lose me either. Same with Luanne and how her father basically wanted out from her life. It wasn't fair. The town was changing too—everything you and I talked about how San Francisco inspired and welcomed all, well I knew Marietta could be a place like that."

She sighed, seeming at peace with this answer. "From what I've heard, you helped keep a lot of its beauty alive. And you never thought I'd ever see it, did you?"

He chuckled. "No ma'am! I really did think that you were just my imagination. You couldn't have existed, with how you disappeared."

"Simon, I wish I could do everything possible to make it up to you for that evening." She pressed her lips together before asking her next question. "Did you ever meet anyone else?"

"No. I might have talked with a few ladies or gone out to dinners, but no. I was never concerned with finding anyone else. I didn't try forcing it. I had so much else to figure out in my life."

"I see."

"And you?"

"I couldn't. Silly as it was, I couldn't move on without having known what happened to you. That's why I came to Marietta last year and tried to find you. I thought that with my gift, I might run into you again, and I did! Last summer, I saw you by the train tracks, you were older then, and driving a red car…"

So that wasn't another hallucination. He could still picture her in the sunlight with her white sunglasses and a blue bike, a blank stare flickering between each passing train car, and he was so sure it was all because of the summer heat.

"What took you so long?" he asked. Her shoulders dropped and so did her face.

"Simon Grace? I tried finding your exact name and nothing turned up." She went for her purse and from a side pocket pulled out a folded old paper, the receipt from their lunch at St. Francis where he had signed his pen name. "Why didn't you just use your last name?"

"I did sign that, didn't I? I thought I was being cute. I did go by Simon Grace, though, for a while. I didn't want to get grief from my family over my projects, especially since Mama wasn't exactly pleased with my dropping out of school."

"That's understandable. But it didn't make my search any easier. Still, look at us. I'm here now."

"Yes, you are." Looking down at the paper he held, he examined his own wrinkled hands, skin tight and bony as it brushed her small, soft fingers handing the receipt back to her. She was here, and he was so grateful for this moment to see her again, but sixty years too late. There was nothing that could be changed about that.

"What will you do now, darling?"

"I don't know. I've been here a year, and I've been dreaming of this moment. And now it's finally come." Suddenly, she couldn't hold her tears back any longer. Frantically wiping at her face, she lowered her head to sob. "I wish there could have been more."

"Marjorie, darling—"

"Simon, I'm so sorry about everything."

"No! There's nothing to be sorry about. I don't regret anything. I've been happy. I really have. But are you happy? I only hope that everything since then has been all that you've wanted."

She looked up to him. "I only ever wanted you."

"I did too, darling. I still wish it was different. But look at you! Lovely as ever at such a young, fun age. Don't waste your time now wishing for what we could never have. Just be happy now. Be happy that we did find each other again."

Simon pulled her close as she lay her head on his shoulder. He closed his eyes and almost like magic, it was as if he too was traveling back in time. He felt twenty-five again, uncertain about what his tomorrow would be and nervous to be holding a wonderful girl like Marjorie in his arms, frantically thinking about how they could stay here forever in this moment. But it was only a feeling. He opened his eyes and gave her a last kiss on her head.

"Thank you for coming back to me, Marjorie," he softly said to her. "And now you know, I am always here."

They sat together for some time in silence, the birdsong that had been gone for months now coming clear through the trees again, a few bees now buzzing by toward the azaleas.

Finally, Marjorie sat up, wiping her eyes once more, and exhaled. "We should probably go back to Luanne," she told Simon.

Still arm in arm, they made their way back to the back porch. "I almost forgot," Marjorie began again. "The record."

"You can keep it. I may have been able to sing once, but God, I can't stand my voice."

"It's so smooth! The world really did miss out on you."

"It only matters that you heard me."

"Does this mean we can't listen to it now?"

"I wish we wouldn't. Luanne's never heard me sing."

"The cat's already out of the bag, *Uncle*."

He was laughing again, they both were. And once more, Simon felt young—staring back at the woman who had found her way back to him. His silent wish come true on the luckiest day.

Chapter 20

"As a parting gift, what'll ya have?"

Nelson was hunched over the dark-stained counter where the soda shop was open for business—well, open next Friday. The counter was set, a new sink installed in the back, and the original mint backsplash tiles were polished to their former glory. The headaches of Northfield's threatened lease hike and the scrambling fight that ensued felt so long ago. Marjorie was more than thrilled to be the first customer in, even as she was on her way out from her job at Nelson's. By next week, she and Doc would both be welcomed to their first day at the Museum, Marjorie appointed as their new community relations manager. Nelson wasn't sad to see her leave—she was more or less being promoted.

"I'll keep it simple," she said, sitting down at one of the new mint-upholstered stools. "Just chocolate, please. Heavy whip."

"Heavy for a simple order," scoffed Nelson as he went to work with a smile. Wednesdays were generally slow, but as Marjorie looked around from this corner of the salon, the place was in no way quiet. Each stylist was finishing their last foils or blow-drying the crown of their client's head, with the light flooding in from the front windows and illuminating the reception desk in a lovely glow. Marjorie would miss her station, but she always knew that it was a stepping stone—and now it was time to move forward. She'd finish her shake and then go meet Benny for a few Sun Glows as she spilled the details about her first date in over a year. It seemed as if everyone was moving on into the sunshine of these longer days.

As Alex finished her last client of the day, she came over to sit down by Marjorie at the bar and waved playfully at Nelson. "I'll take a banana shake, spiked, boss," she called out.

"You're still on the clock, missy," he retorted without looking up.

"I kid! But I could use a drink before tonight." Marjorie nodded and patted Alex on the back—it wasn't any dinner she was going to with Stephen tonight. After weeks of dating, he'd felt the time was right for her to formally meet his parents. Alex was still in shock. "I don't even know what I'll be wearing," she confessed to Marjorie.

"The offer's still on the table if you need to stop by and borrow a dress," said Marjorie. "A-line is always classic, and your figure would be great!"

Alex shook her head. "Your stuff is gorgeous but too bright and bubbly for me. I need to be authentic, and if I don't wear something black, I'll be a mess."

"Fair enough. Regardless of whatever black or velvet you choose, you're gonna look incredible and besides, Art already knows you, so that's a plus."

"He's always been polite in a work setting, but this is outside of work—and going over to the fanciest restaurant on the Square? Fuck."

"It's gonna be fine! Remember months ago we didn't even think you'd get to this point." Alex jerked her head back and smiled.

"I still give him shit about how much of a pussy he was to not break it off with her. But I mean, he's considerate, and he does see the good in people. It's been a while since I've met someone really good like that, you know?"

"I do."

The chocolate shake was laid out in front of Marjorie with a gracious amount of fluffy whip that bounced as she moved it closer to her. She placed her lips to the mint-striped paper straw and took it in, closing her eyes—all of a sudden it was Dion singing across the air, a chill of a winter back in 1959 and the kind smile of Curtis that flooded her mind, memories from that first moment she'd been back in time in Marietta and had set in motion a lovely little life she couldn't believe was now hers. But as she opened her eyes, she would have thought she was still back in the fifties if she hadn't met Nelson's gaze, brows arched high over his thick glasses awaiting her approval. She sat up, smiling at him.

"Yesss," she responded, drawing it out into a hiss. "If this is just the chocolate, I can only imagine how the other drinks will be!"

Nelson's sigh was followed by a laugh. "I've spent twenty-seven years as a hairdresser, one trade is enough to learn. It doesn't matter who makes the shakes so long as they keep coming. Christopher's a fast learner, from what I've seen."

Thanks to Caroline, Christopher now had a steady job. He was training in the evenings after the salon was closed, and Marjorie hoped that she'd catch him and Mikey on her way out. She sipped on the shake slowly and looked out toward the front door. "It'll be nice to have a dog still here," she said to Alex and Nelson. "But not much is going to change! I'll still be popping in here, especially if I can get one of these shakes while I color my hair or get a blowout."

Alex let out an uneasy laugh. "Please come hang out, but I beg you," she paused, reaching out to gently stroke a long lock of her friend's dark, wavy hair. "Don't change your hair color. Ever. Not because I don't think you could do any other shade, but your hair is healthy. Keep it that way."

Marjorie raised a brow. "Even if I'm a good tipper?" she teased.

"You could offer to pay my next rent and I'd still refuse. I couldn't bear the thought of destroying this mane."

Marjorie scoffed and turned to Nelson. "You'll be losing money if you keep this one around!"

Nelson, whipping up a second shake for Alex and laying it before her, responded, "I only hire the best. The best know when someone's got a good thing going for them and not to mess with it."

"Can you tell that to Art, Nelly?" Alex pleaded. But Nelson stared back at her, softening his expression in an amusing way, a rare sight caught between the long hours of the salon.

"I don't need to. He's happy for you guys. Otherwise he wouldn't have talked my ear off hundreds of times about how much he hated Stephen's ex."

"He *did*?"

"I swear. It's going to be fine."

...

Marjorie popped her head out the window, and the beauty of May awaited her. The world was right back where she loved it most, wrapped in the quiet warm air of the late Southern spring and soon to be swept up in magic of the twilight fireflies. Still in her satin slip, she brushed out her rolled hair, the blue polka-dot swing dress she chose for the evening draped over the armchair in the corner. She'd been eyeing the vintage piece for months from Etsy, and now that it was finally hers there wasn't a more fitting occasion than tonight's Pie Night.

Doc watched her getting ready, on the foot of the bed with his head bowed between his front paws while his tail sleepily wagged side to side. He was much improved from his scare back in January, but any long walks to the Square were no longer ideal. Thankfully, Pie Nights were right here at home, always his favorite days since making this new life with this younger human whom he loved, in spite of her occasional stares off into the distance that sometimes stopped her in her tracks during their walks.

With the smack of her lips after applying her favorite red shade, she grabbed the dress and went over to change in the bathroom. She only had a few hours to kill before everyone arrived, leaving time for taking Doc on his long evening walk and setting up the porch. It was going to be another full evening, with Benny and Morgan, Alex and now Stephen, and even Danny.

She still couldn't believe that Danny was coming tonight. It was only two weeks ago that they really began talking again, and had she not decided to stop back into Westside Antiques, she wasn't sure how much longer it would have been before she felt comfortable reaching out to him. But after her first year in town and finding Simon, she was sure it was fate. Stumbling upon Miss Roberta at the front register talking with Westside's owner not only made her smile, but got her heart racing, even faster when she mentioned her nephew was just in the back clearing out the booth.

Doc followed her out to the porch and sat next to her on the wicker bench while she pushed the stack of records on the coffee table to the side to make room for the porcelain plates and utensils. In a little over a year her favorite spot was heaven—the mismatched furniture, potted pink geraniums along the steps, and the baby blue gingham pillows that were scattered on the floor near her red Crosley that was propped up on an old planter. As she admired the setup, she could feel Doc's tail thump into her side to let her know he was ready for a walk. "Ready, baby?" she asked him, leaning in to kiss his wet nose as he opened his mouth like a smile. His breath smelled like the stale creek that ran through the edge of the cemetery—very fitting.

She was just hooking on his leash when a chill began to fall over her. She started rubbing her arms and looked up, knowing what was about to happen; the bright afternoon sky even seemed to swirl from blue into a soft periwinkle as the dusk of another decade seeped in. But then, "Marjorie?" a voice suddenly called out.

Marjorie swung her head to where the sunlight flooded behind the shadow of someone standing at the bottom porch steps—Simon. At least, in the glare of the sunshine she thought it was him, his relaxed silhouette and his hair a bit outgrown and blowing in the wind and what she thought was that sheepish smile that had melted her heart in that summer back in San Francisco. Was he a ghost?

But no—it was Danny, with a bouquet of red tulips in one hand and a bottle of wine in the other, slowly moving toward her as he asked, "Are you OK?"

Doc stretched out, his thumping tail only quickening at the sight of Danny coming closer. He set the wine down on the steps and ran his hand through his loose hair to push it off his brow before kneeling to pet Doc on the head. "Hey buddy," he softly greeted him. Marjorie still hadn't answered.

"Oh!" she finally said. "I was just lost in thought about something. You're here early."

"I thought I'd come by and see if you needed any help getting the place together."

"Thank you, but I got the pies and we're good on drinks. While you're here you can just take it easy and keep Doc company. You're all he cares about—and the pie, of course."

"He should know better by now pie is off the table. And not by his own doing." He stood up and looked around. "It's gonna be a beautiful evening—thank you for having me."

"Of course! I'm so glad you could make it out today—it's been too long. I actually was about to take him for a walk, if you wanted to join? We usually just take our time around the cemetery."

"Absolutely. I can hold his leash if you'd want? Let's go!"

Uncertain if it was the small warm breeze that passed or being close to Danny's bare arm as they walked side by side, Marjorie felt a tickle run through her. They reached the cemetery gates and took the winding path up toward the older graves, with Marjorie looking back at the wide hill now behind them. Of all the places in this town, that one made her feel the closest to San Francisco, back in sunny Dolores Park where Simon had first seen her. Simon, the real reason for these warm evenings thousands of miles away from her first love of a city and the time spent dancing between timelines to get back to him in some way. But now, her way was forward, and in the splendor of the new town and people around her she was ready to keep moving.

"Seeing you tonight, I'm really happy," she finally began. "I am sorry for how things have been. I've been in a weird—"

"Please, you don't need to apologize," Danny cut in gently. "I've missed you, though. But I didn't want to complicate things if you didn't want it that way. I want to help—be here for things, whether it's for looking after Doc or moving furniture or anything."

"You're too good to me."

"It's easy to be. It's not every day you walk into an antique mall and actually find something worthwhile."

"Well, dusty and musty seems to be your type."

"I don't mind the dust as much as other guys. But if musty means unique, great music taste, easy to talk to—and probably eighty-five years old on the inside, then I've met my match."

Marjorie snorted and shook her head. "It's been an inner turmoil adjusting to things all in this last year when I decided to move here and stick it out. I didn't mean to take it out on you, and honestly, I'm surprised you would still want to be here with how mad I got on my birthday."

"But I understand. Like I said, I want to make things easier for you while you're here. Not worse."

They were nearing the end of the long path that led toward the east gate, and Marjorie could see the towering angel with its laurel sheath resting atop where the Gartrell sisters lay. Admiring the light seeping through the cedar that illuminated the angel's face, Marjorie thought back to what Lucy Gartrell had said—*Love, my dear. All you can do is focus on the love.* Something about that conversation always calmed her.

"There was something else that I wanted to talk to you about," Danny began again. "This is going to sound weird, but I swear, it's real."

"What is it?" Marjorie asked.

He stopped and took his phone out, pulling up a picture of The Georgian Terrace's lobby where a gallery of photos from the hotel's past hung. In the middle was a particular photograph, black and white, from what looked like a lively evening that took place in the Grand Ballroom.

"A few weeks ago I was in the lobby waiting to meet with one of our vendors when my eye caught this one photo from 1932. I've seen these pictures so many times at work but then—"

Using his fingers to zoom in on the photograph, Marjorie's face grew hot when in view came herself, not looking into the camera but smiling away, in the peach dress and golden headscarf that she wore that afternoon visiting Danny. A quick-miss anomaly among the marcel-waved women and men in dark tuxedos.

"Jesus," she muttered under her breath.

"I mean, I'm not seeing things, am I?" Danny let out a nervous laugh, waiting for Marjorie to say something. "I don't know how that could—"

"But it is," Marjorie finally spoke. "You're not seeing things. Oh, God."

Now she laughed. The sky was slowly dimming, the once vibrant blue faded into a dull hue that seemed like they were still on the porch back at Dogwood. That tickling feeling still pulsated through Marjorie, but somehow, she seemed more excited than anxious. Up until now, only Eileen had known her travels, her burdens, and then Simon—but as she faced Danny, she took a deep breath, and smiled.

"Eight years old," she simply said, opening herself to him and the future she was eager to travel toward. "Let's start there."

THE END

Acknowledgements

There are quite a few of you for whom this story would not exist at all without you.

Uncle Mark, my dad's best friend since 8th grade and always the life of the party at family gatherings. The CD you made for me of various oldies songs really was the playlist of my preteens. Even as my music taste expands, I am always drawn back to the classics.

I wouldn't have been encouraged to pursue a life of literature and creativity if not for my English teachers, Tom Wills, Maureen Allan, Amber Lineweaver, and Kevin Cline at Clayton Valley (Charter) High School, and my supporting professors from the University of San Francisco, Susan Steinberg, Dean Rader, Ryan Van Meter, and Justin Torres, who only cemented I was on the right path of telling my truth through fiction.

And don't get me wrong, I miss San Francisco. Everything about that beautiful city was my first taste of adventure, a place pulsating with colors and sights and people from all walks of life. I am so grateful to have lived there for ten years and figured out who I really was. It was where I met my best friend and #1 cheerleader, Doug. I love that we grew together in such a vibrant city and took this leap into an uncertain new chapter that's proven to be the best years.

Which brings me to Marietta. Everything about you has been an absolute dream, but this whole love letter wouldn't have been possible without the people. The city's charm and beauty are deeper than the buildings and the Square, but comes from the community that shapes it. I'm so glad I could be a part of life here– and for everyone who's been so welcoming since we moved here in 2022, I haven't forgotten. Julia at Marina Marina and Mike and Eric at Park West Vintage. Lauren, Sam, and Vivian at Pie Bar. Stephanie and all your efforts with The Marietta Square Branding Project. Abby, Gina, and Brittney at Visit Marietta. And Elizabeth, Caroline, and Dominic, thank you especially for bringing The Reading Attic to The Square. There's really no bookstore like it! Working there set me back on this path, seeing other local writers blissfully live out their dreams with every live reading and book signing. If they're doing it, then why couldn't I?

It's also where I met Jennifer, my editor and fellow Janeite with whom I entrusted my work and for good reason. It's a real gem now, thanks to your insight, and I'm so happy you approached me during that Sunday in The Reading Attic. Nothing like supporting local creatives, and local editors!

And of course, Len. It's a privilege to have been a part of the team at Lenny's Hair Salon and I know I've only captured a fraction of the magic that really happens inside the business. The music played on vinyl, the blue '62 Bonneville, the wild celebrity encounters, the saltwater taffy and homemade cupcakes, the hair tutorials, the antiques, the bobbleheads, and the fire extinguisher scams. It's a whole other world within Marietta, and only few get to bear witness.

And Christa and Amy, the Marietta I depict wouldn't be the same without your enthusiasm and resources at The Marietta History Center. When I first moved here, the Center was the first place I went to truly get acquainted with my new home. With all the work you and the team have done, the soul of the city is still intact.

For extended research, Old Marietta you've been a Godsend! Davis McCollum, rest in peace and thank you for creating a Facebook page so extensive and filled with more than information, but love for the people who called this place home. And thank you to everyone who contributed to the Facebook page San Francisco Remembered and the database of Open SF History. All the archives helped me piece together remnants of the past I've never known yet feel nostalgic for.

And the friends I've met here. It was lonely at first, but knowing you now is a reminder that the right people will find you. Grateful for you, Chelsea and Annedra, for our love of vintage, and Sara and Nicole, for our love of our hometown. And Annedra, I hope your Aunt Connie and Uncle Doug will enjoy this read, as certain Marietta scenes and local jargon used wouldn't have been possible without their own unique memories that they shared over lunch on that beautiful spring day last year.

But the friends who are still here, who've always been around, I love you guys. Alyssa, my oldest and most cherished one, even when I can be too much you're still there for me. In fact, having your read through of the very first drafts of this story really helped a lot! And Gaby and Giuliana, college wasn't an easy time for me but graduating with you both as my friends and constant source of literary humor keeps me going down this magical path. I'll always remember the night before our Senior presentations, workshopping and editing together and really getting to know you both by the heart you put into every word, on each page. The right people make you shine brightest, that's for sure.

All my family, I love and miss you all from Georgia. Mommy, Daddy, Milan, I know it's been a strange and at times painful last few years since this move. But I love this story so much and it wouldn't have happened without this leap. It's not easy, but I love your endless support and thank you for understanding and letting me see this through. Even as I come to visit, nothing changes. I am a better version of myself, more confident and inspired and the joy I experience now I want to bring into every second we spend together, especially for Bentley, Porsche, Logan, Berlin, and London.

Lastly, back to you, Peaches. I don't regret anything about this life you and I have built out here with our silly but darling boys Duke and Bingley. Our family is a unique one, in a lovely house filled with lots of dog hair and late night music before bed and too many mosquito bites on the back deck as we sit and watch fireflies and think about everything we've done to get here. Here's to the many more wonderful things to come our way, we're so close. This book is proof of that!